FEB 0 1 2015

MW01134262

rae of sunshine

MICALEA SMELTZER

For my family.
Thank you for believing in me.

rae of sunshine

chapter one

THE THING ABOUT STARTING OVER is it isn't as easy as people say.

It's impossible to become a completely different person.

You can change your hair.

Your makeup.

Even your name.

But at the end of each and every day you're still the same person you were yesterday, and the day before that.

I'd spent the last year trying, and failing, to become a different person. The shitty events of my life had certainly changed me and I wasn't the same carefree girl I used to be, but I was still Rachael—or Rae as I preferred to be called now—because no matter how far we run we can never escape ourselves.

It might've been stupid but I felt like hiding behind the new nickname gave me a bit of anonymity. Not that anyone at Huntley University was going to know who I was or what I'd done.

My eyes fluttered closed as I felt the breeze tickle the skin of my cheeks and I inhaled the scent of lilac.

For the first time in a year I felt peaceful and centered. Like maybe I was where I belonged—which was funny, since I hadn't wanted to even go to college after everything that had happened.

I opened my eyes and grabbed one of my duffel bags from the car and my camera case.

My camera had always been like a limb to me—an extension of who I was. Even after everything that happened last year I'd never been able to give up photography. It brought me peace when everything else in my life was chaos. I slammed the door closed and locked my car, since I'd have other stuff to get later and I didn't want anyone trying to steal something. For now, I just wanted to get to my dorm and check things out.

I pulled the piece of paper out of my pocket with the housing information on it. I already had it memorized, but for some reason I found it necessary to read it again. It brought me some strange sense of peace. Like it was a lifeline or something.

With my head bowed I stepped onto the sidewalk.

I hadn't taken more than two steps before I fell.

Only, I didn't fall—I was knocked to the ground by the force of a very heavy male body.

I could smell his sweat—even more potent than the lilacs dotting the campus—and it wasn't the stinky kind of sweat, oh no, he smelled delicious. Like he'd been rolling around the sheets naked for hours having the hottest sex imaginable.

"Fuck, I'm so sorry!" The guy exclaimed, rolling off of me. He reached down to pull me up, and when he did I ended up plastered against his chest. It was hard and smooth, not a blemish in sight. He kept a tight hold on me so I couldn't scramble away. "Are you okay?" His eyes roamed over my body as he surveyed any damage he might've caused. His eyes lingered longer than necessary on my body.

"I'm fine," I assured him, finally looking at his face and—holy-hotness, it should be illegal to be that good looking. Brown hair hung in his eyes, eyes that were so blue that they could only be categorized as cerulean. Stubble dotted his defined jaw and his lips were kissable. They didn't make guys like this where I was from. Not. At. All.

Clearing my throat I took a step back, bowing my head so that my hair hid my suddenly flushed face. I couldn't believe I was ogling the guy who'd just knocked me down. Or any guy for that matter. I hadn't allowed myself to look twice at any guy in over a year. Not since...

I shook my head free of my thoughts and reached down for my camera case. Luckily it was heavy duty and I didn't need to worry about my camera being damaged.

Without a second look at the guy that had knocked me over I dusted the dirt off my camera case and walked away. He might've been hot, but I wasn't going down that road.

He jogged after me. Of course. "Whoa, whoa, whoa," he grabbed my arm, "you're not getting away that fast."

I looked at him and then at the spot where we'd fallen. There was a football lying there and I assumed it was the reason he'd run in to me.

"Uh," I pointed to the fallen ball, "it looks to me like you have a game to get back to." My pulse thudded in my throat at the feel of his hand on my arm. I felt a light sweat break out across my skin. I couldn't understand my body's reaction to the stranger. For the first time in a year I felt...*alive*. It made no sense.

I pulled my arm from his hold, since he still hadn't let go. Unfortunately it did nothing to alleviate the feelings he produced inside me.

He saw the ball and looked behind him. That's when I noticed the other sweaty guys watching us. They were all good looking but they had nothing on the Adonis in front of me.

"They can wait," he grinned, looking boyish. "What's your name?"

I couldn't understand why Hottie-McHot-Pants was talking to me. I was nothing special. From the looks of him he had to be a junior or a senior and I was a freshman. Besides, if he was interested in an easy lay he needed to look elsewhere.

"Why do you want to know?" I countered.

He chuckled. "I mean, I did lay on top of you, so I figured I should at least know your name."

My cheeks heated further and I bit down on my tongue. Something told me he wasn't going to leave me alone until I told him my name. "Rachael," I answered automatically. "But I prefer to be called Rae," I hastened to add.

"Rae," he repeated, a small smile causing his lips to crook at the corners, "I like it." He held out his hand. "I'm Cade."

I looked at his hand and then at his face before taking a step back. "I didn't ask for your name."

He let his hand fall and smiled like he wasn't at all upset by my actions. Chuckling he said, "Well, now you know it."

Giving him an awkward smile, I turned to leave.

I only made it three steps before he called, "Rae?"

I swiveled around to face him and tilted my head to the side. "Yeah?"

"I'll see you around."

It wasn't a question. It was a statement. I could tell Cade was the very determined type. Unfortunately for him, I was very determined not to know him or anyone for that matter. I was here to get my education and disappear again. I wasn't looking for any connections. Connections meant feelings, and feelings meant attachments, and attachments made you do stupid things.

I'd lost the piece of paper with my dorm information and I almost went back to get it. But since I had it memorized, and going back meant taking the chance of running into Cade again, I decided not to.

The amount of people bustling around campus made me feel a bit uncomfortable, but it was easier to blend in and appear normal so I'd have to learn to deal with it.

I jogged up the steps of my dorm building and breezed inside.

I was nervous, but you wouldn't know it if you saw me. I was a master at concealing my emotions.

Muttering my room number under my breath, I stopped outside the door when I found it.

I took a deep, steadying breath, and wrapped my hand around the knob.

This was it.

This was the moment that would forever change my life.

I knew it.

And then I walked into an explosion of Pepto-Bismol.

"What. The. Fuck?" I gasped, looking around at all the pink.

Pink bedspread. Pink rug. Pink pillows. Pink blanket. Pink chair.

Pink everything.

"My eyes!" I cried as I slapped a hand over my face.

"You must be my roommate!" An overly chipper voice sing-songed.

I lowered my hand and— "Gah!" I gasped in shock. The pretty strawberry blonde in front of me even wore a pink shirt. Thank God her shorts weren't pink or I might've had a heart attack. Death by Over Exposure to the Color Pink—now that was a headline.

I couldn't believe I was going to have to live with *this* for the next ten or so months of my life. Kill. Me. Now.

I looked down at my dark hair and black clothes. I didn't see how I was going to get along with the Barbie Doll in front of me. We were clearly polar opposites.

"I'm Thea," she held out a hand. What was up with everyone wanting to shake my hand today?

Skirting around her, I headed towards the plain side of the small room.

She followed me, either oblivious to the brush off or ignoring it. "You must be Rachael."

"Rae," I corrected her, dropping my bag on the bed and refusing to turn around. "I prefer to be called Rae."

"Oh, okay. Rae is a pretty name. I mean, so is Rachael, but Rae is cooler. I—"

"Do you ever stop talking? Or breathe?" I wheeled around to find her all up in my personal space.

"Sorry," she frowned. "I'm nervous."

"Obviously," I muttered. "Look, Thea?" She nodded. "I'm not here to make friends. So, don't expect any late night talks with me, or nail painting, or whatever else it is you've conjured up in your head."

"Oh." Her face fell.

I turned back to my duffel bag and dumped my clothes on the bare bed. I needed to go back out to my car and get everything else. My mom had made sure I had everything I needed, since she knew I'd never do any shopping on my own. I had changed a lot in the last year, and I no longer cared about much of anything.

I hadn't always been such a depressed person, but then life dealt me a pretty shitty card and I handled it my own way. Nothing I did could make me forget that day.

Once all my clothes were put away, I headed towards the door.

"Where are you going?" Thea spoke up from where she lounged on her bed. I still had to repress my gag reflex from all the pink.

"To my car," I answered, glaring at her.

"Cool, you want some help?" She asked, bouncing up. Before I could answer, she invited herself by saying, "Okay, good."

She was like an over eager golden retriever. I didn't quite know what to do with her peppy personality compared to my doom and gloom one. Something told me this was going to be a long year.

As we walked through the building, she said, "My brother goes to school here. He's kind of a big deal."

"Is that so?" I asked, not interested at all in hearing about her brother.

"Yeah, he's the quarterback of the football team," she bounced along.

"Is that important? I don't really like football."

She stopped walking and grabbed my arm. Her mouth hung open in shock. "How do you not like football?"

I shrugged. "I just don't."

In another lifetime I had liked lots of things that I didn't anymore.

"Are you from here?"

Here happened to be Colorado.

I huffed, irritated with all her questions. "Yes."

"And you don't like football?" She gaped. "But it's like...necessary to the way of life."

I snorted and tilted my head. "*Oxygen* is necessary for life, not football."

She shook her head and started walking. I didn't know where she was going since she had no idea which car belonged to me.

I pointed to my car when we reached it. "It's that one."

"It's cute," she smiled.

I laughed at that. Cute was certainly not the word anyone would ever use to describe my clunker of a car. Looking at Barbie I was pretty sure she probably drove a cute little Volkswagen. I had a cute car once, but that had been before.

Before what?

Before I destroyed everything.

With Thea's help it wouldn't be necessary to make another trip out to my car. We walked back to our dorm and I noticed the guys playing football were gone. Maybe if I were a normal girl I'd tell Thea about Cade. Then we'd laugh and talk about how hot he was. But I wasn't normal, not anymore.

Luckily, Thea didn't talk much on the way back.

She ended up spending several hours on her computer while I fixed up my side of the room. There was nothing personal on my side. It didn't scream *This is Rachael Wilder's Room!* It could have been any girl's room on any campus at any school. The day that ruined my life effectively stripped me of my identity. I ghosted along, a fragment of the girl I used to be. I think my parent's had hoped college would snap me out of this 'phase', but day one was a resounding failure.

"I like your comforter," Thea said, looking over at my side of the room.

I eyed her bubblegum confection of a bedspread and looked down at my gray and yellow one. "Yeah, it's the life of the party."

She let out a laugh and looked around at all the pink. "I guess we can't all be as bright and colorful."

"And thank God for that," I cracked a smile, smoothing my hand over the bedspread before sitting down. "One of us has to be tame."

"So," she bit her lip, closing the lid on her laptop, "I was wondering if you'd want to go to a pool party with me?"

I narrowed my eyes. "How on earth is there already a party at this place? Isn't today the first move-in day?"

"It's not tonight," she corrected me. "It's Sunday, and it's kind of a big deal around here. Only certain people get to go, because it's invite only. Since my brother is, well my brother, I was invited, but I won't know anyone but him and his friends and I don't want to be alone. Please, come?"

A pool party was *not* my thing, and I hadn't worn a bikini in a year. Looking at her pitiful face and pleading eyes made it impossible to say no.

"Fine, I'll go on one condition," I warned, staring her down so she didn't get too excited.

"Thank you! Whatever it is, I don't care!" She clapped her hands together.

"I'm not swimming," I told her. "I *can't* swim," I added, to avoid any possible questions about why I didn't want to swim.

"What do you mean you can't swim?" Her perky nose scrunched together. "Everyone knows how to swim."

"Not me," I sighed. I *could* swim, but I wasn't the strongest swimmer. The real reason for not swimming had more to do with not wanting anyone to see the scar on my abdomen than with my weak swimming abilities.

She frowned. "Well, that's fine. Most girls lounge around anyway or at least that's what my brother said, but he probably just doesn't want me to wear a bikini. He gets all pissy when guys look at me," she rolled her eyes. "Typical brother."

I didn't have a brother, so I didn't know. I shrugged, because she seemed to want some kind of response.

Thea stood from her bed and stretched her stiff muscles. "I'm starving. Do you want to grab something to eat?"

Food. I'd completely forgotten about dinner...and lunch for that matter. All I'd had at breakfast was an apple. My mom would've clucked her tongue and given me a lecture for already failing to take care of myself on the first day of school.

I was a bit afraid to agree to go with Thea, though. Despite my warning, she seemed all too eager to band together and become besties.

But I'd hate myself if, God forbid, I let her go by herself and something awful happened to her. I didn't need a fourth death on my hands. Yes, fourth.

"Fine," I agreed grumpily. "Let's go."

She smiled and tucked a piece of her strawberry blonde hair behind her ear. She grabbed her purse—and guess what? It was pink. Of course. Its bright color was a stark contrast to my skull and crossbones messenger bag.

Thea and I headed to the dining hall. I was surprised when she didn't fill every second with chatter. Instead, it was almost peaceful walking across campus with her at my side. She didn't know who I was or what I had done. We were strangers and she couldn't judge me for my sins. There was something comforting in that. For the last year I'd hated myself and the looks from others hadn't helped in that—seeing the judgment in their eyes. My parents and therapist always assured me that what happened wasn't my fault, but that was a lie. I might not have been in prison but I was stuck behind bars of my own creation.

I missed the old Rae—or Rachael as I was called then. I missed the girl that laughed and smiled with her friends. I missed the girl that loved her parents and didn't resent them. I missed the girl that always looked for the positive in life. I missed *everything* about the old me, but I killed her when I killed *them*.

"Rae!" Thea called and I halted in my steps. I turned around to look at her and found her standing outside two glass double doors of a brick building. "The dining hall is this way," she nodded at the building.

Oh.

I backtracked hastily.

"It's okay," Thea smiled, despite the fact that I hadn't apologized from my mistake, "I wouldn't know where anything is if it wasn't for my brother." She opened the door and I followed behind her.

"You talk about your brother a lot, don't you?" I commented, heading to the counter. I wrinkled my nose in distaste at the cheeseburger they were serving for dinner. If that was a cheeseburger than I was a duck. I picked up a bowl of salad. That seemed like the safer of the two options. Thea picked that as well.

I followed her to a table and took the seat across from her.

"I love my brother, so why wouldn't I talked about him?"

I lifted my head, confused at first until I realized she was answering my question. I shrugged indifferently and took a bite of salad.

"You don't talk much," she stared at me.

I shrugged again. "I don't have much to say."

"Everyone has something to say." She countered with a raised brow.

"Not everyone."

She sighed heavily and tossed her salad around with the fork. She was growing frustrated with me and I didn't blame her. If roles were reversed and I had to deal with me I'd get huffy too.

After a few minutes of tense silence she spoke. Her pale green eyes seared me as she stared at me, her lips turned down in a frown. "You know, we don't have to be best friends but we do have to live together. We should at least try to make it as civil as possible and try to get along."

"I thought I was trying," I grumbled. I looked away from her eyes and began to pick at the silvery polish on my nails.

She blew out a breath, causing her bangs to flutter against her forehead. Finally she cracked a smile. "If that's what you call trying then you're doing a pretty lousy job."

"So...I don't get an A for effort?"

"Definitely not." She rested her head in her hand. "No stickers for you."

"Stickers?" I asked with a raised brow.

"Yeah," she laughed, and it was light and musical sounding. "You know, like teachers give school kids stickers when they do something good."

I screwed my face up in displeasure. "What kind of school did you go to? No," I held up finger, "let me guess, some preppy private school."

Her cheeks turned pink—her favorite color, how appropriate.

"How'd you know?" She asked.

I narrowed my eyes at her fancy clothes. "You have rich kid written all over you."

I left out the part that I was one of those rich kids. I just didn't dress or act like it anymore.

"Is it really that obvious?" She paled, her hands fluttering over her body.

It was almost funny. *Almost.*

"No," I said to put her out of her misery. It really wasn't as obvious as I made it sound, but since I came from an upper-class family I could always pick out people who ran in the same circles.

"Oh good." She visibly relaxed and we finished our meal in silence.

It had been twilight when we left our dorm but on the way back it was completely dark. Luckily, there were lights every few feet so you didn't have to worry about monsters lurking in the shadows. I don't know why I was worried. After all, all the monsters lived inside me now.

"I'm going to bed," Thea announced when we stepped into our room, "it's been a long day."

I nodded in agreement. She grabbed some pajamas and went to change in the bathroom. We were lucky that our bathroom was only shared between the two of us. I wouldn't have been pleased if we'd had to share with another dorm. I didn't like people in my space and it was bad enough that I'd been stuck with a double.

I'd begged my parents to pull some strings to get me a single, but they refused. They told me I needed to stop locking myself away in suffering and make new friends. "Live your life, Rachael," my mom told me before I left, her hands on my shoulders, "just because they're dead doesn't mean you are."

But she was wrong. I was dead.

chapter two

THEA AND I HAD BOTH BEEN EXHAUSTED after moving in and went to bed early. When I woke up on Saturday morning it was still dark outside.

I couldn't remember the last time I ever slept in. My body ran on very little sleep. Sometimes I thought it was a miracle I hadn't fallen over dead yet. I knew that living, and suffering for what I'd done, was my punishment. It's why I was still here. Living while my friends were dead.

I tried so hard not to remember anything from *before*, but it was impossible.

That day was always going to haunt me. There was no flushing it from my memory. I had to learn to live with it—to survive.

I scrubbed my hands over my face and let out a soft groan so I didn't disturb Thea. The last thing I wanted to do was deal with her at this time of the morning. I needed some time to myself before she woke up.

I slipped out of bed and into my running clothes as quietly as possible.

Rachael didn't run, but Rae did.

I found that when I ran I couldn't think about anything else. My thoughts ceased to exist. When I ran I was free from my sins.

I opened the door and eased it closed so that she couldn't hear the lock click. Hopefully she'd still be sleeping when I got back. Classes didn't start until Monday, so it wasn't like she'd have to get up early.

I moved through the building like a ghost and out the double doors.

I stopped on the steps and inhaled the crisp morning air. It was chilly, but I didn't mind. Unfortunately, I knew that meant there wouldn't be many mornings left where I could run outside. I'd have to use the school's gym—I wouldn't like it, but I refused to give up running.

After a few stretches I took off.

Immediately I felt that rush I always got—like I was in control. I hadn't been in control of my life in a long time.

My feet thumped against the concrete sidewalk as I jogged around campus. I kept my pace steady, but a little on the fast side. When I first started running I used to run so hard and fast that I'd throw up. But now my body was used to it and I could run for hours without getting tired.

I began to sweat, despite the cool air, and my hair stuck to my damp forehead.

My breath was heavy and the steady beat of my heart in my chest soothed me.

I was so absorbed in the humming of my body that I didn't notice when someone fell into step beside me, but soon their presence became overwhelming.

I flicked my gaze over to the stranger and found that it was no stranger at all.

It was the tackler. *Cade*, he'd said his name was.

My steps faltered and I tripped.

Down I went, scraping my knee against the cement. I hissed between my lips at the sharp sting.

Jesus Christ. All I did around this guy was fall. Granted, the first time he knocked me to the ground so that didn't really count.

"Are you okay?" He asked, dropping down beside me. His voice was a husky gasp as he inhaled sharply, his chest heaving with each breath. His t-shirt was damp with sweat. As was his hair. Clearly he'd been running for a while before he joined me.

I glared at him with heat in my eyes. "Why the fuck were you running beside me?"

"You looked lonely," was his response.

I narrowed my eyes. "I wasn't."

I clumsily came to my feet and started to walk, trying to shake off the stiffness in my limbs from the fall.

"Are you mad?" He asked, catching up to me easily with his long-legged stride.

I stopped in my tracks and looked up at him. "Yeah, I'm mad. That's twice you've made me fall. If this is how you pick up girls you need to try a new method. This one is seriously lacking."

He threw his head back and laughed—the kind of laugh that shakes your whole body. I liked the sound of his laugh too. It was warm and happy sounding. I never laughed anymore and I wondered if I did, would it sound like Rachael's? Or would it be different?

"You're funny."

"I was serious." I tilted my head, putting a hand on my hip.

He grinned down at me and I saw that he had a dimple in each cheek. The heavy scruff on his cheeks helped to camouflage them, but they were still there. They gave him an almost boyish appearance.

A lock of brown hair swept down to hide his blue eyes. He grinned at me, completely unfazed.

"You're different."

I looked up at him and nodded. "You're right."

He narrowed his eyes with his hands on his hips. He looked at me like I was some intricate puzzle he was trying to piece together. When he didn't say anything I started to walk away again. My legs felt okay so I started jogging.

Cade joined me once more and I wasn't even surprised.

When we circled the fountain that sat in the middle of campus I was tempted to push him in, just so he'd leave me alone. But I didn't.

Cade continued to run with me—even though I knew from his appearance he had to have already run *a lot.*

Neither of us spoke, but when you're running hard there isn't much breath for small talk.

My dorm appeared in front of me and I ran harder. I didn't say goodbye to Cade as I jogged up the steps and into the building. I felt his eyes on me though.

I swore I wasn't going to look, but when the doors closed behind me I allowed myself to turn.

He stood on the sidewalk outside the dorm, staring at where I stood—although I doubted he could actually see me.

I wondered what Cade found so fascinating about me.

Most people were afraid of me, and I didn't blame them. They should be afraid. I was a killer.

I stepped away from the door and headed up the steps to my room.

Thea was still sleeping, a light snore echoing through the room. I shook my head and grabbed my stuff so I could shower.

By the time I was done in the bathroom Thea was stretching her arms above her head and blinking sleep from her eyes.

"Did you get up early?" She yawned.

I nodded, heading to my side of the room to make my bed.

"I hate mornings." She ran her fingers through her wild and tangled hair. "Would you mind waiting for me to shower, so we can get breakfast together?"

"I can wait," I assured her.

"Great." She slowly peeled her body out of bed and grumbled unintelligibly all the way to the bathroom.

While Thea was getting ready I spent the time unpacking the last of my things—which was mostly my clothes. I hadn't brought much with me decoration wise. Looking at Thea's side of the room I thought I might have to remedy that fact, because I wasn't sure I could handle all the pink.

Thea took her sweet time doing her hair and makeup. I was about ready to throttle her by the time she said she was ready. I was starving and she was holding up progress.

I followed her out of the building and instead of turning to head towards the dining hall she went the other way.

"Where are you going?" I asked.

She shrugged. "My brother told me about this neat little diner on campus. I thought we'd check it out. My treat," she smiled.

When she looked at me like that I found it impossible to say no.

I didn't want to like her. Hell, I wanted to *hate* her. But something told me it was impossible not to like Thea. She was one of those people that were so vibrant and full of life that they were impossible to ignore.

Five minutes later we stood in front of the diner. Thea pushed open the door and a bell chimed pleasantly.

"Take a seat anywhere!" One of the waitresses called as she bustled behind the counter.

I followed Thea to a booth in the corner. The place was busy, but not too crowded.

Menus were already on the table and we each picked one up.

"Hmm," Thea hummed, "everything sounds so good. I don't know what to get."

"I think I'm going to get the waffles," I shrugged, setting the menu aside.

"Those do look good." She licked her lips as if she could taste them already. "I think I'll get them too."

By the time a waitress finally made it to us we placed our drink and food order.

When the waitress left I longed for her to return, because her departure meant I was going to be forced to talk to Thea.

"So," Thea drummed her fingers against the table, "I guess we should get to know each other, since we're going to be living together and everything."

I crossed my hands on the table and sat back. "Is that really necessary?"

Her lips quirked. "Yeah, it kind of is." Leaning forward, her voice lowered. "I know you said you don't want to be friends, but frankly I think that's stupid, Rae. We're going to be living together for quite a while and we should try to get along. I can tell you're the type of person that pushes people away and while I can respect that to an extent, I refuse to tiptoe around my roommate."

Whoa. This girl was nothing like what I thought when I first met her. I'd thought then that she was a clueless bimbo, but she saw more than I gave her credit for.

"Okay, then," I shrugged, hoping I wasn't making the wrong decision, "what do you want to know?"

"What are you studying?"

Easy enough. I hadn't expected that. I figured she'd go right for the jugular and ask me why I was so fucked up. Thea was full of surprises.

"Photography. You?" I didn't see the point in going into deeper details with her. The less I said the better.

She bit her plump bottom lip and looked down at the table. "Undecided." Her eyes flicked up to meet mine. "Yeah, I'm one of *those* people."

I gave her what I hoped was a reassuring smile. "There's nothing wrong with not having it figured out yet. You'll get there."

She cracked a small smile in return. She reached over for the saltshaker and slid it back and forth across the table between her hands. "I hope so. Sometimes it really sucks living in my brother's shadow. He's got it all figured out and he's good at everything. I'm just me...and sometimes I don't even know who I am."

I tried my best to hide my surprise at her honesty, but I failed.

She let out a soft laugh that held no humor. "Sorry to get so deep on you." Her eyes flooded with sadness. "I don't have many friends...actually, I don't have any real friends. Most girls just want to get close to me because of my brother. But you...you don't know him. I feel like I can trust you."

"I'm not a good person," I told her, swallowing thickly. "You don't want me as a friend. I've done things. *Horrible* things. I—"

Thea shook her head. "No. I think you're wrong. I think you're beating yourself up over something that's stupid."

I doubted killing three people counted as stupid, but I wasn't telling her that. I didn't want to see the fear in her eyes, or the hatred. I'd gotten enough of that back home. The whispers and glances had often become overwhelming. It was why I spent the majority of the last year locked inside my bedroom.

"I'm not a good person, Thea," I repeated. I needed her to understand that.

Her eyes softened and she reached for my hand where it rested on the table. I flinched at the touch, but refused to pull my hand back.

"You say that, Rae, but I think you're wrong. Often times it's all too easy to dilute ourselves into believing one thing than it is to see the truth in our own eyes. I may not know you that well, but I do see you. I see the pain in your eyes and I know something haunts you. We all have demons, but the thing is we usually think they're worse than they really are."

I opened my mouth to reply, but was cut off by the waitress appearing with our food.

While we ate Thea chatted about random things—the campus, her brother, how nervous she was for classes. I think she hoped she could distract me from our previous conversation, but it wasn't working.

I wanted to dismiss her words, but I couldn't, because a part of me wondered if she was right.

I knew what I'd done was wrong, horrible, despicable, and a bunch of other things, but was I torturing myself because it was easier than moving on?

chapter three

SUNDAY STARTED MUCH THE SAME as Saturday had. I got up early, before the sun rose, and went outside to run.

Cade joined me halfway through.

We didn't speak today and I tried my best to ignore him. I was learning that Cade wasn't easily ignored, though.

Just like yesterday, I turned to look at him once I was safe in the dorm.

He stood watching me, arms crossed over his chest and his head tilted to the side.

I backed away and up the steps, and still I felt his eyes on me. It wasn't an unpleasant feeling and while it should've been creepy, it didn't seem that way. I wished I could figure out what he wanted from me, but I didn't dare to ask.

I was considering changing my running schedule, but after some deep thought about it I decided against it. I wanted to run in the mornings and I wasn't going to let Cade ruin my schedule. I could ignore him or avoid him. Problem solved.

Back in my room I grabbed my towel, clean clothes, and my shower caddy.

If yesterday served as the norm, Thea wouldn't be up for another hour or two.

I was dreading this afternoon—aka The Pool Party.

I hated myself for agreeing to attend. Parties were not my thing. Especially ones involving water and half-naked people.

I pushed all thoughts of the hell I'd have to endure later out of my mind and let the hot water relax my sore muscles.

Soapsuds clung to my skin and hair before swirling down the drain.

Around and around.

Away.

Gone.

I stared at those white suds like they held the key to the universe.

I wished I could leave so easily.

Just disappear and cease to exist.

My fingers absentmindedly rubbed against the scar on my abdomen. I should've died, but I didn't.

Miracle, the doctors said.

Curse, I chanted.

Most days the pain of my past was crippling. I'd learned to deal, but it didn't make the memories any easier to bear. I'd lost my whole life in one instant—seconds was all it took to shatter my life, and I was the one to blame for it. *I* did this to myself. I was responsible for everything. At least I could own up to it unlike some people. I accepted what I'd done. I didn't try to put blame on anyone else. Nope. This was all me.

My body began to shake as I cried.

In the safety of the shower was one of the only times I'd ever allow my emotions to get the better of me.

The water washed the tears away and the spray helped dull the sounds of my sobs.

I didn't cry much about it. Tears didn't solve anything. They didn't have magical healing powers that made everything better. They didn't erase the past, but sometimes I had to let them out.

Eventually I turned the shower off and stepped out onto the cold tile. It was brown and dingy. The whole dorm needed a good cleaning. Maybe after the pool party I could stop at the store and get some cleaning supplies.

Cleaning, like running, was good for me. It was mindless and numbing. It allowed me to focus on what was in front of me and not the horrors that haunted me every minute of every day.

I reached out and swiped my hand over the mirror, wiping away the condensation. My hazy reflection appeared before me. My eyes were red rimmed and purple shadows bruised the skin beneath them. I rarely slept these days and when I did nightmares haunted me. Well, not *nightmares*. Memories.

Memories were crippling.

In the last year I'd often wished for a magic wand that would erase my memory and take away all the painful things. The problem was *everything* was painful—the good, the bad, *all of it*.

I turned away, not able to take another second of looking at the girl in the mirror. I hated her and I didn't want to be her.

I wanted to be someone new.

With a sigh I got dressed. Despite the last of the summer heat lingering in the air I dressed in ratty black jeans, a black t-shirt with a band name on it—a band I didn't even know if I liked or not—and tied a checkered black and red shirt around my waist.

I lined my eyes in heavy black eyeliner—a shield from the world around me.

My dark brown hair curled around my shoulders.

I was ready to face the world, even if I didn't want to.

I pushed open the bathroom door and found Thea sitting up in bed. She stretched her arms above her head and yawned.

"Morning," she smiled brightly.

I nodded in acknowledgement.

"Are you still coming to the party?"

"Yeah," I sighed. It would be rude to ditch her now and I was working hard at trying to be nice.

"I'm going to shower and go get something to eat. You wanna come with me?"

"Sounds good," I forced a smile, sitting on the end of my bed. I knew if I was smart I would've left without her. I didn't need Thea complicating my life. But selfishly I didn't want to have to face the crowded campus alone, so that's why I agreed.

She got up and gathered her stuff before going into the bathroom. A moment later I heard the shower come on.

I sat back on my bed and grabbed my computer. I flicked through some old photos, marking ones I wanted to edit later.

An hour later Thea was ready to go.

I laced up my boots and followed her out the door.

The dining hall was as loud as a concert when we arrived. Although, a concert I would've enjoyed. This...not so much.

I grabbed an orange and a bowl of cereal—Trix, because those delicious things weren't just for kids.

Thea and I sat at a table with a few other people. They didn't acknowledge us, and we pretended like they didn't exist. That was college for you.

I didn't mind being ignored, though. In fact, I preferred it. I didn't like having to fake being interested in conversation when I wasn't. I was *trying* to make an effort with Thea, to at least keep things civil since we had to live with each other, but there was no way we'd ever be best friends forever.

After all, forever never lasts.

"So," Thea started, taking a bite of blueberry muffin.

I raised a single brow, waiting for her to continue.

"Are you wearing that to the pool party?" She eyed my clothes.

"Yeah." What was wrong with what I was wearing? I wasn't going to swim.

She wrinkled her nose with distaste, but didn't say anything for which I was thankful.

"I'm glad you're coming with me," she smiled genuinely, seeming to forget my clothing choice. "Parties like this aren't my thing," she sighed heavily. "They're not really my brother's thing either, but he has a part to play. At least that's what he tells me."

I pushed my bowl of cereal to the side of the table and started peeling my orange. "Do I get to meet this mysterious brother of yours?"

She laughed, flipping her curly strawberry blonde hair over her shoulder. "Of course."

"You seem fond of him," I commented.

"I am."

Something told me those were the only words I was going to get out of her. She didn't know, but those two words gave me a wealth of knowledge. They told me that her parent's probably weren't great. Either they were abusive or strict. Thea had obviously come to rely on her older brother. She looked up to him.

Sometimes I wished I had a sibling I felt like that with, but then after everything that happened to me I'm sure I would've pushed them away like I did everyone else.

I couldn't bear to be close to anyone anymore.

Emotions were complicated and messy.

"Do you have any brothers or sisters?" Thea asked suddenly.

I shook my head and grinned. "Nope. I'm perfect. My parent's had no need to reproduce a second time."

Thea's lips quirked into a smile and finally she laughed. "Wow. I didn't know you had it in you," she sobered. "You actually made a joke. I'm impressed. I'll have to tell that one to my brother. He'll argue that he's the perfect one and I'm the pesky little sister."

"I doubt that." I might not have met her brother yet, but from everything she said it was obvious that they were close and he loved her.

We finished eating and headed back to our dorm so Thea could get ready.

The fact that she needed to primp again baffled me. She'd already spent an hour getting ready before we could get breakfast. I couldn't fault her too much. Rachael had been the same way—concerned about having her hair perfect, her makeup done, and her clothes pristine. Rae didn't give a shit.

She came out of the bathroom with a tank top and jean skirt overtop of a bikini. Thank God it didn't take her another hour to get ready or I might've lost my mind.

"What time do we have to go?" I asked.

She looked at the clock beside her bed. "Now."

"Great." There was no enthusiasm in my tone.

Since Thea didn't have a car, I drove. That was fine by me. It put me in control. If this thing sucked I could leave whenever I wanted.

We ended up at a community pool that had been closed off for the party. The place was already packed and I felt my anxiety grow. My hand tightened around the steering wheel—like as if I could sear myself to it and not have to go. This was the last place I wanted to be. Why had I agreed to this? Oh right, I was trying to be a good person.

Taking a deep breath I slipped out of my car and followed Thea over to the fence. She batted her eyes and told the guy standing there her name.

He waved us inside.

What the hell was this? A club? The guy was literally holding a clipboard and crossing off names.

Thea said hi to someone and then hissed under her breath to me, "God, I hate her. She's such a bitch."

"Oh look!" She clapped her hands together excitedly and pointed at two lounge chairs that were free. "Perfect spot!"

"Yippee," I groaned.

She looked at me over her shoulder and laughed. "Most people would die to be at this party."

"I'm not most people."

"No, you're not," she agreed.

She dropped her tote bag on one of the lounges and I took the other. I looked extremely out of place in my grunge clothes compared to all the preppy hipsters surrounding me. Several people gave me dirty looks. I resisted the urge to show them my middle finger.

"Ignore them," Thea said, catching on to what was happening.

"I am," I told her.

I didn't mind people staring at me when they didn't know me. It was when they heard my story and looked at me with pity or horror that I couldn't stand it.

"Oh! Look! There's my brother!" Thea cried. "Cade!" She called. "Cade! Come over here and meet my friend!"

Ice slithered through my veins, wrapping around my heart and nearly stopping it.

First off: Cade? It couldn't be...but I didn't imagine there were very many Cade's.

Secondly: friend? Since when were Thea and I friends? I didn't know much about her besides the fact that she had a brother, didn't have a major, and had horrible taste in colors.

"Hi," a warm voice chuckled softly, "I'm Cade Montgomery."

I knew that voice. Fuck.

I looked up slowly and there he was. "Cade." He stood there smiling cockily, those dimples winking at me. His blue eyes sparkled with laughter—and I wasn't sure if he was laughing *at* me, or with me, at the irony that he was Thea's brother. Seriously, what were the freaking odds?

His smile widened as I stared at him. Despite introducing himself he'd known it was me sitting here. "Rae," he replied. His eyes skimmed over my dark heavy clothes, but he made no comment on my lack of swimwear.

Thea's mouth dropped as she looked between us. "You two know each other?"

Cade started to reply but I cut him off. "If being tackled to the ground by this ogre counts as knowing each other then the answer is yes."

Thea's brows furrowed. "You tackled her? I'm confused. Ohhh, is 'tackled' a code word for sex? I'm not good at reading between the lines."

I shook my head. "He tackled me. As in the normal sense of the word tackled."

"Why'd you do that?" She turned to glare at her brother.

"It was an accident," he chuckled, scrubbing his hand through his longish hair. "I can see that you've recovered just fine." He looked me up and down.

I rolled my eyes.

"So," he smiled slowly, "how've you been Rae?"

I resisted the urge to snort since he'd seen me this morning. True, it wasn't like we had chatted while we ran, but his question was still ridiculous.

I stretched my legs out on the lounger and closed my eyes. "I've been just dandy, and right now I'm in need of a nap." I wasn't one for small talk. Small talk led to long talk—was that even a thing?— and I wasn't here to make friends.

I cracked on eye open and found Cade grinning down at me.

"Stop staring at me," I groaned, opening both eyes. "I can't sleep with you watching me."

He chuckled and lifted his arms, encompassing the chaos around him. "How can anyone sleep with all this noise?" He crouched down beside me, in the space between the lounger I occupied and the one Thea was stretched out on. Lowering his voice so that there was no chance of Thea hearing, he said, "You can't avoid me, Rae."

"I'm not trying to," I glared.

He stood up slowly and smiled crookedly. "See you in the morning," he whispered.

And then he was gone.

Air whooshed out of my lungs. I hadn't even realized I was holding my breath.

"What the hell is going on between you and my brother?" Thea asked, slipping her sunglasses down her nose so that I couldn't avoid her gaze.

"I have no idea."

And that was the honest to God truth.

"I'm going to get a drink," Thea sighed, standing up and adjusting her bikini top so that her ample chest was covered. "You want anything?"

"Something strong."

She laughed. "I'm sure that won't be problem."

I received more stares once Thea left my side, but no one bothered me. I leaned back on the lounger and took several steady breaths to calm myself.

Once upon a time this had been my scene. My friends had been just like these people. And I'd been the girl over there in the pool clinging to her boyfriend's shoulders.

But not anymore.

Apparently I'd been too happy and life had seen fit to toss a bucket full of misery my way.

The sunlight bathed Brett in a halo, making his red hair glow. He smiled at me and walked forward.

"I was beginning to think you weren't coming."

"I'd never miss your birthday." I smiled as he wrapped his arms around me and kissed me squarely on the mouth in front of everyone.

"Stop sucking face," Sarah groaned, "the rest of us want to party."

With a laugh Brett pulled away, keeping a hold on my waist. "It's good to see you too, Sarah."

"It's hot and I'm going swimming. Are you losers coming?" She looked at Brett and me, then at Hannah who hovered somewhere behind us shyly. "Come on," she coaxed, stripping off her clothes down to her bikini.

Without waiting for any of us to respond she ran forward and jumped into the in-ground pool at Brett's house. The pool was large, but with all the people at the party currently swimming it seemed smaller.

Brett grinned down at me. "You ready, Rachael?"

I smiled nervously. Brett knew I wasn't a very good swimmer and it always made me nervous getting in the water.

"You won't let go?" I asked, a slight begging tone to my voice.

"I'll never let go," he promised.

I nodded and he took my hand. Together— because the two of us had been inseparable since we were in diapers—we ran forward and jumped into the water.

Beneath its cool depths Brett's arms wrapped around me and his lips smashed against mine.

For the first time in my life I wasn't afraid to drown.

Thea sat down, a peculiar look on her face. "What's wrong?" She asked.

"Nothing," I sighed, taking the drink she offered me, and shaking off the remnants of the memory.

I took a sip. I wasn't sure what it was, but it was definitely strong.

"Cade said not to accept a drink from anyone but him unless you get one yourself."

I raised an eyebrow at her and lifted my drink. "Am I safe accepting this one from you?"

She laughed. "Yes. You're hot and all, but I prefer guys."

Laughter bubbled out of me. It felt strange and foreign, but good at the same time.

Thea's smile was pleased, almost as if she sensed I didn't laugh often.

I hadn't wanted to make friends here.

I wanted to lay low, get my degree, and get the hell out of here.

But watching Thea and the other rowdy college students around us, I couldn't help but wish for more. The real college experience. Not what I had planned to do which was basically shut myself up in my room when I wasn't in class.

I knew it was stupid, but I felt like if I went on and lived my life that I was betraying the people I lost. Their lives were cut short, so shouldn't mine be?

My therapist disagreed. Like my parents, he'd spent the last year or so trying to convince me to move on. I couldn't.

I knew I had disappointed my parents with my inability to let it go. I hated seeing the pain etched on their faces, knowing that I was responsible for putting it there.

I knew they hoped that college would be good for me—that getting away from home and the glares from everyone that knew what I'd done would give me a chance to 'spread my wings and fly'. My mom's words, not mine.

Being away did help, but I still couldn't escape the crushing memories. Not just what happened on that fateful day a year ago, but what happened before. I couldn't escape the good times or the bad times and it was crippling.

"Do you ever think about the future?" Brett asked as we lay in the tall grass, gazing up at the stars.

I curled my body around his, resting my head against his chest where I could hear the steady thumping of his heart.

"What do you mean? Like, college?" I asked.

"No, about us..." He whispered, his fingers tangling in my hair.

Brett and I had been best friends since we were infants. We grew up in the houses next to each other, and since neither of us had siblings and were the same age we'd always played together. As we grew older that friendship turned into more. I couldn't imagine my life without Brett in it.

"Well," I wiggled, trying to get comfortable, "I see myself marrying you one day, preferably after college, and having cute little redhead babies," I laughed, reaching up to tangle my fingers in his hair.

"I want that too, Rachael. I want to grow old with you by my side." Maybe it was a strong declaration to make at sixteen years old, but I knew Brett meant it. I never doubted his feelings for me. I knew he was it for me. I would never love another guy the way I loved Brett. It just wasn't possible. This was once in a lifetime.

"Hey," Thea snapped her fingers in front of my face. Once she had my attention she asked, "Where'd you go?"

"Nowhere," I sighed, looking away so she couldn't see the moisture in my eyes. I didn't know what was making the memories so much worse today, but I had a pretty good idea that it had something to do with Cade and the feelings he stirred inside me.

She sat back on the lounger and eyed me. "You zone out a lot," she stated.

It was true.

"Yeah," I agreed. There was no point in lying.

She stared at me as if she was waiting for me to elaborate. She shouldn't hold her breath.

Luckily I was saved from saying anything more thanks to the guy who showed up beside Thea. He grabbed a chair and smiled at me before turning his attention to her. Immediately her fair cheeks flared with a blush. She sat up and leaned towards him. I didn't think she even noticed that she was trying to get closer to him.

I couldn't blame her though. The guy was gorgeous, but he didn't compare to Cade in my opinion.

He had light brown hair and heavy scruff covered his cheeks and chin but it wasn't enough to be considered a beard. He had searing brown eyes and an easy smile. He seemed friendly enough and not a creeper. Thea seemed to know him.

"Hi, Xander," she looked up at him and—I kid you not—batted her lashes.

"Thea," he nodded, fighting a grin. "You are?" He lifted his gaze to me.

"Rae," I answered, looking between the two. "Thea's roommate."

"Ah," he nodded. "I'm Xander."

"Oh," She shook her head, as if just now realizing I was still here. "This is Xander," she looked at me and pointed at the guy.

I laughed. "Yeah, he just told me."

"Oh," she said again and her cheeks reddened. "Right." Biting her lip she looked at Xander and back to me. "Xander is a friend of Cade's, we grew up together."

Now I understood. Someone was crushing on her brother's best friend. That sounded messy and complicated, but from the looks he was giving her the feelings were reciprocated.

"Interesting," I commented when it became obvious I needed to say something.

Satisfied, Thea turned back to Xander and began chatting away.

It wasn't long before another guy showed up. His name was Jacen but he went by Jace. He was good looking—I was beginning to think that was a requirement to go to this school—with straight blond hair. He had piercing green eyes and an overall broody vibe to him. A colorful tattoo covered the whole sleeve of one of his arms. He sat in a chair beside Xander, a beer bottle dangling from his fingertips. Apparently he was a friend of Cade and Xander's. Like me, he didn't seem to belong here. Not in his black jeans and white shirt. He kept glaring at anyone that stared at him for too long.

It wasn't long until Cade joined us. I didn't even see him approach. I *felt* him. His presence was that potent.

It bothered me that without even trying he'd managed to needle his way under my skin.

Instead of grabbing a chair he sat down on the end of the lounger I occupied.

I promptly pulled my legs up to my chest.

He chuckled, his gaze flicking my way as a strand of hair fell into his eyes. A knowing smile tugged up his lips.

He didn't acknowledge my reaction for which I was thankful.

He fell into easy conversation with the others and I ignored them for the most part. While they chatted I looked around at all the people gathered. There had to be at least a hundred people. I'd been to large parties before, but now I just felt out of place. I wasn't sure where I belonged anymore. I was lost, floating away at sea.

Eventually I brought my attention back to the group gathered around me. The last thing I wanted to do was look like I'd zoned out again. Thea was going to start thinking I was weird if she didn't already.

I was uncomfortable in my current position. I turned so I was sitting sideways on the lounger.

Cade used my movement as an opportunity to scoot closer to me.

My body tensed up at his proximity.

His arm brushed against mine and I shivered.

I wasn't sure if I loved or hated my body's reaction to him. I was going with hated, because it was completely unfair that one guy could affect me in such a way.

Not even Brett—I cringed as I thought of his name—had made my body react like this. I was drawn to him like a fly to honey—which only ended in disaster.

I wasn't dumb or naïve enough to believe that Cade saw something in me. Guys like him—hot jocks—wanted one thing and one thing only and that was an easy lay. He wouldn't get that with me.

"So, Rae," Cade turned to look at me, his blue eyes sparkling, "what brings you to Huntley University?"

What a stupid question.

"Uh...I wanted a degree and college seemed like the most logical place to achieve that."

Jace's lips quirked in a smile and Xander chuckled.

"You're a sassy little thing, aren't you?" Cade grinned.

Thea watched her brother and I with a careful gaze.

Little thing? Considering I was five-foot ten I couldn't remember the last time I'd been described as *little*.

I eyed Cade, but he was unfazed by my glare. He was something else.

"It was a compliment," he finally said.

"If that's what you call a compliment then you're really shitty at them."

Xander snorted and Jace actually cracked a full smile.

"Excuse me," I stood up. I didn't know where I was going. I just knew I had to get away. Cade was making my brain fuzzy.

I hadn't made it far when some idiot bumped into me. A small scream escaped my throat as I stumbled.

There was no ground to break my fall.

I went straight into the swimming pool.

I heard Thea's scream just before my head submerged.

Water stung my nose and since I hadn't been prepared to go face first into the pool, water entered my lungs.

My vision grew spotty and I floated down.

Sinking.

Drowning.

Gone.

The light was bright and the pain was intense.

For a moment I thought I was dead, but then I realized if that was the case everything wouldn't hurt so bad.

I slowly blinked my eyes open and the room came into focus.

A hospital.

Why was I in a hospital?

What happened?

Why couldn't I remember?

"Oh thank God!" My mom cried and crashed into my arms.

I winced and she immediately let go, apologizing profusely. "Oh, Rachael, I thought we'd lost you."

"Wh-what happened?" I tried to get my voice to work, but it came out all crackly sounding. By some miracle she understood. She appeared reluctant to say anything, but at my insistence she finally told me. With each word that left her mouth I retreated farther and farther into myself.

~e~

I gasped, coughing up water. Even once the water left my lungs I kept coughing. I knew people surrounded me but I was too embarrassed to look at them for the moment.

I slowed my breathing and tried to take steady breaths.

"Are you okay?" A warm hand landed on my shoulder.

I turned to look at Cade. He was soaked and water dripped from his shaggy hair onto my shoulder.

"Are you okay?" He asked again.

I nodded. "D-did y-you?" I stuttered, still trying to catch my breath. "Did you jump in after me?"

"Thea said you couldn't swim," he shrugged, "so of course I jumped in after you. A bit too late though. You'd already sucked down a lot of water. I had to give you mouth to mouth."

Mouth to *what?* Oh hell no. You had to be freaking kidding me. I'd been unconscious for my first kiss with Cade? Not that I wanted to kiss him, but it was still completely unfair and embarrassing. And all these people had been a witness to this. Great. I'd be the laughing stock of the whole college before I even had my first class.

Cade seemed to sense my embarrassment.

"Back up everyone," he warned with a voice that brooked no argument, "you're crowding her."

After a pause everyone backed away, except for Thea. I found myself thankful that she was still crouched by my side. I didn't know what to make of this new feeling of fondness towards my roommate. Thea had this calming quality to her and an overall sweetness that made it impossible not to like her. I wasn't looking for a friend, but something told me Thea wasn't going to stand for that.

Cade grabbed the back of my neck, his hand warm against my chilled skin, and slowly lifted my head. "Are you okay?" He asked for a third time since I'd never answered him.

I nodded slowly. "Yeah, I'm okay." I was still struggling to catch my breath, but I was otherwise unharmed. Thanks to Cade. Great, now I was indebted to him.

He wrapped his muscular arms around my shoulders and helped me up. My legs were shaky. I think I was still stunned from the events that had transpired.

"I have some spare clothes in my Jeep," he explained, guiding me towards the gate with Thea on my heels. "I don't expect you to stay, but I don't want you going back to your dorm soaking."

It really surprised me that Cade seemed to have such a caring heart. I'd always assumed jocks were selfish cocky assholes. Not this guy.

He led me over to a black Jeep Wrangler. It was jacked up on large wheels with no top on. "Hold her," he commanded Thea.

She grabbed ahold of my arm and steadied me. I kept shivering.

Cade reached into the backseat of his Jeep and pulled out a red duffel bag. He shuffled through it and pulled out a heather gray shirt. "I have some shorts in there if you want those too."

"This is fine," I said, reaching for the shirt.

He wouldn't relinquish it and I was too weak from nearly drowning to put up much fight. He laid the shirt on the driver's seat of his Jeep and reached for the one I wore.

"What the hell are you doing?" I swatted his hand away.

"Helping you," he looked at me like I'd lost my mind. Turning to Thea he asked, "How'd you guys get here?"

"Rae drove," she answered.

"Get your stuff and go get her car and bring it over here. I want you guys to go back to the dorm."

My eyes widened. I didn't want Thea to leave me alone with her brother. The guy was dangerous in a too-sexy-for-his-own-good kind of way and I didn't need any kind of temptation.

"I don't want to drive Thea away from the party," I said.

Cade grinned slowly and I knew I was in trouble. That smile spelled dangerous. "I can take you back to your dorm. Thea grab Rae's bag." I'd completely forgotten I'd left the bag where we'd been sitting.

Thea nodded, eyeing her brother and I with a shrewd look. She couldn't seem to figure us out. I saw Xander waiting for her by the gate. She seemed reluctant to leave me alone, but eventually she went to do as her brother asked.

Cade tugged at my shirt and this time I was unprepared since I'd been watching Thea abandon me.

He managed to get it off of me before I could stop him and I knew the moment he saw.

Air hissed between his teeth and his fingers hesitantly brushed against the raised pink skin on my stomach.

"What happened?" He asked. I was surprised that there was no disgust in his tone.

"Something I don't want to talk about," I growled angrily. I didn't like for people to see the scar. It raised too many questions I didn't want to answer.

Cade sighed and his damp hair fell over his forehead. "Okay."

I balked in surprise. I couldn't believe he was letting it go so easily. He helped me into the dry shirt that was much too large. It smelled like him—fresh cut grass and rain. He pulled his own shirt off and tossed it into the duffel bag. He didn't put a dry one on which meant that his perfect chest was on display for me. A man's chest shouldn't be a work of art, but Cade's was.

"I don't have another clean shirt." He explained when he saw me staring. Somehow, I doubted that.

Thea returned with my bag and handed it to me.

"I can take you back to the dorms if you want me to," she said timidly.

"I'm fine," I assured her. "I can drive myself." I was already pulling my car keys out of my bag.

"Nice try." Cade snatched the keys from my hand and tossed them to his sister. "*You*," he pointed at her, "can drive her car home when you're ready to leave. I'm taking Rae back to the dorms."

I resisted the urge to stomp my foot like a child. I did not want to be alone with Cade Montgomery.

But nobody argued with Cade, that much was obvious. What he said was law around here.

Fuck that.

He could take my keys but he couldn't take my legs. I was walking back to school. It might've been an eight mile walk but I didn't care.

While he was distracted with talking to Thea I walked away.

I hadn't even made it off the property when he caught up to me.

He grabbed me around my waist and tossed me over his shoulder.

"Put me down!" I beat his back, trying to wiggle out of his grasp.

He chuckled. That's right, he *laughed*. That was his only response.

He opened the passenger door of his Jeep, sat me down, and buckled me in.

He climbed in the driver's side and sped out of the parking lot before I could finagle my way out of the car.

"Who are you?" I snapped.

"I'm Cade," he answered with a smile. "Did your tumble into the swimming pool cause you to lose your memory?"

"There's nothing wrong with my memory. I was just assuming you were the President or some member of the royal family with how fucking bossy you are."

He chuckled, speeding towards the dorms. "I have never met a girl like you before."

"I can't figure you out," I muttered, not even bothering to comment on his previous statement. Of course he'd never met a girl like me. Most girls weren't murderers.

"Elaborate." He glanced my way with a crooked smile.

I huffed a sigh and glared at his profile. Handsome or not, he was currently pissing me off big time. "It's obvious you're a big deal on campus. Guys want to be you and girls want to fuck you, just to say they did. And yet, you're following me around like some lost little puppy dog. If you're trying to make up for knocking me down that day, consider yourself forgiven. It was an accident. And I don't like you running with me. You need to stop that. I like to run by myself."

"No can do." He shook his head.

I bit down on my tongue to contain a scream. "Why?"

"Because I like running with you. I like *you*. Like I said, you're different. Even now that you know who I am it doesn't matter to you. It's refreshing. I'm used to people only wanting to be close to me because of my name or because of where I might be going with football. You. Don't. Care."

"You're right. I don't. You mean nothing to me."

He smiled, his blue eyes twinkling. "You don't mean that. You like me. Admit it."

"I don't know you, how could I like you?" I countered, my arms crossed over my chest. Thank God we were almost back at campus and I could get out of his car and out of this shirt that smelled a little too good.

"Then let me take you out."

"No."

"No?" His brows lifted with surprise. "I don't think anyone's ever told me no before," he whispered, rubbing his hand over his heavily stubbled jaw.

"There's a first time for everything. I'm not interested."

"You will be," he said with surety.

"You're really cocky, you know that, right?" I glared at him. True, he was gorgeous with that shaggy brown hair and blue eyes and that smile and...I needed to stop, because I was pretty sure I could go on for days about him.

He chuckled huskily and smiled. "And you really know how to cut a guy down, you know that, right?" He mimed my words.

I rolled my eyes and let out a sigh of relief when he turned into the parking lot. Freedom was in sight. I could get away from Cade and pretend this whole mouth-to-mouth thing never happened.

But when I got out of his Jeep he followed.

Instead of stopping at the steps of my dorm he sauntered inside like he owned the whole damn place.

"Hi Cade," a smooth and sexy sounding female voice called after him.

"Hey," he replied, flashing her the same smile he gave me. I rolled my eyes. Right there was proof that I was nothing special to him. I was a challenge and that was all.

I shook my head and my wet hair swished around my shoulders.

Cade continued to follow me. At the top of the stairs I turned around sharply and came face to face with his bare chest. No wonder the girl downstairs had been so keen to say hi.

I pushed all thoughts of his bare chest out of my mind, though. "You can go now. I'm at my dorm. I'm alive. I don't need your help."

"Don't be silly, Rae. I'm your friend and I'm not leaving until I know you're okay."

"You are *not* my friend," I seethed, slashing my hand through the air.

"Yes, I am," he grabbed my hand and dragged me down the hall.

He stopped in front of the right door and I almost asked him how he knew which was mine when I realized that Thea was his sister, so of course he'd know.

I opened the dorm door and didn't bother protesting when he followed me inside. I didn't know Cade but I knew enough to see that he wasn't going to leave until he was ready.

"Sit," he pointed at the bed that was obviously mine.

"Um, I live here. Stop bossing me around." I purposely refused to sit even though I was exhausted.

He narrowed his eyes. "God, you're frustrating."

"So I've been told." I lifted a shoulder in a small shrug.

He shook his head and headed into the bathroom. A moment later I heard the shower turn on.

He poked his head out of the doorway. "Come on."

I blanched. "No way. I'm not showering with you. Are you crazy?" Cade was clearly off his rocker. I had never in my eighteen years of life met a guy like him.

He threw his head back and laughed. "Did you seriously think I meant for us to shower *together*? I'm not that presumptuous, but if you'd like for me to join I'm happy to accommodate your fantasies."

My mouth fell open in shock. I stepped into the bathroom and pushed him out. "Get out!" I yelled before slamming the door in his face.

His answer was to laugh. I could hear him through the closed door.

I stripped off my damp jeans and pulled his shirt over my head.

The hot water did wonders to revive me and I took extra time washing my body and hair—just killing time in the hope that Cade would be gone when I was done.

When I finally stepped out of the shower the small room was steaming. Since I'd been flustered earlier I hadn't grabbed clothes. I slipped Cade's shirt on once more and opened the door.

I let out a scream when I saw him lying on my bed, arms crossed behind his head, and smirking like he owned the place. "Why are you still here?"

"You have my shirt."

My face turned red. "You're ridiculous," I shrieked. Before he could say anything else I grabbed my clothes, went back into the bathroom, and changed.

This time when I opened the door, ready to throw the shirt at him, he was gone.

He was infuriating.

I walked over to my bed and found a note lying on top of the pillow. I reached out and picked it up.

I was only kidding. The shirt looks better on you anyway. Keep it.

-Cade

I stared at the note, dumbfounded.

Cade Montgomery was the most annoying and infuriating person I'd ever met.

So why couldn't I shake him?

chapter four

SOMEONE WAS SCREAMING. I thought it was Hannah.

"Rachael, stop!"

I looked up and the world disappeared, replaced by a blinding white light.

The screeching of metal was worse than the screaming.

Pain lacerated my side and I sucked in a sharp breath. I tasted blood on my tongue.

The world that had been filled with noise just moments before was now eerily silent.

"Brett? Sarah? Hannah?"

Nothing.

And then, just when the darkness threatened to take me I heard their voices.

"You did this. You killed us. You'll pay for this, Rachael."

I woke up with a gasp, the nightmare clinging to my skin in the form of sticky sweat. My heart thundered in my ears. I'd had the same nightmare since...since it happened, but it always had the same effect on me.

An alarm blared through the room—the reason for waking me—and Thea covered her head with her pillow.

"Turn it off," she groaned.

"It's your alarm," I told her.

"Shiiiiiit," she groaned. "I hate mornings."

She sat up and her hair stuck up wildly around her head. She slapped her hand against the annoying clock, ceasing its cry. It was then that I realized the time.

"Oh crap." I scrambled out of bed, looking for clothes. My first class started at eight and it was already seven-thirty. I wouldn't have time to run. I couldn't believe I hadn't woken up at six or even earlier like I normally did. But after the catastrophe of a pool party last night I guessed that explained my current state of exhaustion.

I shimmied into a pair of jeans and grabbed a t-shirt out of the drawer. I tried to make my curly hair look halfway decent but it was pointless.

I grabbed my bag and ran out the door without even saying goodbye to Thea.

I made a pit stop for coffee and a sandwich, because food was a must at this point and we didn't have anything in our dorm yet. Luckily, I had a few minutes to spare.

I ordered and grabbed my stuff. I didn't even take time to look around the place. I had a one-track mind and right now I was focused on getting to class.

That would be my downfall.

When I turned to head out the door I collided with a solid chest and stumbled back. I knew that scent. I'd become intimately acquainted with it yesterday while wearing his shirt.

He reached out and grabbed my elbow to steady me. I looked up into his too blue eyes that caused me to pause. Why did he have to be so gorgeous with that dark hair and smile? Why did he have to make me feel so good?

"Rae," Cade grinned, his lips quirking up at the corners. "We really need to stop meeting like this." He winked and released my arm.

"Yeah," I mumbled in reply, because I was too busy gawking at the outline of his chest concealed behind a gray t-shirt. He wore a leather jacket on top and his jeans were a dark blue. He smelled like dessert and I wanted to take a bite. I hadn't let myself think such thoughts in a year, and I hated that this one guy could frazzle me in such a way. He didn't know me and I didn't know him. Therefore, this...this *connection* between us shouldn't have existed, but it did. I'd never believed in destiny or soul mates, but I did believe in Cade Montgomery and there was more to him, to *us*, than I wanted to accept.

I shook my head and side-stepped him as I headed to the door.

He followed and I wasn't the least bit surprised. I could feel him hovering behind me, his body a heavy and warm presence.

I looked over my shoulder at him as we stepped onto the sidewalk and the door closed behind us. "Weren't you getting coffee?" I asked, walking away.

"Can't we share?" He jogged after me.

"Uh..." I looked at him like he'd lost his mind.

He continued to speak, completely unfazed by my dumbfounded expression. "I mean, I did give you mouth to mouth, so my saliva has already been in your mouth. It's not like sharing a cup of coffee would be gross or anything."

Fucking Montgomery. I couldn't find a sound argument for that and he knew it.

"Fine," I agreed, stopping in my tracks. As we stood there I took several sips of the heated liquid and handed it to him. "Your turn."

He chuckled and took the paper cup. As he sipped, he started to walk. "You coming?" He called over his shoulder.

I rolled my eyes and followed. After all, he had my coffee.

"You know," I told him, as I fell into step beside him, "you're like that annoying homeless dog that shows up at your house and won't go away once you give it a little attention."

He snorted and grinned down at me. "Are you saying I look like a homeless dog?"

"No, I'm saying you act like one," I explained.

"So, you think I'm good looking?" His eyes sparkled with mischief.

I wanted to smack my forehead. *Walked right into that one, didn't you, Rachael?*

I decided to not even bother trying to talk my way out of this one. Instead, I said, "Oh please, you're very aware of what you look like. Don't act like you're clueless to the effect you have on the female population. Unfortunately," I looked him up and down, "your charm and looks don't work on me. I'm saving you the trouble here, Cade. Leave me alone. You're not going to get anymore from me than this right here," I waved a hand between the two of us.

He tilted his head slightly to the side and studied me. "I never said I wanted to fuck you, Rachael." His voice lowered and he stepped forward. I shivered as he reached up to play with a piece of my hair. "Although, if that's what you wanted, I doubt you'd resist. I see the way you react to me." His lips brushed my cheek and I gasped. "Just. Like. That." He stepped away, his point having been proven. "And while I'd like to fuck you until neither of us can walk, that's not the reason I talk to you. I want to be your friend, Rae."

"I don't need friends," I spat, like the mere idea was repulsive.

An elegant brow rose on his forehead. "Everyone needs friends."

"Not me."

"Even you." His eyes narrowed.

I snatched the coffee cup from his hand and gave him the most withering glare I could muster—which frightened most people, but of course Cade just continued to smile like I'd handed him a damn lollipop.

"You're determined to make me not like you, which makes me even more determined to like you."

"Wow, that was quite the mind bender, Cade," I started walking away. "I'm late for class, so please stop wasting my time."

"Hey," he called after me and I turned, "you're the one that talked back. You don't have to talk to me, Rae. But you do."

With that, he turned on his heel and sauntered away, his point having been made.

꒰ℯꙐ꒱

I walked into my first class with not a moment to spare. I slid into a seat beside a guy with spiky black and blue hair just before the professor walked in.

If Cade Montgomery had caused me to be late I might've lost my ever-loving mind. Like a full-on Toddlers and Tiaras kind of hissy fit.

After what happened last year I gave up on my dreams of photography and going to college. I killed three people. I didn't deserve my life, whether or not I was technically guilty of their deaths or not. I still felt I needed to be punished and I'd done it by closing myself off from everything and everyone. However, my parents and therapist had been persistent in the fact that I needed to go to college. I had to admit now that I was here I was glad they'd been so pushy.

I thought this might be exactly what I had needed all along.

A fresh start.

chapter five

My first two weeks of classes flew by and I began to settle into my new life. Despite my thoughts on first walking into my dorm and meeting Thea she was actually pretty cool. In fact, I kind of even liked her. I hadn't wanted to make friends here, but Thea was pretty impossible to ignore and she was determined to be my friend. We met up for lunch and dinner every day and often hung out in our dorm and around campus together.

I hadn't seen Cade at all in the last two weeks—not since our run in at the coffee shop.

That should've been a good thing, but instead I found myself looking for him every chance I got. From whispers on campus and what I'd gathered from Thea, he was like a superstar here. I thought guys like him—you know, the super hot jock types—*craved* attention, but Cade stayed hidden. He was a pretty unusual guy.

Since he seemed to have disappeared that meant my morning runs had been relatively quiet and pretty boring. I never thought I'd like having someone run with me, but leave it to Cade to ruin it for me. Now running didn't seem as much fun without him. On the few mornings we'd run together we hadn't even spoken much, but Cade seemed to calm and center me. He had a weird effect on my body. I wanted to hate it, but I didn't. Cade made me feel alive when I'd been dead inside for far too long.

I knew it would be better if I stayed away from him—far, far away—but I wasn't sure I was strong enough for that. Something about him drew me in and I was too weak to resist—just like I couldn't seem to resist becoming friends with Thea. The Montgomery siblings were pretty impossible to dislike. They both had a magnetism to them and it was nice to have people in my life that didn't know what I'd done. Back home, I'd been judged and looked down upon—not that I could blame anyone for their hatred. What I'd done had been wrong, so very wrong. But I was human and I craved normalcy, and for the first time in a year that's what I was finally feeling. Normal. I'd almost forgotten what it felt like.

I knew I was being silly to even be thinking about Cade. After all, I hadn't seen him in a while, but the jock had invaded all my thoughts.

Realistically, he was probably avoiding me and had found someone else that actually returned his feelings—because while he might've made me *like* him, it didn't mean I wanted him in that way. You know, a sexual way, because I so wasn't going there. Sex complicated things, and when feelings were involved...yeah, that was a bomb I wanted to avoid at all costs.

"Hey," Thea smiled, appearing in the doorway of the bathroom where I stood brushing my hair. "We should go out tomorrow. We've been cooped up on campus for too long. I'm bored."

I resisted the urge to wince. "Going out isn't exactly my thing."

"Is anything your thing?" She countered. She had a valid point there.

"Not really," I replied honestly. Once upon a time it had been, but not anymore.

She jutted out her bottom lip and brought her hands together in a pleading manner. "Please," she begged, "Please, please, please? We don't have to go to a club or anything like that. Ooh! Ooh!" She suddenly raised one arm excitedly, like a little kid in school desperate to be called on because they knew the correct answer to the teacher's question. "I know! This weekend is the end of the carnival! Let's do that! It'll be fun!"

I wanted to say no, but I found myself saying, "Okay." Apparently it was impossible to say no to Thea. Actually, it was more than that. Despite my vow to not make my friends here, I was actually desperate for it, and I wanted her to like me. Yeah, I was weird, but at least I was aware of it.

She let out a shriek and wrapped her thin arms around my neck. "Thank you, thank you, thank you!" She chanted. "This is going to be so much fun!"

You would've thought I told her that her favorite actor was going to be sleeping in our room with how excited she was.

"Yay." I shook my hands around, feigning excitement.

Thea backed away, into the dorm room, and grabbed up her bag. "I better go, I'm going to be late for class."

I looked down at my phone and paled when I saw the time. Crap. I was going to be late too. I was losing track of time more often thanks to my wandering thoughts.

I grabbed my bag from the room and ran out the door. Thea hurried behind me and once we exited the dorm we headed our separate ways. She tossed a cheery, "See you later," my way, but I didn't reply.

I breezed into class with a few minutes to spare. I took a seat next to a girl name Novalee. She had purple hair, a sprinkling of freckles across her nose, and a pierced eyebrow. I'd seen some of her photos and she was amazing—the kind of photographer I was envious of.

She glanced up when I sat down and I forced a smile. She did the same.

Our professor came in and began the lesson. Before it was over he started discussing a project that would run all semester long and we were to work with a partner. He was hoping since each of us had such a distinct style we would be able to learn something from each other and at the end of the semester we were to turn in a collage showcasing our collaborated work.

"Find someone to work with," he waved his hands dismissively, "and then you can get out of here."

I turned to Novalee and she was already looking at me. A single brow arched on her forehead, but she didn't say anything.

"Want to work together?" I asked.

"Sounds good." She shrugged, picked up her bag, and left.

I think I'd finally found someone that hated talking as much as I did.

⁓e⁓

"I don't know what to wear." Thea pouted with her hands on her hips as she stared into her overflowing closet.

I quirked an eyebrow and peered over her shoulder. "It looks to me like you have plenty of options."

She wrinkled her nose. "Not really."

I sighed. She'd already been standing there shuffling through clothes for a good thirty minutes. It was safe to say that she was tap-dancing across my last nerve.

"Come on, Thea," I groaned, not even bothering to try to hide how irritated I was. "Just pick something and put it on so we can go."

"Okay, okay," she intoned, picking a random dress off a rack.

Despite the fact that I was standing there she stripped down to her underwear and slipped the dress on. It was a pretty pale blue with flowers on it. She fluffed her hair and touched up her makeup.

"Reeeadddy," she sing-songed.

I stared at her for a moment and then glanced at myself in the floor-length mirror she had on her side of the room.

It was safe to say I looked like a piece of crap next to Thea. I was dressed in a worn pair of jeans and a black t-shirt. My curly hair was all over the place and I'd smeared on the bare minimum of makeup.

True, Thea had taken a lot longer to get ready than me, but she looked stunning.

"Why are you staring at me?" She asked. "Do I have lipstick on my teeth?" She swiped a finger over her teeth.

"No, you're good," I assured her. "I was just thinking that it's completely unfair that you look like that, and I'm well...me." I waved to my drab attire.

She smiled slowly. "Why don't you let me dress you? I'm sure I have something that'll work for you."

Considering I was five-foot ten and Thea couldn't be more than five-foot four I doubted she had anything that would fit me. I was slender all over and she had the kind of curves girls envied and guys drooled over.

"I doubt your clothes would fit me," I told her.

She waved a hand dismissively. "We'll make it work."

She shuffled through her clothes once more. "Aha," she grinned, producing a short and flowy mint green dress.

"I don't think that will cover my ass," I stated. The thing was really that short and it would be even shorter on me.

She rolled her eyes and thrust the dress into my hands. "Just put it on. If it's indecently short then that's what tights are for."

Clearly there was no arguing with Thea. She had an answer for everything.

I slipped into the dress and surprisingly it wasn't *that* short on me. It still exposed a lot of leg, but I wasn't worried about flashing anyone my lady bits.

"See?" Thea clapped her hands together. "I knew it would work. Now sit." She pointed to the bed.

I did as she asked and she began to braid my unruly hair to the side. A few shorter pieces escaped and framed my face.

"You're so pretty, Rae. It's not fair."

I resisted the urge to snort at those words coming from Thea.

After she finished with my hair she raided my closet for shoes. I didn't have many options that would match the dress so she settled on my lone pair of black flats.

She handed them over and gave me a look— the kind of look that said I was in trouble.

"We need to go shopping. Like at a mall. You need real clothes."

I let out a small laugh as I slipped the shoes on. "Last time I checked, those were real clothes."

"You know what I mean. You need some more...sparkle, and less doom and gloom." She wiggled her fingers like she was doing jazz hands.

I paused and quirked a brow. "Did you seriously just use the word *sparkle?*" My eyes widened. "Oh, let me guess, you were one of those girls that paraded around on stage in a tutu for a pageant?"

Her cheeks heated. "They're not tutu's, they're dresses, and I only did that till I was like..." She paused, thinking. "Twelve. Then I put a stop to it."

"Do you have any crowns with *sparkles*?" I giggled. Whoa, I actually giggled. That was new.

She put her hands on her hips. "Stop making fun of me."

"Alright, alright," I relinquished, standing up. I smoothed my hands down the front of the dress. "Are you ready to go?"

She nodded. "Yep...oh, and I probably should've told you..." She bit down on her bottom lip and gave me a sheepish look.

"Told me what?" My eyes narrowed and my heart pumped faster with fear at her next words.

"My brother will be there."

Oh, shit.

I schooled my features and stood up straight, feigning that I was unaffected by what she told me.

"Oh...that'll be...fun?" It came out sounding like a question. Since I hadn't seen Cade in two weeks, not since the coffee shop incident, I wasn't sure where we stood. It looked like I was about to find out.

"Yeah, when I told him we were going he wanted to tag along. Jace and Xander are coming too," she shrugged, "so it won't be just the three of us."

I let out a breath I didn't know I was holding. "No worries. It's fine."

"He keeps asking about you," she whispered, her lashes lowering. "I'm sorry for being nosy, but did something happen between you guys?"

My mouth fell open in surprise. "Absolutely not. I'm not the kind of girl that jumps into bed with every guy that walks by me."

"Okay," she said the word slowly, staring at me, "then what is going on? And don't tell me nothing, because I know there's something?"

"Honestly?" I shrugged and she nodded. "I don't know. He knocked me over within my first ten seconds on campus and then there was the pool thing and the coffee thing and..." I trailed off, purposely not telling her about the times he ran with me, because my runs were *my* thing and for some reason I didn't want her to know. It was one of the only times I was ever free of my thoughts and I didn't want to share that with her. "Yeah, that's about it. He asked me on a date one time and I said no. I don't want a relationship and he's your brother. That would be majorly awkward. He's not my friend...I don't really know where we stand."

She eyed me for a moment and let out a soft sigh. "He likes you."

I shrugged again. "So?"

"My brother doesn't like many people or trust them. I mean, he's nice to *everyone*, but it doesn't mean he likes them...not in the way he likes you."

"Cade doesn't like me in any different way," I replied easily.

Her expression said 'yeah right'. "I've known my brother a lot longer than you have, and trust me when I say he *likes* you." Her face softened. "He's a nice guy and he deserves to have someone in his life. Someone like you."

"Whoa, whoa, whoa," I held my hands up in defense. "Get that look out of your eyes right now. I can see you planning our wedding already. I've only been around your brother a few times and yes, he's nice. But he's also ridiculously cocky and annoying. I don't want or need a boyfriend. I'm just fine on my own."

She sighed. "Whatever. But I seriously wouldn't be mad if you liked him back."

I buried my face in my hands. "What is this? Elementary school?"

Thea's eyes lightened and she grinned. "College. Elementary school. Same thing."

I cracked a smile at that and we finally left.

The carnival was only about fifteen minutes away from campus—but it took us another ten minutes to find a place to park. It looked like everyone else had the same idea we did.

Thea's phone chimed with a text message and she looked down at the screen.

"Cade said they're at the entrance."

I nodded because I didn't know what else to say.

I followed her to the entrance, tugging at the bottom of the dress. I suddenly felt very naked and I kinda wanted to run back to my car and hide.

"Stop fidgeting," she scolded.

"Sorry," I mumbled, and let my hands drop. My arms felt awkward at my sides so I crossed them over my chest, which only served to make me look grumpy.

"Honestly, Rae." Thea groaned. "At least try to smile."

I tried to force my lips up.

She wrinkled her nose. "On second thought, don't smile. That looks even creepier."

Thea, Queen of the Blunt Comments.

I finally lowered my arms and took a deep breath.

I could do this.

It was just a carnival and I was going to have fun. It didn't matter that Cade was here.

The entrance came into view—a silly arch made of balloons—and there stood the three guys waiting for us.

Xander and Cade had their heads bowed together in conversation while Jace stood a few feet away smoking a cigarette and tugging at the beanie he wore.

Cade looked up then, almost like he sensed us, and a huge smile spread over his face making his eyes crinkle at the corners. That smile...it was like a kick to my gut. It reminded me of everything I could never have again.

"Hey," he chuckled, stepping forward, "look who it is. My Rae of Sunshine."

I rolled my eyes at his jest-filled comment. "Ha, ha, ha," I fake laughed.

"Come on," he grabbed my wrist, "admit that it was a good one. In fact, I think it might be your new nickname."

I tried to pull away from his grasp but he was too strong for me. He wrapped a paper band around my wrist and secured it. Seeing the question in my eyes he explained, "You have to wear a band to get in." He held up his own wrist and wiggled it around.

"Oh," I nodded. Of course. "You didn't need to get one for me. I could've bought my own."

"That's what friend's are for." He shrugged, smiling lazily.

"You're not my friend." I said the words firmly.

He chuckled and scrubbed a hand over his jaw. "I beg to differ, but if you say we're not then I'll have to work that much harder to convince you that we are."

I felt flustered by his words and very confused. I hadn't seen him in a while and he was acting like we were close, which most definitely wasn't the case. He baffled me.

"I don't understand you." The words tumbled out of my mouth before I could stop them. I wanted to smack myself in the forehead for saying anything, because I *knew* he'd make me explain.

"Why is that?"

As we walked forward, beneath the balloon arch, I shrugged. "It's just...I haven't seen you in a while and you're acting like..."

"Like what?" He prompted, shoving his hands in the pockets of his jeans and gazing down at me.

"I don't know," I shrugged.

He chuckled. "Oh, you know."

Ugh. I stopped in my tracks and tilted my head back to look at him—which was saying something since a lot of guys were shorter than me. "You act like you know me and you don't. I haven't even seen you in two weeks."

His eyes lightened and he smiled. Over his shoulder I saw Thea watching us closely. "Someone's been keeping track."

I rolled my eyes. "Definitely not."

He shrugged off my words. "I've been busy. Coach has us practicing morning and evening. Plus, I have classes. As for the not knowing you part..." His voice lowered and he took a step forward and cupped my cheek. I shivered at his touch and backed a step away so that his hand fell away. "I really want to get to know you."

"Why?" I asked, incredulous. There was nothing special about me. I was just...Rae. Rachael Wilder. The girl who killed three people. The girl who was angry at herself and the world. The girl who should've died that day. The girl who should not be standing here having any sort of conversation with the likes of Cade Montgomery.

"Why wouldn't I?" He gave me a significant look and sauntered away, catching up with Jace and Xander.

I stood there in shock. Cade confused me like no one else. I truly couldn't figure him out. I shouldn't even want to know anything about him, but I did. I so did. Damn him.

Thea scurried to my side. "Still want to tell me there's nothing going on with you and my brother?"

I gaped at her for a moment. "I have no idea what just happened."

"Mhmm," she hummed in disbelief.

"I swear," I assured her, as we started walking once more. The whole place smelled like popcorn and funnel cake. I felt my stomach do a flip at the thought of all the buttery and sweet goodness I could devour. "You know, your brother is kind of strange."

She laughed. "So are you. Maybe that's why he likes you."

I gave her shoulder a light bump with mine. "That wasn't funny."

"I thought it was," she smiled.

The carnival wasn't that big and it wasn't long until we'd ridden everything. Despite my best efforts, I was actually having fun. In fact, I was downright giddy with excitement.

"I'm going to get a bottle of water," Thea told me, after we got off one of the spinning rides. I felt dizzy and pressed a hand to my forehead to steady myself. "You want anything?"

"Water is good," I replied, leaning against one of the game booths for support.

"I'll be right back," she called over her shoulder before bleeding into the crowd.

My skin was warm despite the cool temperature and I felt almost drunk—drunk on life, maybe, because for the first time in a long time I was happy to be *alive*. I guess having fun could do that to you. I would have to remember to thank Thea for this. I'd been reluctant to come, but this had been the best thing for me. In fact, I was starting to think that Huntley University was going to change my life. Maybe it already had.

For some reason I found myself spinning around with my arms spread wide. I couldn't stop grinning and since the sun had gone down all the colorful lights blended together in a swirl.

It was beautiful. Magical.

"What are you doing?" Someone laughed at me.

"Living."

I'd forgotten what it was like to be so happy and carefree. To be just a girl. It was amazing and I didn't want to lose this feeling. I didn't want to go back to feeling so morose, but I knew that just like Cinderella at the ball my time was almost up. I was determined to enjoy this and hang onto this feeling for as long as I could.

I finally stopped spinning and when I stopped it was Cade that stood in front of me. I was surprised I hadn't recognized his voice since it usually filled my body with such warmth.

"Hi," I said stupidly with a goofy grin on my face. I seriously felt drunk but I hadn't had anything to drink. I swayed unsteadily again and he reached out to steady me. "Thanks," I mumbled, clinging onto him. I was glad I hadn't eaten anything yet. Between the ride and my own spinning adventure I was starting to feel sick to my stomach.

"No problem." He didn't let go. In fact, he drew my body even closer to his. Where I was soft, Cade was hard. I fit perfectly against the side of his body and I resisted the urge to rub myself against him like a cat.

I really needed to get away from him, because in my current state there was no telling what I might do or say to him.

"I think we should go on the Ferris Wheel," he suggested, his hand lowering from my elbow to my wrist. He chuckled when he felt my pulse jump.

I'd been in love once. I thought Brett was my forever, my everything. I thought we'd get married and have kids. Grow old together. But that couldn't happen anymore.

Right now, with Cade touching me, and the way my body reacted, I couldn't help but wonder if everything with Brett had been a lie. Well, maybe not a lie, but just not...*right*. Because this? This felt right. Perfect even. Cade made my pulse race and Goosebumps dot my body. I didn't even know him but he pushed all my buttons and made me want him when I shouldn't. After what happened to me I'd vowed never to love anyone ever again. Loving someone and losing them was too painful. But staring up into the depths of his blue eyes he made me want to take the plunge. I'd never known that someone you'd just met could have such a hold on you, but Cade did. I didn't want him to, but that didn't stop the feelings.

"Did you hear me, Rae?" He reached out and plucked the end of my braid.

"What?" I asked, blinking rapidly to clear my thoughts.

His lips quirked into a smile. "I said we should go on the Ferris Wheel."

That was probably a really bad idea, but right now it sounded like the best thing ever. "Sounds good." My voice seemed to catch in my throat as I stared up at him. I was trying to make sense of my feelings, to find some explanation, but there was none.

Cade nodded towards where the Ferris Wheel sat in the distance. "Let's go." I nodded and followed along.

I completely forgot about Thea and the fact that she was supposed to be coming back and would worry when she found me gone.

Cade and I stood in line side by side. I leaned my head back and looked up at the clear night sky. I took a deep breath and felt my heart begin to slow, the high from earlier beginning to disappear.

Slowly, I came back into myself and I turned to look at Cade. He was watching me closely with narrowed eyes. Back home, when someone looked at me like that I used to duck my head and run away, but Cade didn't know what I'd done so I stared right back at him. Now that my mind was clearing I was angry at myself for agreeing to go on the Ferris Wheel with him. This only spelled trouble. The kind of trouble that used to be fun, but I wanted no parts in anymore—no matter how nice or good-looking Cade was.

"Go out with me," he stated.

I snorted. "Didn't we already have this conversation?"

"We did," he grinned. "But that time you said no, and today is a new day so maybe you'll say yes."

"No."

He put a hand over his heart and winced. "You wound me."

"I don't date, Cade." I looked away and stared at the back of the head of the girl in front of me. She had pretty chestnut hair and she was smiling at the guy beside her who I assumed was her boyfriend. My stomach dipped. That used to be me. I looked at Cade again. That could still be me if I allowed myself such things.

"Okay...so how about we go out as friends then? No date." He raised his hands in mock surrender.

I let out a laugh that held no humor. "We're not friends." I said for what felt like the hundredth time.

He sighed heavily and for the first time since the day he knocked me over I could sense his frustration with me. Good. Maybe he'd leave me alone. He should. I was no good for him and the sooner he learned that the better.

"Why don't we go grab a burger next weekend as *acquaintances* getting to know one another?"

Jesus Christ, he wouldn't let it go.

"Fine," I relented. I could use this as an opportunity to show him how fucked up I was and why he should run the other way.

His eyes widened in surprise. "Great. I'll text you a time when I know something."

"I never gave you my phone number."

He grinned. "I'll get it from Thea." Of course he would.

I was about to make an excuse to leave, and forget the whole Ferris Wheel thing, but then it was our turn to take a seat. Cade put his hand on my waist and I lost all rational thought. He guided me forward and I sat down.

He took the spot beside me and since he was so large and the seat wasn't that big we ended up plastered together. Maybe that had been his plan all along.

My heart picked up speed and I grabbed ahold of the railing to hide the shaking in my fingers.

Up we went and I felt his eyes on me, but I refused to look at him. I kept my eyes focused on the stars above and prayed he couldn't see my heart pounding in my throat.

The wind was cool on my face and I found myself shivering.

Cade lifted his arm and wrapped it around me, drawing me even closer. His warmth enveloped me and my breath left me in a shaky gasp.

"I'm not trying to make a move," he whispered, like he sensed my unease, "but I could tell you were cold and it's not like I can take my jacket off and give it to you." He lifted his shoulders in a small shrug and used his free hand to point to where we were strapped in.

"Where are your friends?" I asked, desperate to steer the topic away from the fact that his arm was wrapped around me.

"They were getting something to eat."

"Thea was getting us water," I blurted, "she's probably worried about me."

Cade chuckled and his breath stirred the hair on top of my head. "We'll have to find her once we get off this thing then."

I nodded in agreement.

It grew quiet between us and neither of us seemed to know what to say. It surprised me that for once Cocky Cade seemed to be at a loss for words.

I looked around us and I'd thought the kaleidoscope of colors had been brilliant on the ground, but from above like this it was even better.

My mouth was gaped in awe like a small child. I'd been to carnivals before, but I'd never let myself appreciate one. I'd been too focused on other things.

Too soon we were getting off the Ferris Wheel and going in search of Thea and the guys. A part of me wanted to get back on and escape the world for a little bit longer.

Cade didn't try to hold my hand—which I was thankful for, but also found surprising.

After five minutes of looking we found all of them sitting at a picnic table eating hotdogs. My stomach rumbled at the sight.

I sat down beside Thea and tried not to drool on her food like a hungry dog.

"Here," she handed me a water bottle, "got this for you."

"Thanks." I replied, twisting off the lid.

"I couldn't find you, but it seems someone else did." Her eyes flicked across the table to her brother who grinned in response.

I shrugged. "Yeah. He wanted to go on the Ferris Wheel."

"Of course he did," she muttered, dipping a fry in...was that mayonnaise? Ew.

Cade drummed his hands against the table. "I'm going to get some food, you want anything?" He asked me.

I turned away from Thea to face him. "I can get my own food."

"I'll get you a hotdog." He grinned and pushed away from the table.

Jace and Xander looked up from their food at me. "Can you believe it?" Xander asked Jace.

"Nope," Jace replied, shoving a fistful of fries in his mouth.

"What?" I asked, since it was clear whatever they were referring to had something to do with me.

"Nothing," Xander shrugged.

"Bullshit," I muttered.

Jace snorted. "I like you." He took off his beanie and laid it on the table. His blond hair stuck up in every direction but he didn't seem to care.

"Don't let Cade hear you say that," Xander chided. "I think he just might punch you."

Jace grunted in response. "She's a cool chick. Just voicing my opinion." He raised his hands.

I turned my attention to Xander. "What did you mean by your first comment? The whole, 'can you believe it?' thing."

Xander sighed and set his hotdog on the paper plate. "It's just that Cade would never normally do that for anyone. I'm not saying he's rude to everyone else...he just..."

"He distances himself from people he doesn't really know," Thea inserted. "But with you he doesn't. He's just Cade...there's no façade around you. He lets you see the real him."

"I'm still kinda lost." I frowned, looking between the three of them.

Thea tried to explain. "Cade is used to people wanting something from him because of who he is. He has to keep a shield up or he'd lose his mind. Do you have any idea how many girls have thrown themselves at him in the hopes of getting pregnant because they think he's going to go pro and they want to trap him?"

I absorbed her words. That had to be hard. "I'm just not interested in your brother that way." Lie. My body definitely was, but my mind was firmly against it.

"Then maybe you could at least try to be his friend," she spoke softly. "He needs more of those."

Friends? Cade's *friend*? Could I do that?

I wasn't so sure.

I wasn't sure I could be anyone's friend anymore, but...I felt like maybe Thea and I were friends now. So maybe I could try to make the effort with Cade. After all, my plans to lay low and keep to myself had failed miserably.

"I'll try," I sighed and Thea brightened at my words.

"Try what?" Cade asked, putting a plate down in front of me

"It's not important." I smiled at him in the hopes of distracting him. "Thanks for this."

"No problem." He waved a hand dismissively.

We all ate and made idle chat. When we were finished everyone was ready to leave. We headed back to the parking lot and started to go our separate ways.

"Rae?" Cade called when Thea and I parted from the group.

"Yeah?" I turned around, my brows raised in question.

"Thank you."

I opened my mouth to ask him what he was thanking me for, but before I could respond he turned his back to me and disappeared into the darkness.

chapter six

THE ALARM ON THEA'S NIGHTSTAND pierced the room.

She sat straight up, her hair puffed around her head like a fluffy cotton ball, and groaned. "I swear that alarm is the spawn of Satan." She smacked her hand roughly against the top. "Die motherfucker. Die."

I snorted, pulling my damp hair back into a bun. I was already back from my run and freshly showered.

"You know what else should die?" She turned sleepy eyes my way and then answered before I could respond. "Monday. Monday should die a fiery and painful death." She flopped down on the bed and covered her eyes with the crook of her elbow. "I fucking hate mornings."

I laughed. "I think we've established that."

"And you don't help," she continued. "You're always so chipper in the mornings."

"Chipper?" I questioned. That wasn't a word I'd ever use to describe myself.

"Okay, maybe not *chipper*, but you're definitely a morning person." She lowered her arm and cracked her eyes open. "Look at you dressed and ready to conquer the world. It's not fair. I don't even feel like brushing my teeth."

"Ew, Thea. That's gross." I moved across the room for my backpack and camera case. I was hoping to get a morning shoot in. The campus was so pretty in the early hours.

"Hey, at least I'm honest." She rolled over then, but rolled too far and fell face first on the floor. I slapped a hand over my mouth in the hope that she wouldn't hear me laughing at her. "If this is a sign of what's to come today," she mumbled, turning onto her back, "then I want a fucking do over."

"Sorry," I offered her a hand, "life doesn't work like that." *I wish.*

She took my hand and I helped her up. "Thanks," she grumbled, heading for the bathroom. "I'll see you for lunch."

I nodded even though she couldn't see me. "See you later," I called, heading for the door.

Since I had a while before my first class I spent my time walking around campus, snapping pictures here and there when something piqued my interest. I didn't know why, but the moment I raised the camera to my eye I always saw the world in a different light. The chaos diminished and I saw only the beauty.

In the distance I saw a guy sitting against a tree with a book in his lap. He was completely absorbed in the words on the page and nothing around him seemed to matter. I focused on him and snapped his picture.

He looked up then and it was like someone kicked me in the gut. It was Cade. He grinned and I smiled in response as he raised a hand to wave me over.

I stood still for a moment, reluctant to join him. But I didn't see how I had much choice unless I ran away.

I closed the distance between us and he smiled up at me from where he sat on the ground.

He lifted a hand to shield his eyes from the morning sun. "Well," he chuckled warmly; his blue eyes making my stomach flip, "if it isn't my morning Rae of Sunshine."

"Still with the silly nickname?"

"Always," he shrugged, causing his gray sweater to pull taut across his shoulders, "I like it."

"It's stupid." I muttered, still standing there looking at him.

"That's your opinion." He patted the spot of grass beside him. "Join me for breakfast. I'll share."

That's when I noticed he had a to-go box of breakfast food from the diner Thea and I had gone to a while ago.

When I didn't move, his voice grew stern. "Sit, Rae."

I sat. He was rather bossy and I couldn't seem to ignore his orders.

"Eat. You're too thin." He pointed to the smorgasbord of food he had.

"You know," I picked up a piece of buttered toast, "most guys think there's no such thing as too thin."

"Bullshit," he chuckled. "That's something girls believe because they're often times way too self-conscious. Guys like curves. We want something to grab ahold of." He raised his hands in the air, miming that he was grabbing some invisible breasts. "No one wants to cuddle a twig."

I shook my head and nodded at the book in his lap. "What are you reading?"

"Do you really want to know?" He chuckled, bowing his head so that the longer strands of his hair hid his face from sight.

"Yeah." I picked up the fork and took a bite of scrambled eggs. I wasn't worried about using the same fork as Cade. After all, he already drank my coffee and we couldn't forget the mouth to mouth incident.

He lifted the book in the air and I tried to hide my surprise.

"Harry Potter? Interesting choice of reading material," I commented.

"I like fantasy books," he admitted. "Historical ones too, like old westerns, but mostly fantasy. I mean, who hasn't at least once wished they could be a wizard?"

I bowed my head and a small smile graced my lips. "I will admit to at one time thinking it would be really cool if I could do magic."

"Ah, something we agree on," he grinned, setting the book in the grass.

I don't know why but I lifted my camera and took a picture of the book. It looked so pretty lying there with the grass sticking up around it and a few fallen leaves.

"What's with the camera?" Cade asked, picking up a bottle of water and taking a sip.

"You know how you like to play with a ball?" I smirked. Waving my camera around a bit, I explained, "This is my toy. My life actually." I lowered the camera into my lap and stared down at it.

"So...is that what you're studying?" He picked at a piece of toast.

I nodded and tucked a piece of hair behind my ear. "Yeah. I mean, I know realistically I'll probably never be able to travel the world and take pictures like I want and I'll more likely be stuck doing weddings and family portraits, but as long as I have my camera and can use it I'll be happy." I let out a breath and looked up for his reaction. He watched me with a calculated gaze, thinking deeply. Before he could say anything, I asked, "What are you studying?"

"Architecture."

"Really?" I reeled back in surprise. I hadn't expected that. "I thought you'd say like sports medicine or something like that."

He threw his head back and let out a bellowing laugh. "Is that all you think of me? That I'm some dumb jock that only thinks about football?" I nodded, because it was true. He chuckled lowly and shook his head. "You don't know me at all, Rae. I'm quite looking forward to getting to know each other better this weekend," he winked.

I picked at a piece of grass, ignoring his comment about this weekend because frankly I was trying to forget about it.

"Why architecture?" I ventured to ask.

He shrugged, playing with the lid of the water bottle. "You know Xander?" He waited for my nod. "Well, his dad owns a company and we've been friends forever. When I was little, and I'd go to his house, I was always fascinated with the blueprints. Cooper, his dad, picked up on my interest and he started taking Xander and me to sites they were working on. It always astounded me how this building would start out as lines on a piece of paper," he spoke passionately, "and turn into this real place that people used." He shrugged. "I knew then that's what I wanted to do for the rest of my life."

"Where does football come into it?" I asked.

He grunted unintelligibly and looked away. "I like football. I don't *love* it. But...but my dad does. He started me young and I just continued with it because that's what was expected of me and I wanted to make him proud." His face grew sad and he looked away.

"He wants you to go pro," I stated. I'd heard enough from Thea to know that Cade was talented enough to make a career out of football.

Cade looked back at me and nodded.

"But you don't want that."

"No," he sighed, running his fingers through his longish hair. "I don't want that life. I just want to be normal. The spotlight? It's not my thing."

"You're a strange guy." And he was. I thought most guys in his position would be ecstatic at the prospect of going pro. The money. The women. The lifestyle. But not Cade. He was right when he said I didn't know him at all and I'd passed too many judgments on him. Maybe...maybe I could be his friend.

"You're a strange girl," he countered with a small smile.

"Touché." I laughed lightly, plucking a piece of grass from the ground and twisting it around my finger.

"You know," he said, and lay on the ground, crossing his arms behind his head. The movement caused his shirt to ride up exposing the lower muscles of his smooth stomach. A light dusting of hair started at his naval and disappeared beneath the top of his jeans. I looked away hastily, my cheeks heating, and prayed he hadn't seen me staring. "It really sucks how people judge you by what you do and not by who you are."

I winced, because that's exactly what I'd done with Cade, and look how wrong I'd been. And people judged me the same way too.

"I'm sorry," I whispered, surprising us both. "I hate when people judge me that way and it's exactly what I did to you."

He turned his head towards me. "I didn't expect an apology, Rae, but thanks. It's not just you though. *Everyone* judges me. Even the professors." He sighed heavily. "You have no idea how many classes I've walked into and they take one look at me and make some smart ass comment, because of what I do. They think that I just want a free ride, and that's not what I want at all. I *want* to work hard and get my degree. I want to be an architect and build someone's dream home or an old fashioned church that will stand the test of time. I don't want to be that guy they think I am. I'm *not* that guy."

"I know." And I did. I saw it now. I stood up and dusted loose grass off my jeans. "I'm glad we had this conversation and I don't mean that in a sarcastic way. I'm truly happy we did." I backed away slowly and he watched me. When I was far enough away that he'd barely be able to hear me, I said, "I'm looking forward to this weekend."

And I was.

Thea dropped down into the seat beside me, her backpack slamming on the table. "Monday's suck and I need a cupcake. Or a brownie. Or ice cream. Something loaded with sugar, stat."

"That bad, huh?" I frowned, picking some of the extra bread off my sandwich.

"Yes," she groaned, smacking her head against the table. Raising her head, she said, "You know, maybe it wouldn't be so bad if I actually knew what I wanted to do with my life and I wasn't taking all these stupid classes that bore me half to death."

I felt bad for her, because that really had to suck. "Surely there's something you like that could be a potential career."

Her plump lips turned down into a frown and she pouted. "Nope. Nothing." She lowered her head to the table once more in the shelter of her arms. Her body began to shake. "I'm such a failure."

"You're not a failure," I assured her. My hand hovered above her back, not sure whether or not I should try to offer her comfort. Eventually I gave her a small pat and pulled my hand away hastily.

She peeked her eyes up at me and sniffled. "I totally am. This is *college*. I'm supposed to have it all figured out and I'm clueless."

"You *will* figure it out," I assured her. "Give it time."

I'd known I wanted to be a photographer from the moment I first picked up a camera at ten years old, so I'd never been in Thea's position, but I could imagine it was pretty miserable.

"You really think so?" She sat up, wiping her hands beneath her eyes.

"I know so." I nodded reassuringly. "Don't get yourself too worked up about it. One day something will happen and you'll know what you want to do. Don't stress yourself unnecessarily."

She nodded at my words and then surprised me by hugging me. I slowly lifted my arms to hug her back. "You're a good friend, Rae."

I opened my mouth, ready to tell her that we weren't friends, but that would've been a lie. Somehow, Thea had weaseled herself into my heart and become my friend. I hadn't had one of those in a long time—I'd come to deny myself such things. But it felt good knowing I had someone like her in my life. I hugged her back with renewed force. I wasn't alone anymore.

"You're a better friend," I whispered in her hair, because it was true. She could never know the real me and what I had done, but she could know the me that I was now.

She pulled away and gave me a shaky smile. "I'm sorry for crying on you."

I cracked a smile. "It's okay. But seriously, you need to stop stressing yourself."

"I'll try to be better." She straightened her clothes and stood up. "I better get something to eat. Class on an empty stomach is not fun." She forced a smile and flounced away with a little more pep in her step. Now that was the Thea I knew.

By the time she returned she was in a much better mood.

She set her food down, and eyed me. "So...my brother asked me for your phone number?"

He'd told me he was going to, but that news still sent a shiver down my spine.

"He did?" I acted like I was clueless.

"Mhmm," she grinned, peeling the top off her yogurt. "Would you like to explain *why* to me?"

I shrugged and squirmed in my seat, reluctant to tell her of our plans. I mean, it wasn't like it was a date or anything, but if I told her the truth it would certainly sound that way.

"Rae?" She pleaded, giving me puppy dog eyes. Damn her.

"We're going out for lunch or something. I really don't know the specifics." When she brightened I hastened to add, "It's *not* a date." Nope. Definitely not a date.

She grinned like the Cheshire cat. "Yeah, right."

"Seriously," I assured her. "Ask him."

"I will." She turned to her food and the subject, thankfully, dropped.

I finished eating and looked at the time on my phone. "I better go," I told her. I still had time before my next class but I was supposed to meet up with Nova so we could discuss our project.

I walked across campus and stood by the bench she'd told me to wait at. My head swiveled in every direction, looking for her purple hair. At least she wouldn't be hard to miss.

When she didn't appear in a few minutes I sat down on the bench, checking my phone to see if I'd missed a text from her canceling our plans, but there was nothing.

The whirl of a motorcycle caught my attention, streaking across the parking lot.

It screeched into a spot a few spaces down from where I sat. The rider removed their helmet and purple hair tumbled forward.

Holy crap.

It was official, Nova was not only the weirdest person I'd ever met, but the coolest as well.

She caught sight of me and waved. I slowly lifted my hand and wiggled my fingers. I was still in shock.

She walked over to me, swiping her fingers through her hair.

I stood up, shaking my head. "Let me get this straight. You're a photographer, you have purple hair, *and* you drive a motorcycle?"

She laughed, squinting from the sunlight. "Yeah."

"Can I be you when I grow up?" The words tumbled out of my mouth.

She laughed, a real genuine laugh. It surprised me at first since I'd barely ever seen her smile.

"Sorry, I don't think it works that way." She hopped up on the bench, sitting on the part where your back rested.

I sat down once more. "So, this project..." I started. "My photos are typically people or nature and very straightforward. Yours...are...wow." I'd seen several pieces of Nova's work in class and to say I was envious of her talent was an understatement.

She cracked a smile. "My photos are conceptual. I see things that aren't necessarily there. When I take a photo I don't just see a bench," she waved her hand to where we sat, "I see what I can do with the bench. Maybe I want it floating or in a tree or upside down." She shrugged. "You get the picture...no pun intended," she laughed.

"What do you think we should do then?" I asked, nervously wringing my hands together. Conceptual photography was *way* out of my comfort zone, but I'd always wanted to try.

"Marry the two concepts, obviously. You'll dull me down and make my photos more realistic and I'll help you spice yours up."

"Thanks...I think." I mumbled.

"Sorry," she let out a small laugh, "I meant no offense."

"I know," I replied. It was pretty obvious that Nova was a blunt type of person. She didn't sugarcoat things. I kind of liked that about her, but I knew it could become annoying.

"Will you be free this weekend?" She asked.

"Uh..." I started. Cade hadn't told me which day he wanted to go out or given me a time. "I should have some free time but I'm not sure when yet."

"You can let me know then," she hopped off the bench. "I don't have any time after classes this week but I should next week."

"Sounds good," I nodded, and stood. "We'll figure something out."

She unzipped her leather jacket and nodded. "See you later." She turned on her heel and disappeared around the corner of a building.

I headed to class, hoping this project didn't turn into a disaster.

chapter seven

I WAS STARTLED ON WEDNESDAY morning when I walked outside for my morning run and found Cade sitting on the top step.

He seemed lost in his thoughts and didn't hear me approach.

I sat beside him and lightly bumped his shoulder with mine.

He pushed his hair out of his eyes and smiled. "Hey, Rae of Sunshine."

I sighed, but made no comment on the nickname. "What are you doing here?"

He shrugged. "Coach gave us the morning off. I thought we could run together."

"Don't you want a break?" I questioned. If this was a chance for him to relax and sleep in I didn't understand why he was here.

He shook his head, his lips curving up. "Nah, I'd rather run with you."

I started at his words. He wanted to run with me? Even though it shouldn't have, his words pleased me. I stood up, hiding my smile, and descended the rest of the steps. "I guess we better start running then." Without giving him a moment to join me I took off. It didn't take him long to catch up. He shortened his strides to match mine. I didn't mind having him run with me this time. In fact, I found his presence almost comforting. I hadn't liked him, didn't *want* to like him, but just like his sister he'd weaseled his way into my life and made it impossible to resist him.

By the time I would've normally started heading back to my dorm, Cade slowed to a walk. He grasped my arm and tugged slightly. Nodding his head in the other direction, he said, "Come this way."

I followed him, because apparently all rational thought had been flushed down the toilet the moment I saw him sitting on the steps.

He found a grassy spot and sat down, drawing his knees up and draping his arms overtop.

I sat down too, plucking at my damp top.

"Why are we here?" I asked, my breath coming out as a pant.

"No reason," he shrugged, flicking his hair out of his eyes. "I just wasn't ready to say goodbye to you." He grinned boyishly.

"Hey, you shaved." I couldn't believe I'd just now noticed.

He chuckled and scrubbed a hand over his bare jaw. "Yeah, coach doesn't like us to look homeless when we have a game and interviews, so it had to go."

"Homeless?" I laughed.

"Coach's words, not mine." He held his hands up defensively.

"So you have a game coming up?" I wasn't into football so I never kept track of such things.

"Yeah, on Saturday." He looked away briefly at a spot where a flock of birds were fighting over a crumb. "Will Sunday work for our...non-date?"

I laughed at his terminology. "Sunday is fine."

He stared at me for a moment, his blue eyes like twin flames. "Will you come to my game?"

"I-I-" I stuttered. I hadn't been expecting him to ask that and I didn't know how to respond. "Football isn't my thing."

"Please?" He begged. "I want you there."

I didn't know what to make of that.

When I didn't reply immediately he said, "If you won't come for me, will you at least come for Thea? It's a home game, obviously, and I don't want her being harassed because of who I am."

Cade knew exactly what to say to weaken my resolve. Damn him.

"I'll go," I finally relented. "For both of you," I added, and he grinned. I liked Cade's smile. It lit up his whole face and softened his chiseled features.

"Thank you." He reached for my hand and grasped it briefly before letting go.

My hand tingled with warmth where he'd touched it. I schooled my features so he couldn't see how much that single touch effected me.

A part of me wanted to believe that the reason Cade had such an effect on me was because I'd spent so long without human contact like this. But I knew deep down that wasn't the case. It was just Cade.

"What are you thinking about?" He asked.

"Nothing." I lowered my head.

"Liar," he chuckled warmly. "That wrinkle between your brows says otherwise." He waved a finger towards my face. "Come on, tell me. Don't make me beg."

I shrugged casually. "I think about lots of things."

"Not going to tell me?" He pouted.

"No," I laughed. "I'm not."

"Does that mean you were thinking about me?" His eyes sparkled with laughter and he fought a smile.

"You're really full of yourself," I muttered, suppressing a laugh as I shook my head and looked away.

"I'm right, aren't I?" Even though I wasn't looking at him I could feel his smile like a caress on my skin.

"No," I said defensively.

His answering smile said he didn't believe me.

"I'm hungry." He rubbed his stomach.

"Okay?" It came out as a question.

"Let's go to the dining hall and get something to eat," he suggested.

When I started to protest he pressed a finger against my lips, promptly shutting me up.

"There's no harm in breakfast."

He was right, but still...

I looked down at my sweaty clothes and back at him. "I'm kind of gross."

"So am I." He plucked at his white t-shirt. "Come on, Rae, we can be sweaty together."

I snorted in a very undignified manner. "That sounded kind of perverted."

He tapped my forehead with his long fingers. "I think you have a dirty mind, because that was a completely innocent comment."

He hopped up in one lithe movement that I was instantly envious of. It was amazing that a guy his size could move like that. He certainly wasn't small—not with his height and those muscles, but he moved so gracefully.

He held his large hand out for me and after a second of thought I took it. He hauled me up and against his chest. My breath left me in a gasp. My body curved against his hard lines and my eyes flicked up to his. Time seemed momentarily suspended. He stared at me for a moment and then his eyes darted to my lips. My tongue flicked out to moisten their surface. Blood roared in my ears as it rushed through my body. I couldn't think about anything other than Cade and how good this felt. He reached up, smoothing his fingers against my cheek. My eyes closed and my breath came out in a shaky gasp. His touch felt heavenly and forbidden all at the same time.

When I opened my eyes and looked into his I saw that they'd darkened into a stormy blue.

Neither of us moved or even breathed.

Then he released me and the spell was broken.

I looked down at the ground, hoping to hide my embarrassment.

He grasped my chin and forced my head up. "You feel it too." His eyes seared into me, leaving a brand.

I gasped, but didn't get a chance to reply. He turned and walked away. When he realized I wasn't following he turned around, his hands shoved in the pockets of his basketball shorts. "You coming?"

"Yeah," I shook my head and jogged after him.

I made no comment about what he'd said. I figured that was better, because I wasn't sure I could lie. I did feel it—whatever this thing between us was.

When we arrived at the dining hall it was relatively empty.

I fixed a bowl of Froot Loops and Cade got Captain Crunch. I couldn't help smiling at our childish choices.

We sat across from each other at one of the many tables.

When Cade wasn't looking at me I studied him. I noticed dark circles beneath his eyes and wondered what had caused them. Loss of sleep, obviously, but *why*?

Before he could notice me staring and make a cocky comment I looked away.

The silence between us was oddly comfortable. I'd never been this content to sit with someone and not speak, but with Cade it was okay. He felt like someone I'd known forever which was weird since I'd known him no time at all.

When we'd both finished eating Cade grabbed my bowl and threw our trash away.

I expected to head separate ways, but he fell into step beside me.

"Thanks for having breakfast with me. I'm sorry I wasn't feeling very chatty. I just..." He twisted his lips. "I have a lot on my mind right now." He forced a smile.

"I can relate to that," I assured him.

"I didn't want you to think I was being rude since I'm normally so chatty," he chuckled.

I grasped his arm briefly and squeezed it in comfort. "You don't need to explain anything to me. I get it. Trust me, I do. Probably better than most people. And honestly, I'm kind of surprised you even like me and want to spend time with me. I haven't exactly been the nicest person to you." Taking a shaky breath, I told him, "I'm going to work on that."

His smile turned genuine and then to a full-blown grin. "Is that so?"

I nodded, smiling because his grin was so damn infectious. Everything about Cade was infectious—no, magnetic.

"Yeah. Be patient with me, though. I've...I've been through a lot." I knew that was probably admitting too much, but I needed him to know I had a reason for being so standoffish before. When you went through something like I had, and then had to deal with the aftermath, it made you skittish and untrusting of other people.

"Patience is my middle name," he winked.

"Of course it is," I laughed, bowing my head a little.

My dorm came into view and I started up the steps.

"Rae?" He called.

I turned around and smiled. "Yes?"

"This dinner on Sunday...are we really still going as acquaintances?"

My smile widened. "No, Cade. We're going as friends."

And then his smile lit my world on fire.

chapter eight

"ARE YOU REEEAAAAADY for some foooooooootball?" Thea chanted, coming out of the bathroom. She took one look at me, wrinkled her face in disgust, and grunted, "You are *so* not ready for some football. What the hell are you wearing?"

"Uh...jeans and a sweatshirt." I looked down at my attire wondering what she found so appalling about it.

"But it's all black! You can't go to the game like that! You'll stick out like a sore thumb! You need to wear our school colors!"

Since she looked like blue and gold had thrown up on her, I tended to disagree. Seriously, she had on little blue shorts with a fitted yellow short-sleeved top. Blue and yellow ribbons were wrapped around her ponytail. Even her eye makeup was blue and yellow.

She headed for the closet and started rummaging around. It wasn't long until she was throwing clothes at me that I somehow managed to catch. "Thea!" I groaned. "I'm not wearing this!"

"Yes, you are!" She turned around, hands on her hips. "I am not letting you walk out that door looking like you're going to a funeral! This is a football game and you're going to support your school! Team spirit, Rae! Team. Fucking. Spirit."

Jesus Christ, I was never going to win this argument.

"Fine," I stripped off my shirt. "I'll wear that," I took the yellow shirt from her hands that was emblazoned with the school's mascot—a wolverine. "And I'll ditch the black jeans, but I'm wearing *blue* jeans, and not...whatever that is." I waved a hand at the blue cotton shorts she held that I was sure were a twin of the ones she wore. No way was I leaving the dorm with my ass cheeks hanging out. That was not acceptable.

"Fine," she tossed the shorts back in her closet, "as long as you wear the shirt I'll survive."

My lips quirked in amusement at her melodramatics.

Once I was changed and dressed to her satisfaction it was time to leave.

I was shocked by the flow of students when we stepped out of the dorm. Everyone seemed to be heading to the game and I had no idea how we'd even get seats.

"This is crazy." I hissed under my breath where only Thea could hear.

"No, this is football."

"Same thing," I mumbled.

The walk to the stadium took forever thanks to the crowd.

I had to admit that the energy was infectious.

"I don't have a ticket," I gasped, when I realized they were checking slips of paper up ahead.

Thea turned her gaze my way. "Chillax, did you really think Cade wouldn't have us covered?" She held up two tickets. "Best seats in the whole place. We'll be able to smell their sweat." She said the last part like it was the greatest thing in the world.

"I'm not sure I want to smell sweat," I wrinkled my nose.

"Oh," she grinned, "trust me, you do."

"Tickets?" A voice interrupted our conversation.

Thea handed them over and pointed to me so the man would know the second ticket was for me. He studied our seat numbers and gave her directions. She appeared bored by his explanation and I figured Thea had been to Cade's games often enough, even though she hadn't been a student here until this year.

Since Thea obviously knew where to go I followed her.

At one point we came close to being separated and she grabbed ahold of my arm, dragging me behind her.

Our seats were close to the front and in the middle of the field. The benches where the players would sit were in front of us.

Thea sat down and clapped her hands together, doing a little dance in her seat. "I'm so fucking excited!"

"I gathered that." I laughed, leaning away from her flailing her arms before she smacked me in the face.

"This is my first time attending a game as an actual student!" She grabbed my arm and gave it a shake, like she was trying to force her excitement into me. "Aren't you excited, Rae?" Her eyes were large, ready to pop out of her skull. I was pretty sure she'd had too much sugar this morning.

"Ecstatic," I said, trying to force some enthusiasm into my voice.

Thea seemed to buy it, or at least she pretended to. "God, I love football season." I swore her whole body was shaking with excitement at this point. I didn't know how I was going to make it through the next few hours if she kept this up. I wished I had a tranquilizer to give her—yeah, she was that bad.

"You really love football," I laughed.

"Yep," she nodded, threading her fingers together so they'd stop tap-dancing across her knees, "I've grown up with it."

A few minutes later I asked, "When do they come out?"

She looked down at her phone. "Anytime now."

I wanted to ask her what number Cade was, but I figured she'd get the wrong idea, so I kept my mouth shut.

The stadium was large and packed. The sounds of that many voices all speaking at once sounded like a roar. The energy was contagious. I could feel it vibrating through my body.

"Here they come!" Thea grasped my arm, her fingernails digging in to the point that she drew blood.

Our team—and I only knew that since they were wearing blue and yellow—ran out on the field. They were huge, all tall and muscular. It made for an intimidating sight.

And then the atmosphere changed. Everything became hushed and music—some rock song or something—started to play through the speakers.

The last player slowly walked out onto the field, his shoulders straight. When the music picked up he turned to face us, as he walked sideways. He lifted his arms in the air and jumped up and down a bit, hyping the crowd up even more.

I *knew* it was Cade. It sounded crazy, but I felt that it was him.

The antics he was pulling on the field with the crowd didn't seem like the Cade I knew, but what did I really know about him?

After he had the crowd worked into a frenzy he ran over to his teammates. I made sure to memorize his jersey number. Eighty-three.

"Isn't it incredible?" Thea asked me with wide eyes.

"Spectacular," I agreed. And it was. I couldn't deny that even if I had no idea what the hell was going on.

The opposing team came out without the pomp and circumstance ours had.

When they started playing I watched with awe. For the first time ever I wasn't bored out of my mind watching football. My dad had been obsessed with it and every weekend during football season it was the only thing on our TV. I'd never cared about it then. But now I had someone to root for.

At one point Cade was tackled to the ground, rather forcefully from what I could see, and I winced, hiding my face behind my hands. I didn't like seeing him hurt.

During halftime when they were about to walk off the field, I watched Cade remove his helmet and turn to search the stands. His shaggy hair was damp with sweat and he pushed his fingers through it, forcing it away from his eyes.

His gaze landed on me and his grin spread. He slowly lifted an arm and pointed right at me.

Thea squealed, "I knew it!" She kicked her legs excitedly.

With a wink, Cade lowered his hand and ran off the field.

People in the stands looked around wildly, trying to find whom he'd been pointing to. I knew it was impossible for them to figure out it was me, but I still found myself trying to blend in and not try to catch their attention.

"You are so dating my brother you little liar," Thea said from beside me. I turned to her and let out a sigh. She wasn't mad at the idea of me dating her brother, oh no, she was so dang excited, which made it difficult to keep telling her that nothing was going on.

"I'm not, I swear," I told her. "I know you're probably already planning our wedding and excited over the idea of us being sister-in-laws, but Cade and I are *not* dating." I slashed my hands through the air. "We're just friends."

Thea sighed, her eyes growing sad, but she quickly brightened. "For now." She let the subject drop and turned her attention to one of the people walking the stairs selling food. Once she'd bought enough food for ten people she shoved most of it at me and demanded that I eat. Cade might be Cocky Cade, but Thea was Bossy Thea. It didn't have quite the same ring to it, but it was the truth.

I couldn't believe that only a few weeks ago I'd told this girl I wasn't here to make friends, but yet I was sitting beside her at a football game, and it was safe to say that we were friends. My plans never seemed to work out.

"So," I asked, munching on some popcorn, "where are Xander and Jace?"

"Xander plays football," she explained, "and Jace is...Jace. This isn't his thing."

"He seems kind of...odd. Nice," I assured her, "but odd."

"Like you?" Her eyes sparkled with laughter.

I laughed, tossing some popcorn at her. "Yes, like me."

"I don't really know how to explain Jace. We grew up with him too, but he didn't really become friends with Cade until high school. I don't know the story there."

"So...what's going on with you and Xander?" I asked and watched her cheeks flame with color.

"Nothing."

"Nothing? Do you want there to be something?" No way was I letting her get off that easy. Not the way she pestered me with questions about my nonexistent relationship with Cade.

"Yes. No. I don't know," she shrugged. "It's weird, because we're friends, but he's Cade's *best* friend. We grew up together and I don't think he sees me like that. I'm just Cade's sister to him."

I begged to differ. "I've seen the way he looks at you, and trust me you're not just Cade's sister to him."

She turned her gaze to me, her eyes full of hope. "Really?"

I nodded and let the subject drop.

We'd finished eating and had wadded up our trash when they players came back out on the field.

Thea became even more energetic as the game progressed, which was saying something since she'd been bad enough before.

When the score tied Thea grasped my hand so tightly it went numb.

In the final seconds of the game, Cade was sprinting across the field with the football cradled in his arm. His long legs almost seemed to blur as he ran.

I found myself standing up, and chanting, "Go! Go! Go!"

Thea grasped my hand and then we were both screaming as guys tried to knock him down.

When Thea screamed in my ear with excitement I knew Cade had made it. "He did it! Go Cade! That's my brother!" She pointed, but no one could hear her. Everyone in the stadium seemed to be screaming.

Cade's team ran over to him and the scoreboard flashed.

We'd won.

I didn't know why but my blood roared at that. This football thing could be addicting and fun when I had someone to cheer for.

"Aren't you glad you came now?"

Yes. Yes, I was. "It was okay."

"Whatever, Rae." Thea rolled her eyes.

The stands began to slowly empty out, but the energy level was still high. I was sure there were bound to be lots of celebratory parties popping up along campus. People would want to draw out this win for as long as possible.

"Think you'll come to another game?" She asked, a knowing smile on her lips. I wasn't fooling her. Not at all.

"Maybe," I shrugged, as we walked back to our dorm. I was a little bummed that I wasn't going to see Cade, but I didn't let that show. I knew he probably had a lot of stuff to do with his team. "I'd love to bring my camera next time."

She grinned. "So there will be a next time?"

I groaned. I hadn't meant to let that slip out. "Yeah, there will probably be a next time."

She smiled, clasping her hands together as she danced ahead of me humming pleasantly under her breath.

For a moment, I was envious of Thea. I wished I could see the world as beautiful and simple as she did. I used to. Now I just saw the darkness and the pain that lurked around every corner.

chapter nine

I DIDN'T KNOW WHAT TO WEAR.

Shocker.

But seriously, what did one wear on a non-date? I guessed I should dress like I normally did, but that seemed too easy.

I tapped my fingers against my lips.

"What are you doing?" Thea asked, walking into our dorm. The door slammed closed behind her—Thea never did anything quietly.

I'd hoped to be gone by the time she arrived. Of course my luck wasn't that good. Actually, I was pretty sure my luck was nonexistent.

"Trying to find something to wear," I mumbled, frustrated with myself for getting so worked up over this. What I wore shouldn't matter, but right now I was being a typical girl.

"Oh, yeah. That's right, you're going out with Cade."

"It's not a date," I spat.

She smirked. "I didn't say it was."

My cheeks colored. "It's really not."

"Hey," she lifted her hands, "you don't need to defend yourself to me." She dropped her bag on her bed. "Do you want any help?"

No. "Yes."

Thea walked over and perused my closet. "Here." She shoved torn black jeans into my hands a loose gray sweater that hung off my shoulders. "And these." She bent down, picking up a pair of chestnut colored leather boots. "Cute and simple and not trying too hard."

"I don't want to try at all."

She huffed. "There is nothing wrong with that outfit. It's cute and something you'd wear around campus. It's not a skintight dress that has your boobs hanging out asking for some attention, so pull your panties out of that wad."

My lips twitched with the threat of laughter. "Okay," I agreed.

I changed into the outfit and looked in the mirror. Thea was right. It was perfect.

Cade had texted me hours ago, telling me he'd pick me up at six. After arguing that I'd meet him at the restaurant, instead of going with him, I'd finally given in when he threatened to carry me out of the dorm and to his car if I didn't cooperate. I knew he wasn't lying.

"Are you nervous?" Thea asked.

My head snapped in her direction. "Why would I be nervous?"

"No reason," she shrugged innocently. I was going to throttle that beauty queen one of these days.

My phone vibrated in my pocket and I pulled it out to see a text from Cade telling me he was in the parking lot. Stupidly, my heart sped up.

When I looked up from my phone Thea was watching me with a knowing smile.

"See you later," she sing-songed.

"Mhmm," was my only reply, as I grabbed my bag and left.

It wasn't easy to miss Cade's black Jeep Wrangler sitting in the parking lot. The thing was huge.

He hopped out of the truck and my breath faltered.

Holy hell.

His hair was brushed back away from his forehead, which only served to accentuate the curves of his cheekbones and the cut of his chiseled chin.

He wore a light blue button down shirt that made his eyes pop even more. His shirt was tucked into a nice pair of jeans and held up by a thin black belt.

Cade was good-looking. Period. But right now...he was almost god-like.

When he chuckled I realized I'd stopped walking and stood staring at him. Such a great way to start off this non-date.

I shook my head and forced my feet forward.

He opened the passenger door for me and I climbed inside. I couldn't help being reminded of my first date with Brett.

My heart raced in chest.

Thump. Thump. Thump.

I'd had a crush on Brett for longer than I'd care to admit and I'd been shocked when he asked me to go to the movies with him tonight.

At first I'd been excited, then scared, and finally I was just plain worried.

Worried about what to wear.

Worried about how to fix my hair.

Worried about what to do or say.

The last thing I wanted to do was make a fool of myself. I'd been on dates before, and kissed guys, but none of them were Brett.

They didn't make my heart pound like he did.

Or a light sweat break out across my skin.

I took a deep breath and finished smoothing out the curls in my hair. I did my makeup, making sure not to do it too heavy. After all, we were going to the movies. This was meant to be casual and I didn't want to get carried away.

"Stop freaking out, Rachael," I scolded myself. "You're being stupid."

And I was. I'd known Brett my whole life, but a part of me felt like tonight was monumental— like my life might never be the same again.

I fluffed my hair one last time and went into my closet, trying on four different outfits before settling on a pair of skinny jeans, a flowered peplum top, and boots. It was nice, but not like I was trying too hard...I hoped.

"Rachael!" My mom yelled up the stairs. "Brett is here!"

My heart jolted with excitement.

I took my time going downstairs, not wanting to appear too eager.

I couldn't help smiling when I saw Brett waiting for me in the foyer. His red hair was gelled back stylishly and he was dressed in jeans and a green polo shirt that made his eyes appear even greener. He grinned when he saw me and as his eyes perused my body I felt my cheeks heat.

I'd never been one to act so shy and girly before, but Brett made me nervous.

My mom and dad stood back a ways, watching us. Finally my dad cleared his throat and looked between the two of us. "Have her back by ten."

"Daaaaad," I whined. "I'm sixteen. I can stay out later than that!"

"Fine," he sighed, scrubbing a hand over his beard, "eleven. But any later," he warned, "and I'm calling the police."

Brett chuckled. "Don't worry, Mr. Wilder. I'll have her back in time."

My dad narrowed his eyes and made a grunting sound that said: I'll believe it when I see it. I knew my dad was just messing with Brett, though.

"Come on," Brett said to me, "we don't want to be late for the movie."

My body hummed when he put his hand on my waist, guiding me to the door. My insides were a jumbled mess of excitement.

We walked to his car in silence and he opened the door of his hand-me-down BMW for me to slip inside. "Thanks," I smiled.

He smiled back. Once he was seated, he admitted, "I didn't think you'd agree to go on a date with me."

"What? Why not?" I gasped, astonished.

He shrugged. "Look at you, you're beautiful, and smart, and amazing."

"You're all those things too," I countered.

He grinned crookedly and lowered his head so that his hair brushed his forehead. "Not like you," he chuckled, starting the car.

It didn't take us long to get to the theater. He took me to the old one in town. Most people preferred the fancy new one attached to the mall, but not me, and Brett knew that. There was something so real about this one and it reminded me of a time when I believed people were happier— when life was simple.

"Is this okay?" Brett asked.

"It's perfect," I smiled. Our date had barely started and it was already better than I imagined.

Inside we ordered popcorn and soda.

The theater was pretty empty. Most people didn't come to this one. I liked that it allowed us to have a little more privacy.

We took our seats towards the back.

The lights dimmed and I swore my heart sped up even more, if that was possible.

When Brett reached to hold my hand halfway through the movie I thought I stopped breathing.

Once the movie ended and he still didn't let go of my hand I thought I might burst from happiness.

We walked out of the theater and Brett looked at his watch. "We still have an hour before you have to go home, do you want to walk around town for a while?"

"Sure," I smiled. I wasn't ready to say goodbye.

We hadn't walked very far when Brett pointed to a diner lit up down the street. "They have the best pancakes I've ever had. Are you hungry?"

I wasn't, but I nodded, because if Brett wanted pancakes then we were going to have pancakes.

He grinned and pulled me into the diner. His smile was wide as he looked at me across the table. We placed our order and as soon as the waitress was gone Brett started asking me questions.

We spent the next forty minutes laughing about random things that happened in school and stories from our past.

Brett paid for our meal and we headed back to his car.

On the drive home he kept a tight hold on my hand. His was warm and soft. Comforting.

"I want to do this again...if you'd like that." He bowed his head, as if he seemed unsure of what my reaction would be.

"I'd love it." I probably agreed a little too eagerly, but it was too late to take my words back.

He grinned. *"Good."* He parked in my driveway and I started to get out of the car, but his hold on my hand tightened and he wouldn't let go.

"Rachael?"

"Yeah?" I turned back around to face him and our faces were only inches apart. In the dim light I could see his pupils dilate.

He tilted his head to the side and closed his eyes.

I did the same and when our lips connected I felt like a fireworks explosion had gone off in my body. Kissing a guy had never felt this...magical. I melted against his touch. I grasped his shirt in my hand, moving my lips with his. When his tongue nudged my lips they parted with a gasp.

He pulled away and placed a tender kiss on my cheek.

"See you later, Rachael."

"Bye." My voice came out sounding breathless.

I eased out of the car with shaking legs, looking at him over my shoulder. I knew that something had changed between us tonight and there was no going back—I didn't want to.

I shook my head, coming back to reality. I hoped Cade didn't notice me zoning out, but since he was just easing into the car I figured I was safe.

He looked over at me and smiled. "You look beautiful, Rae."

"Thanks," I squeaked.

Despite my demands that this not be a date it was really starting to feel like a date.

Cade backed out of the parking space and headed off campus.

I didn't bother asking him where we were going, because I doubted he'd tell me. The day at the carnival I remembered a mention of burgers.

Cade reached over and fiddled with the radio. "What kind of music do you like?"

"This is fine," I told him. "I'm not picky."

Cade nodded and tapped his long fingers against the steering wheel. He hummed the song softly under his breath.

I sat back in the seat and looked out the window. I hadn't gone exploring yet, but the town surrounding campus looked surprisingly quaint.

"Do you like it here?" Cade asked, breaking the silence between us. "College?"

I shrugged and then nodded. "Yeah, I do. It's nice being on my own." Not being judged. Having a real life.

"I probably shouldn't admit this," those dimples popped out in his cheeks when he smiled, "but I had trouble my first year away. I *really* missed my mom's cooking," he chuckled.

"Yeah, the food on campus is a bit..." I wrinkled my nose.

"Lacking?" He supplied.

"That's a nicer word for it," I laughed, tucking a stray curl behind my ear. "I drive Thea crazy because I eat cereal for most of my meals. But the food looks so gross."

"It doesn't taste much better than it looks," he winked. That wink made my stomach stir in ways it never had before. "Don't worry though, where we're going you won't be eating cereal. Get ready to feast upon the best burger of your life." Ducking his head slightly he chuckled. Lifting his hands from the steering wheel he held them apart. "I swear they're this big. About the size of your head."

"Are you implying I have a large head?" I kept my face neutral so he wouldn't know I was joking.

"I didn't mean—wait, you're messing with me aren't you?"

Of course my lips had twitched, giving me away.

"Yeah."

"Wow," he chuckled.

"What?" I asked, tilting my head slightly in wonder at his statement.

"It's just...I don't think I've heard you make a joke. It's refreshing." He gave me a serious look before returning his eyes to the road. "You're full of surprises, Rae."

"Something tells me you are too," I countered. "Everyone has secrets."

A muscle in Cade's jaw twitched. "Yes, yes they do."

⁂

"Marty!" Cade cried when we walked into the restaurant. I stood awkwardly behind him as he addressed the older man I assumed was Marty. "Long time no see. I've missed you." Cade slung his arm around the man's shoulders and turned to introduce me. "Rae, this is Marty the owner of this fine establishment. Marty, this is Rae."

"A girlfriend?" Marty's fuzzy gray brows shot up so far they disappeared beneath his bushy gray hair. "You've never brought a girl here before."

"I'm not his girlfriend," I growled.

Cade gave Marty a sad look. "Unfortunately the lovely Rae here doesn't like me that way. Such a shame, right? We could be great together."

Marty chuckled and looked at me. "I can understand not liking this goon. He can be a bit much."

"He can," I agreed.

"Go sit down," Marty ordered, "I'll send someone over to get your drink order."

"Come on," Cade nodded towards the corner of the restaurant that wasn't as busy.

The place seemed a bit shady from the outside...and the inside too. The walls were crumbling and the floors looked dirty. I had to admit the food looked delicious—at least what I'd seen in passing.

Menus were already on the table and I picked one up, looking it over.

"Everything is good," Cade told me, not even bothering to look, "you can't go wrong."

I pointed to the menu and leaned forward a bit. He leaned in too and there was barely any space between us. Up close I could see flecks of gold in his blue eyes. "It looks like everything is not one of the items on the menu."

He bellowed out a laugh. "Joke number two. This night is shaping up to be very interesting."

"If that's what you call interesting," I sat back, "then you really need to look up the definition of the word."

He smiled, scratching his jaw. "You're not like other girls, Rae."

"No, I'm not," I agreed. I wasn't most like people. Not anymore. My innocence had been stolen a year ago when I ruined everything.

"So, where are you from Rae?"

I squirmed. Why did he have to ask that question? "Not anywhere near here." I answered vaguely. Vague was always good.

"I figured that." He stared at me, waiting for me to say something. I knew I needed to give him some kind of information, but I didn't want to lie. Lying only made things worse and my life was already fucked up enough as it was.

"What can I get you to drink?"

The sound of the waitress' voice was akin to angels singing. I was thankful for the reprieve.

"Water for me," Cade said.

"Water for me as well," I smiled at her.

"I'll give you a minute to look at the menu and I'll be right back with your drinks." She tapped her fingers lightly against the wood tabletop and then she was gone.

Cade's eyes seared me when I looked up. "Why don't you want to tell me where you're from?"

"Because it's not important."

He sighed and I felt kind of bad for sounding like such a bitch. "Look," I placed my hands on the table and leaned forward, "there are things that happened there, bad things, and I just don't want to talk about it. Okay?"

He absorbed my words and I thought for a minute he was going to protest. "Okay," he agreed.

I let out a sigh of relief.

"What *can* I ask you?"

"I don't know." I laughed. "Something easy."

"What's your middle name?" He asked.

"Madison. Yours?"

"Paul. Favorite color?"

"Purple. Yours?" I smiled at our back and forth. This, right here, was simple and easy. I needed more of this in my life.

"Gray, I guess. I don't really have a favorite. Favorite movie?"

I had to think about that one. "Titanic. It's romantic and heartbreaking. What's yours?"

"Ghostbusters. Favorite band?"

"One Republic. Yours?" I rested my chin on my hand, fighting another smile.

"Fall Out Boy. Favorite—"

"Here's your water. Are you ready to order?"

I jumped at the sound of the waitress' voice. I hadn't realized it but while we were talking Cade and I had leaned closer and closer together. I sat back, tucking my hands onto my lap.

Cade ordered and I muttered, "I'll have the same." I hadn't even really bothered to scrutinize the menu.

"Good choice," Cade grinned.

"Of course you'd say that." I squeezed the lemon into my glass of water just to have something to do.

"Well, I mean you did order the same thing as me and I have *excellent* taste in everything."

"Is that so?" I asked, raising a brow.

"I mean, I am sitting here having dinner with you. I think that proves I make good choices."

I bit my lip and looked down. My fingers found the paper napkin on the table and I began to pick it apart. "What is it about me that makes you think I'm a good choice?"

His eyes narrowed. "You really don't see yourself the way others see you, do you?"

"I don't know what you mean," I muttered, not meeting his gaze.

"When I say certain things you act like you're a monster." I was a monster, Cade just didn't know it yet. "I don't understand it."

"You don't understand *it* or *me*?"

"You. I don't fucking understand you." His jaw tightened.

I lowered my head and realized that I was ruining our whole evening. "Look," my voice cracked, "you don't know what I've been through. The things people have said to me. The names I've been called. It's been horrible."

"Then tell me," he pleaded.

"I can't. I barely know you."

"Don't you see," he snapped, waving his hand between us, "I'm trying to get to know you but you're making it impossible." He let out a heavy, pent-up breath. "I'm sorry. I shouldn't have snapped at you," he laid his hands on his table. "But I promise you right now, Rae, I *will* get you to trust me and one day, when you're ready, you're going to tell me everything."

I doubted it, but I didn't tell him that.

Our food arrived and I decided to change the subject. I didn't want there to be anymore awkwardness between us because of me. And frankly, I actually wanted both of us to enjoy tonight.

"I had fun at your game," I told him, squirting some ketchup on my plate.

"You did?" He perked up, smiling.

"Yeah. It was cool seeing you play. I've never been into the sport before," I shrugged.

"And now you are?" He questioned, his smile turning into a full-blown grin. The dimples weren't quite showing, but I felt like the tension had dissipated fairly well.

I held my thumb and index finger up with a tiny bit of space between them. "Just a little bit."

"Only a little bit?"

"Okay, maybe this much." I widened the space.

"That's better," he chuckled, taking a bite of his burger.

I did the same. "You know, Thea is extra crazy at football games. I thought she might pull my arm off with the way she kept yanking on it, or maybe bust my ear drum."

Cade chuckled. "Thea is highly enthusiastic."

"Yeah, kind of like a puppy."

Cade snorted and then laughed so hard I feared he couldn't breathe. "Did you just compare my sister to a puppy?"

"Hey," I raised my hands, "don't tell me you haven't thought the same thing. She's a ball of energy. Except in the mornings. That's when she's dreadful."

Cade continued to laugh. "I'm sure it must be interesting living with Thea."

"You have no idea. I'm really tempted to throw everything she owns that's pink out the window. It's just too much. No one should ever own that much pink." Yeah, I *really* hated pink.

"You should see her room at home if you think your dorm room is bad," Cade chortled.

"Oh, God." I slapped my hands over my eyes, like the thought alone was too much to handle.

"In her defense, that's mostly our mom's doing. She always thought Thea should be a princess," he explained, grabbing a fry.

"Like with the pageants?" I questioned, raising a brow.

"She told you about that?" Cade's eyes widened with surprise.

"I guessed. She confirmed." I replied.

"Ah, I see," he chuckled. "She doesn't tell most people about that. She finds it embarrassing. Our mom's a bit...zany."

"That's a kind word for crazy." Shit. I shouldn't have said that out loud.

Cade chuckled. "That's true."

We finished eating while chatting about more random things. It surprised me how easy it was being with Cade. Even when it was rough—like our conversation earlier—I still found myself comfortable in his presence. I might've tried to stay away from him, but that was for his protection. He couldn't see that I would ruin him, but I was growing too weak to stay away. I needed Cade Montgomery in my life anyway he'd give me.

The waitress laid the receipt on the table and before I could react, Cade had already grabbed it with a credit card in his hand.

"Cade," I groaned, "you said this dinner was as friends. Please let me pay my half."

"No can do, Sunshine," he shook his head.

"Caaaaade," I drew out his name.

He stared at me and I stared right back.

The waitress came back by and he handed her his credit card.

"You didn't need to do that," I told him.

"I know," he grinned. "Now just sit back and say thank you."

I sighed, fighting the urge to kick him beneath the table. "Thank you, Cade. The meal was delicious and I enjoyed spending time with you." I meant it too.

His grin spread. "I enjoyed spending time with you too."

My fingers tangled together and I looked away, unable to handle another second of his stare.

The waitress returned with his credit card and after signing the slip we headed out to his Jeep.

"So," he started, shoving his hands in the pockets of his jeans, "does this mean I might get to take you on a real date?"

I stopped walking and leveled him with a glare. "Don't push your luck." I liked Cade way more than I should already, anything that might lead to *more* had to be avoided at all costs.

He chuckled and lifted his arms in mock defense. "Hey, I had to ask." He reached out and opened the passenger door for me. I climbed inside and swore I felt his eyes on my butt.

Once he got in he turned the heat up and rested his elbow on the armrest. His hand was dangerously close to mine. If I was a different girl— one who hadn't been through what I had—Cade would be the perfect guy, and instead of running from him at every turn I'd open my arms and embrace him. I was scared though—terrified, really—of what he would think of me if he knew the truth. The best course of action was to distance myself from him, but I knew it would be impossible. Not only because Cade was unavoidable, but because I'd actually come to like him.

The drive back to campus was peaceful.

He parked the Jeep and unbuckled his seatbelt. "I'll walk you to the door so I know you get in safe." He climbed out of the car and met me on the other side. Together we headed towards the dorm in the distance.

At the door I stopped. "Thanks," I smiled, looking up at him. "For walking me to the door and for dinner. I...I had a good time."

"Good," he grinned. He leaned his solid shoulder against the glass door so I couldn't open it.

I stood still, waiting for whatever he might do or say next, because with Cade you never knew.

Only a few seconds had passed when he lifted his fingers to my cheek. My eyes closed and my lips parted with a breath as his fingers ghosted against my skin. His touch felt like the most delicious kind of torture.

"Goodnight, Rae."

I blinked my eyes open slowly and saw him already walking back to his Jeep.

"Goodnight, Cade," I whispered, lifting my fingers to my cheek. I'd never known a simple caress could make your whole body soar with feelings, but Cade apparently had a magic touch.

chapter ten

"I HATE YOUR BROTHER and he needs to crawl in a hole and die before I kill him myself," I snapped at Thea, as I hunched over the toilet. I'd spent all night sick with stupid food poisoning and I still wasn't feeling better.

Thea stood in the doorway frowning. "I'll give him the memo."

"You do that," I assured her. I flushed the toilet and brushed my teeth for at least the twentieth time since I'd gotten sick. "I'm going back to bed."

"And I'm going to class." She pulled on a jacket and grabbed her backpack. "I'll check on you at lunch and see if you want anything to eat."

I gagged at the mention of food. "That's unlikely." I planned to never eat again.

I burrowed my way into the fort of blankets on my bed. I rolled around until they were wrapped so tightly around me that I'd have to cut my way out. Sleep had been pretty much nonexistent last night and there was no way I'd make it through class today. I was just going to have to suck it up and miss. That was upsetting, but I didn't have a choice.

I was close to drifting asleep when someone knocked on the door.

I held my breath, hoping they'd go away, but then they knocked again.

Dammit. I was going to have to get out of my cozy nest and that was so not cool.

I figured it was probably the RA, wondering why it sounded like someone was dying in here.

I rolled out of bed and pulled on a sweatshirt, trying to tame my wild mane of hair when the person knocked again.

I swung it open and wouldn't you know, there was Cade. Apparently he'd gotten the memo and he wasn't afraid of what I wanted to do to him. I might feel like shit right now and too weak to do anything, but the minute I felt better he was going to suffer for this.

"Thea said you were sick."

"No," I held up a hand, "not *sick*. I have food poisoning."

He winced. "Shit."

"Yeah," I leaned against the doorway for support. "So, if you wouldn't mind, I'm going back to bed now." I started to close the door but he pushed his way inside. "God you're fucking annoying," I groaned, "can't you just go away? I'm not in the mood, Cade."

"You're sick. It's my fault," he put his hands on his hips, nodding at his words, "so I'm going to do the right thing and take care of you."

"No, the right thing would be to get out of my fucking room and leave me alone."

He chuckled. "I'm glad to know that even when you're sick you're still the same, Rae."

"Get out," I pleaded.

"No, I'm staying."

I sighed heavily. I was never going to win this argument. Cade was too stubborn for his own good.

"Fine," I climbed into bed once more. "Then be a good lad and fetch me a Sprite."

He snorted. "Did you just use the words *lad* and *fetch* in one sentence?"

"I did," I declared.

"I feel used."

"Hey," I scolded, cracking an eye open, "you're the one that said you weren't going to leave. Now make yourself useful."

His lips turned up into a smirk. "I'll be right back."

By the time he got back I had already dozed off and he had to wake me. "Here," he slid a straw into the can and held it to my lips, "drink. I'm sure you're dehydrated."

"That's why I asked for the Sprite."

"Such a smart ass," he chuckled. "Now drink."

I did and the cool liquid soothed my parched throat. "That's enough," I told him, when I'd had my fill. He sat the can on the table beside my bed.

"Scoot over," he demanded.

"What? You're not getting in bed with me," I guffawed.

"Yes, I am," he pushed gently at my body, trying to coax me over. "I need to be close in case you need anything."

"Thea's bed is plenty close!" I squeaked.

"Yeah, but if there's an emergency I think it's imperative that I be within touching distance," he argued.

"Where do you come up with this stuff?" I gaped. Before he could answer, I said, "Listen, I don't even want you here, so don't push your luck. Be a good boy and sit on Thea's bed. I'm going to take a nap. Frankly, I'm exhausted and don't feel like dealing with any bullshit."

"Okay," he raised his hands in surrender. "You win." He sat on Thea's bed. "I'll sit here and be a good boy," he waved his hands in the air with a grin as he mimed my words.

"Thank you," I croaked, and I meant it. In fact, I was kind of glad someone was here with me, but I wasn't going to tell Cade that.

"Go to sleep, Rae," he whispered.

The way he looked at me had my throat closing up. It reminded me of a time I'd tried to erase from my memory—of a boy that had stolen my heart and died with it.

❧

"You like him, don't you?" Sarah teased, swinging on the swing set in my backyard.

I tore my gaze away from where Brett was mowing the grass in his yard.

"What? No, of course not," I scoffed. "We're only friends."

"Leave her alone," Hannah defended me. "If she likes him that's her business, not ours."

Sarah and Hannah might've been my best friends—but Sarah was one person I couldn't share everything with. She was a gossiper and if I admitted to having a crush on Brett it would be all over the middle school halls come Monday morning.

"It's pretty obvious," Sarah snorted. "But if you don't like him," she hopped off the swing set, "then I think I'll go talk to him." She tossed a smirk over her shoulder and sauntered through the field that separated my house from Brett's.

I knew she was only doing it to get a reaction from me, but my feelings were uncontrollable. When Brett turned off the lawnmower to talk to her she put her hand on his arm, looking back at me. I saw red.

"Rachael—" Hannah warned, but it was too late.

I was already marching across the field, ready to drag Sarah back by her shiny platinum blonde hair.

"Sarah, what are you doing?" I hissed, leveling her with a glare. I'd never had the desire to claw a girl's eyes out, but right then I was ready to pounce on her.

"I was just asking Brett if he'd like to hang out tomorrow." She batted her eyes innocently.

"He can't. He's busy. We have plans," I spat.

"Plans?" Brett piped in.

"Yes," I maneuvered so I was in front of him, "very important plans that can't be canceled."

"Oh, well forget I said anything." Sarah smiled victoriously and headed back to my house.

"What was that about Rachael?" Brett asked, closing his hand around my arm so I couldn't leave.

I turned around and glanced sheepishly at my feet. I'd always been able to tell him everything, but this was different. I refused to jeopardize our friendship by telling him I liked him.

"I don't know," I mumbled.

His fingers grasped my chin, forcing me to look at him. His stare was intense and I squirmed, trying to get away.

"I really better get back to them." I tossed a thumb over my shoulder.

He stared for a moment longer and released me. "Yeah, I guess so."

I turned and started walking away, pushing the tall grass out of my way.

"Rachael!" He called.

I glanced at him over my shoulder. "Yeah."

"I'll see you tomorrow, since we have plans and all," he winked, turning my world upside down.

"Y-yeah, tomorrow," I stuttered.

He chuckled and the lawnmower started up once more.

I shook my head and went back to the swing set in my yard.

"I knew it," Sarah chimed, clapping her hands together.

I made no comment. Instead I looked over at the boy next door and let myself dream of what a future with him might be like.

&

I couldn't move when I woke up. At first I figured that was because of the way I'd wrapped the blankets around me, but I quickly realized that I was wrong.

Cade hadn't listened to me at all.

That little liar had waited until I fell asleep and gotten in bed with me. He wasn't under the covers, but he'd still managed to wrap his arms around me and put one of his legs between mine. His breath tickled my neck as he slept.

I should of woken him up, but I didn't.

Instead, I stared at him like a complete weirdo. I'd never really allowed myself to study his face, but now that I had my chance I wasn't going to miss this opportunity.

Since he was sleeping the cut of his chin and the angles of his cheekbones seemed softer.

A lock of hair fell over his eyes and wiggled my hand out to brush it away. His hair was surprisingly smooth between my fingers. Unable to help myself I brushed my finger down the straight line of his nose and over the curve of his lips.

"Rae?"

I jumped, pulling my hand back.

"What are you doing?" He cracked an eye open.

"Uh…" I had no explanation for what I was doing and he knew it.

He smirked. "Speechless? That's a new one."

I guessed it was.

"At least you didn't push me out of bed. I was expecting that," he chuckled, raising up to peer down at me.

"There's still time." My voice sounded breathless with want and it pissed me off. I was sick and regardless I shouldn't want Cade. But I did. Oh God, I did. How could I not? He was nice, and funny, and hot, and a million other things wrapped into one. I'd have to be a fucking nun *not* to be attracted to him. It didn't mean I was going to act on it though.

Cade eased out of bed, careful not to kick me with his long legs. He pulled on his boots and my heart froze. He was leaving. Why did that thought fill me with such sadness?

"I'm going to get you some soup. I won't be gone long," he started towards the door.

I sat up, pulling my hair over my shoulder. "Okay." I forced a smile. "Thanks, Cade."

He tapped his fingers against the half-open door, his eyes oddly serious as he looked at me. "It's no trouble at all."

He ducked his head and the door clicked closed behind him.

While he was gone I decided to shower. No way was I doing that with him around.

I took an extra long time washing my hair and scrubbing my body. After being sick all night I didn't smell pleasant. I wondered how Cade had been able to ignore it.

I watched the white soapsuds swirl down the drain before turning off the water. I pulled a towel around my body and brushed my hair so that it didn't tangle and I ended up looking like Medusa. That was something no one wanted to see. I padded into my room and changed into a pair of sweatpants and a baggy shirt. I had just climbed back into bed when Cade returned. Thank God I'd been dressed. I couldn't imagine how mortified I'd feel if he saw me naked.

He sat down on the end of my bed and shoved a Styrofoam cup with a lid on it into my hands. "Eat," he demanded, and this time handed me a spoon.

I plucked the lid off and set it aside. I had to admit the aroma of the chicken noodle soup made my stomach rumble.

"You're not going to feed me?" I joked, dipping the spoon into the liquid.

He chuckled, brushing his hair out of his eyes. "I figured you'd hurt me if I tried. I'm kind of afraid of you."

"You, the big bad star football player, are afraid of me?" I laughed.

"Hey, you can be scary," he defended.

"I feel like I should be offended." I lifted the spoon to my lips.

"Nah, I like the way you are. If I didn't I wouldn't be here right now." His face grew serious and I knew he meant it.

"Thanks," I whispered, lowering my head so he couldn't see my eyes.

"Thanks? For what?" He was puzzled.

I slowly lifted my head and forced myself to look at him. "For staying with me today. I know I was kind of a bitch this morning but I'm glad you're here."

His smiled widened and his eyes lit up. "Anything for you, Sunshine."

"Why do you like me?" I asked. I couldn't seem to stop the words from spilling from my mouth. I wanted to know. I wasn't the nicest person, not anymore, and Cade...he was amazing.

He chuckled and leaned his head against the wall. "Because I see more than you think I do and I like what I see." He turned his head towards me. "One day you'll tell me what weighs so heavily on your shoulders. And you know what, Rae?"

"What?" I whispered.

"It won't change anything for me."

My hands shook and a little bit of soup sloshed over the side. "You don't know me."

"I beg to differ." His blue eyes flicked up to mine. "I think we've done a mighty fine job of getting to know each other the past few weeks. We're friends, Rae, and yeah I want more with you. I'm not going to hide that fact."

"But why?" I gasped. "Y-you could have any girl you wanted, why me?"

He shrugged. "Those girls don't want me for me. Things are different with you."

"How can you be so sure?" I countered. "What if I'm just like those other girls?"

"Are you?" He asked, his lips twitching with the threat of a smile.

"No," I answered, staring down at the soup that was rapidly growing cold.

"Exactly." He nodded. "Being around you, it's refreshing. Even if you never wanted an actual relationship with me I think I could be content with this...with being your friend."

"Really?" I raised a brow in disbelief.

He chuckled, rubbing his jaw. "I could try."

"I-I would like more with you," I admitted and my heart lurched when his face lit up, "but I'm not ready for that."

His face fell and he nodded. "I understand."

"Do you?" I asked.

"Not really," he admitted, "but I can respect that you have a reason."

"You're something else Cade Montgomery," I stated, staring at him in awe.

He chuckled. "What's that supposed to mean?"

"Just that most guys in your position—being a superstar football player—would be a major asshole, but you're not. You're unlike any guy I've ever met." It was in that moment that I realized Cade was an old soul. I'd often heard my mom use the term to describe people who seemed wise beyond their years, and that was Cade. Yeah, he could be cocky at times, but he'd never, not once, been a jerk to me.

He shrugged. "I never asked for popularity and I didn't want it anyway. At the end of the day I'm really a dork," he winked.

I laughed, smiling. "You're not a dork you're just..."

"I'm just what, Rae?" His voice grew husky and desire swirled in the air between us. My rapidly growing feelings for Cade scared me and made me feel like I was betraying my first love. But he was gone and Cade was here, and could I really suffer alone for the rest of my life? My mom always told me one day I'd have to accept the harsh facts and move on from the past. I used to think that was impossible, but Cade, and even Thea, had shown me that I could let go. I was still holding on tight to the past though, but one finger was slipping and it wouldn't be long until I was forced to release it.

"You." I finally answered. "You're just you."

He grinned, his whole face lighting up. "I take it that's a good thing?"

"Yeah," I cracked a smile, "because even when I want to hate you, I like you."

He chuckled. "You want to hate me?"

I finished the soup—or at least what I could manage to get down—and set it aside. "Yes," I answered honestly, "because hating you would be so much easier than wanting you."

"So..." He started, "you know I want you, and now you've admitted to wanting me too, but we're going to do nothing about it?"

I frowned, snuggling beneath the covers—more for a silly sense of protection than actual need for the warmth. "I can't, Cade. You said you could try being my friend and that's what I need from you right now."

"I did say that," he nodded, "and I meant it." He sighed, pinching the bridge of his nose. "This won't be easy for me, but I'll be damned if I can't have you in my life in some way. I'm sick and tired of isolating myself because of fear."

"What do you have to be afraid of?" I asked, suddenly grasping that there was more to Cade than I'd ever realized. Lately, I'd become too blinded by own thoughts and feelings to see other people's problems. But now it was clear, things weren't dandy for Cade.

He slowly raised his eyes to meet mine. The normally bright blue had become a stormy gray. "Monsters."

I made no comment, because I understood his meaning.

With a sigh he kicked off his shoes. "Roll over. It's cuddle time."

"Uh...I don't think friends cuddle." My words fell flat since I was already scooting over to make room for him.

He brushed my hair away from my neck and his breath tickled my skin. "We're special friends, Rae."

If special was code for fucked up then that's exactly what we were, because I knew now that we were two people haunted by very real demons.

chapter eleven

WEEKS PASSED AND LIFE SEEMED to be...not good, but okay.

Cade and I were working on being friends and Thea was...well, Thea.

Cade joined us now for lunch most days, unless he had something else he had to do. Since he was a senior he didn't have many classes, which left him with a lot of free time.

He was already sitting at the lunch table when I arrived. His long legs were kicked up on the table and he had his hands crossed behind his head. People, guys and girls, tended to stare at Cade when he was around. I couldn't blame them. There was something about the sight of him that was mesmerizing. Lord knew he made my brain and body do funny things.

"Hey, Rae of Sunshine," he greeted me. "How's your day been?"

"Boring," I supplied with a shrug, sitting my bag and food down.

"Boring?" His brows rose. "We can't have that."

"Some days just are." I unwrapped my sandwich and looked it over carefully for any mysterious discoloration or oozing—school food could be gross. Since it looked okay I took a bite.

His feet dropped to the ground with a thump. He leaned towards me, flicking his shaggy hair out of his eyes. "What can I do to make this boring day exciting?"

I could think of a million and one ways he could make this day more exciting. Most of those ideas included him naked and sweaty—God, my hormones were in overdrive lately.

I didn't say tell him that, though.

"You could let me take your picture," I supplied. I'd wanted to photograph Cade for a while now, but I hadn't wanted to tell him that—he was already cocky enough as it was.

His eyes widened in surprise. "You want to take my picture?" He grinned slowly. "Oh, this could be interesting."

A lump formed in my throat. Something told me my suggestion was going to earn me nothing but trouble. I knew I should've kept my mouth shut.

Thea appeared at the table and sat down. She was breathless, with her hair blown back. "God, it's windy out there."

"Rae wants to take my picture," Cade announced, not acknowledging her comment.

Thea gave me a sly smile and turned to her brother, her face sobering. "I didn't realize Rae was doing nudes now."

I choked on my sandwich.

Thea reached over and beat my back as I struggled for air. "Thea!" I groaned when I had enough air.

"What?" She shrugged innocently. "It was a good joke. Admit it."

Cade seemed to think so. He was laughing so hard I was surprised tears weren't streaming down his face.

"It wasn't even remotely funny," I huffed.

"Aw, come on, Rae," Cade chortled, "it was funny."

I picked at my sandwich, suddenly not hungry. Nope, I was mortified, because what Thea said had reflected my previous thoughts.

As my humiliation subsided I grudgingly admitted, "It was a little funny."

"See?" Cade grinned. "That wasn't so hard now was it?" Without waiting for me to answer, he asked, "So when are we going to do this?" He tipped the chair back on two legs and waited for me to answer.

"After my last class, I guess," I shrugged, finishing my sandwich. While my appetite might have vanished moments ago I knew if I didn't eat now I'd be starving in an hour. "Around three?"

"Sounds good." He drummed his knuckles against the top of the table. "What do you think?" He over exaggerated a pout. "Will I make a good model?"

"If you don't do that I think you'll be fine." I found myself cracking a smile.

"Oh, man," he groaned, "I thought that was going to be my signature pose."

"Not even close."

"I love it when you get bossy," he smirked.

Thea gagged. "You guys are the most sickeningly sweet couple ever and you're not even a couple. Just do it already so I don't have to continue to watch your nasty foreplay."

Cade chuckled. "The fact that you think this is foreplay is hysterical, but also a good thing, because it means I don't have to kill anyone on this campus for touching you." Oh no. Cade's protective big brother side was coming out. I knew Thea hated it.

She wrinkled her nose. "You realize I'm not a nun, right?"

Cade's face screwed up with distaste. "Let's end this conversation before I do something stupid."

My phone started vibrating in my pocket. I sighed. I knew who it was and the last thing I wanted to do was talk to her.

"I'll see you guys later," I told them, answering my phone as I gathered up my stuff. "Hi, mom." I tried to keep phone calls with my mom to a maximum of once a week. It wasn't that I didn't want to talk to my mom, I'd always been close with her and told her everything, but after last year things changed. She couldn't protect me anymore and she became yet another reminder of everything I lost, because she was so closely tied to all my memories.

"Rachael, you haven't called in a while and I was getting worried. Is everything okay?"

"It's great," I said honestly, throwing my trash away before heading for the glass double doors. As I left I could feel Cade's gaze on my back like a brand marking me. "I've been really busy."

"Oh, of course," she sighed, "I miss you, Rachael. I wish you'd call us more. You've only spoken to your dad once since you left. It's not easy for us having our only baby away at school. Will we see you at Thanksgiving at least?"

I hadn't thought once about the holidays, but the thought of going home was nearly crippling. I stopped and leaned against the wall of one of the buildings, needing the support.

"I'm not sure, mom. The break is only a few days and as busy as I've been I doubt I'll have the time to drive home." I pinched the bridge of my nose, feeling terrible for the lie, but now that I was away from that god-awful town I never wanted to go back.

"Oh, well if anything changes you let me know. I'm sure your dad would be happy to drive down there and get you. It's only three hours from us."

"Mom, we'll see, okay?"

"Okay," she agreed, but she knew I wasn't coming home. I think she was beginning to realize that I may never come home again. "I'll talk to you soon, sweetie."

"Yep."

"Love you."

"Love you too, mom," I hung up, and tears pricked my eyes. I wished so much that I could go back to the days where my mom and dad could chase all the monsters away. But now they lived inside me, where no one but me could see.

"Rae?"

I looked up and saw Cade jogging towards me.

I blinked my eyes to clear them of moisture. "Yeah?"

"I just wanted to check on you," he explained, stopping in front of me. "You seemed upset when you left."

"I'm fine," I assured him.

"Who were you talking to?" He winced. "Shit, never mind, that sounds like a nosy question so don't answer."

"It was my mom," I supplied, suppressing a laugh at his words.

"Oh," he frowned, "are things...rough with you guys?"

I shrugged, not sure how much I should tell him. "We're close, or we used to be. Then shit happened and...I lost who I was. I couldn't confide in my mom anymore. Nothing was really the same."

"Couldn't or wouldn't?" He questioned.

"Huh?"

"You couldn't or wouldn't confide in your mom?" He clarified.

I sighed, glancing down at the ground and away from his penetrating gaze. "Wouldn't."

"That's hard." He reached up and grasped one of the curls blowing in my face.

"W-what?" I suddenly couldn't think, not with him standing so close. It was like my brain had lost all sense of function.

He chuckled, seeming to know what he'd done to me. "It's hard having no one to talk to."

"You speak from experience." It wasn't a question. I'd caught the meaning in his words.

He nodded, tucking the curl he'd been playing with behind my ear. "I do."

"You have secrets," I stated, my eyes flicking up to his.

He nodded and leaned forward. I stopped breathing as his lips brushed my ear. "I'll tell you mine if you tell me yours."

Before I could react he was gone, striding across campus.

chapter twelve

I REGRETTED MAKING THE SUGGESTION to take Cade's picture. This gave me free reign to stare at him and oh Lord my stomach was doing somersaults. After a few pictures he'd stripped off his shirt—despite the fact that it was fifty degrees and windy—and revealed his lickable abs. Yes, lickable, because I was standing here looking through the lens of the camera thinking about how I wanted to run my tongue over all the dents and curves of his stomach.

I needed to get a grip and tell my hormones to calm the fuck down.

Cade had closed his eyes, lying in the grass as multi-colored leaves swirled around him. It made for an amazing picture, but I was still tempted to tell him to put his shirt on. But then he'd know it was bothering me and I couldn't have that. I guess I'd just have to tolerate it. As if it was such a hardship to look at his chest.

"How's the picture taking going?" He asked, cracking one eye open.

I jumped at the sound of his voice. It had been quiet between us for a while and he'd scared me.

"Good," I said. It seemed to be the only word my mouth could formulate at the moment.

"Can I see?" He asked, sitting up and sweeping his hair away from his face—but not before I snapped another photo.

I sat down beside him and he scooted over so there was no distance between our bodies.

His scent was magnetic and I found myself leaning even closer.

My hands shook slightly as I held the camera where he could see. His lips quirked and I knew he noticed.

"These are good," he commented, as I scrolled through the different photos.

I snorted. "Did you think they'd be bad?"

He chuckled. "If you're implying that I might've doubted your abilities, that's a no. I knew you'd be good. I wasn't sure I'd be the best subject."

"Why? You're hot."

Oh. My. God. Crap on a cracker I said that out loud. No, no, no. I wanted to take it back. Why didn't life come with a rewind button?

My cheeks turned an unflattering shade of red and I wanted to crawl away, find the nearest hole, and die in it.

"You think I'm hot?" He grinned, his smile stretching his whole face.

I set the camera in my lap and buried my face in my hands. "You know you're hot," I finally mumbled.

"I very much like the fact that *you* think I'm hot." I looked up to find him nodding with a cocky smile.

"Can we stop talking about this?" I pleaded.

"Why? I think my hotness is an interesting topic. Don't you?" He winked.

I grabbed his shirt and threw it at him. I stood up, gathered my stuff, and tried to get away from him as quickly as possible. I had to get away before I said something even more embarrassing that I couldn't take back.

"Rae! Where are you going? Rae!" He called after me.

I heard his feet thumping against the ground as he ran to catch up with me.

"I'm sorry," he grasped my wrist, and no doubt felt my pulse jump. "I didn't mean to make you feel uncomfortable." He released his hold on me and shoved his fingers through his hair, almost like he was frustrated. "Sometimes I forget how sensitive you are. I was only joking around with you."

Shit, now I felt like crap. Rachael would have never overreacted like this.

I hung my head in shame. "No, don't apologize. You're right, you were only joking and I shouldn't have reacted like that." I let out a pent up breath and admitted, "Sometimes I forget."

"Forget what?" He tilted his head, his brows furrowing together.

"How to be normal," I mumbled. I *wished* I could be a normal girl—like Rachael again. I wanted nothing more than to joke and laugh with Cade and not be so...so *sensitive*, like he said. But I couldn't help myself. It was an automatic reaction and it made me angry with myself.

He chuckled and the sound was rich, warm and husky. "Rae," he smoothed his fingers down my cheek and my eyes fluttered closed, "there's no such thing as normal." My eyes opened when his thumb circled over my bottom lip. He made that simple touch feel like so much more and I had to suppress the urge to moan. "Come with me," he nodded his head in the other direction. "I want to show you something."

I opened my mouth, unsure of what to say.

"Please, don't say no," he pleaded.

The smart thing to do would have been to refuse him and go back to my dorm. But I hadn't done the smart thing from the moment I set foot on campus, so why change now?

"Okay," I nodded.

He grinned boyishly and I couldn't help smiling in return.

I followed him across campus and the amount of times he was stopped by someone wanting to talk to him was insane. I was starting to understand why he normally stayed hidden. And I knew Cade well enough to tell from his body language that he didn't like the attention. Yeah, Cade could be arrogant at times and cocky, but what guy couldn't? Most of the time he was rather shy. I found it endearing.

"Finally," Cade breathed, when we reached a set of doors.

"Where are we going?" I hissed, looking over my shoulder. "I get the impression that we're not supposed to be here."

He chuckled. "Relax, I've got a key." He pulled a key out of his pocket and held it up for my inspection.

"For some reason that isn't providing me comfort right now."

"Oh, Rae," he shook his head, his hair falling forward to hide his eyes, "you need to get out more."

It was true, so I didn't argue with him.

He twisted the key in the lock and reached inside, turning on a light switch.

I stepped inside and looked around. Tile floor. Tile walls. And lockers. Lots and lots of lockers.

"Why are we in the locker room?" I asked as he closed the door.

"This isn't what I wanted to show you, if that's what you're thinking," he nodded for me to follow him. "This is just a shortcut."

"A shortcut?"

"Shortcut. Pitstop. Does it matter?" He quirked a brow and stopped beside a basket. He picked up a football from inside and cradled it in his arm.

"Are we playing football?" I asked, following him once more.

He tossed the ball in the air and caught it. "I suppose, if catch was considered football."

"Catch? Trying to make it easy on me?" I laughed, as he unlocked another set of doors. This time we stepped into what appeared to be a tunnel. I could feel the cool evening breeze flowing around us and see the stadium ahead. A rush flitted through my body. If this was even an ounce of the high Cade felt before a game... wow.

"Aw, Sunshine, I'd never make it easy for you. Then you might win and my pride can't handle that," he winked, bumping my shoulder playfully with his.

Feeling mischievous I reached up and snatched the ball from his hands and started running.

"Cade," I called over my shoulder with a laugh, "I always win."

Our laughter echoed in the tunnel and then I was on the field, still running.

A scream tore out of my throat as Cade caught me around the waist and started spinning me through the air. "Cade!"

We came crashing to the ground in a tangle of limbs.

He rolled so he took the brunt of the fall, but he was quick to roll again and pin me to the ground.

His hair hung in his eyes and we both breathed heavily.

The air crackled between us with electricity.

He reached down, smoothing the hair off my forehead. My breath faltered as his hand then trailed down over my lips.

Things were changing between us.

That much was obvious, and I was too weak to fight it anymore.

The distance between us began to close, becoming smaller and smaller. My heart beat like a drum, my blood roaring through my veins.

This was it.

He was going to kiss me.

And this moment, it was going to change everything.

My eyes closed and I waited, feeling his lips so close to mine. It was an effort to stay still. I knew the smart thing to do would be to move, to stop this, but I couldn't.

I was helpless when it came to Cade. I'd been running and running, and he'd finally caught me. Literally and figuratively.

But then, his weight was gone from my body and he stood above me, holding out a hand for me.

The electricity was gone too, carried away by the wind.

I was stunned. I'd thought...

What I thought didn't matter.

I didn't accept his hand as I stood.

"Rae," he started, reaching for me.

I took several steps back. "I'm okay," I forced a smile. I wasn't sure whether I meant I was okay from the fall or okay because he didn't kiss me. I guessed it didn't matter. Honestly, I couldn't blame him for not kissing me. I was constantly sending him mixed signals. I was surprised he wasn't suffering from whiplash.

Besides, a kiss between us still wouldn't change anything. We couldn't be together. He'd done the right thing.

I took a deep breath, sorting through my feelings and storing them away once more in carefully labeled boxes.

Putting on a playful smile, I pointed at the ball. "So, are we going to play or what?"

He tossed the ball from hand to hand. He seemed to be contemplating something, but finally threw it towards me. "Yeah, let's see what you've got, Sunshine."

I rolled my eyes and caught the ball. "What would you call me if my name was Mary?" I asked rhetorically.

He chuckled. "Gary?"

I threw the ball at him, aiming for his head, but he caught it. "That wasn't nice," he wagged his finger like he was scolding a child. "A Rae of Sunshine isn't supposed to be so naughty."

"I never said I was a Rae of Sunshine. You're the one that made it up," I countered.

He chuckled, furthering the distance between us. "Good point. Are you ready?" He asked, lifting the ball.

"Yeah," I answered, holding up my hands.

He launched the ball at me and I caught it, but the force sent me falling to the ground while the football lodged itself in my stomach. I choked on air.

"Rae?!" He ran towards me and fell to his knees beside me. "I'm so sorry, I didn't think I threw it that hard."

When I managed to get enough air into my lungs, I said, "Do you enjoy knocking me down?"

He laughed at that while looking me over for injuries. "You do seem to fall a lot around me."

"Fall?" I raised a brow, my hand cradling my stomach where I knew I'd end up with a massive bruise. "Falling would mean that I'm just a klutz and trip over things."

He chuckled and started lifting my shirt.

"Hey," I swatted his hands away, "stop that!"

"What?" He looked at me with innocent blue eyes. "I was just looking you over."

"Well, can you not?" I grasped the end of my shirt tightly in my fists.

"I've seen you in a bra before, what's the big deal?" He shrugged. "Besides, I wasn't going to take it off. I was only lifting it," he defended. Suddenly, his eyes widened with understanding. "Is this about the scar?"

"No," I lied, looking away from his eyes that always saw too much.

"I've already seen the scar, Rae. It's not that bad."

"Not that bad?" I repeated. The scar on my abdomen was large, raised, jagged, and a disgusting shade of pink. There was nothing *not that bad* about it.

Cade sighed and his eyes darkened. "Everyone has scars. *Everyone.* Sometimes, you can't see them and those can be the worst."

I closed my eyes and breathed out. "You're right. I'm sorry," I apologized. "The scar is...it's a touchy subject for me."

Cade looked at me and his lips twisted—almost like he wanted to laugh at me. "Most subjects are touchy for you."

It was true.

Since our game of catch had turned into a failed kiss, and now this, I thought it might be best if we headed back to the dorms. "I think we should head back." I pointed towards the entrance we'd come through.

"No way," he shook his head. "It's just starting to get dark."

"That's precisely why we should go back." I sat up, picking grass off my jeans.

He shook his head. "There's something else I want you to see. Please, stay with me a little longer?"

If this 'something else' turned out like everything else had in the past twenty minutes then I was sure it would end in disaster. But I agreed anyway. "Okay."

He grinned like a little boy, his eyes lighting up, and my heart soared. *I* made him smile like that—and that smile of his always made my heart speed up.

"Come on," he helped me up and didn't let go of my hand as he guided me to the center of the field. He sat down and then stretched out on his back, so I did the same. Our hands stayed connected, making my body warm. "Do you feel it?" He whispered. "The energy? Even when there's not a crowd here I still get a buzz in my veins."

"Yeah, I feel it," I whispered back. A few minutes passed. "Why are we laying here?" I mean, this was nice and all, but I didn't understand why he'd begged me to stay for this.

He chuckled and turned his head so that his breath tickled my skin. Even in the dimming light I could still see his eyes sparkling. "You don't have a patient bone in your body, do you?"

"No," I laughed, smiling at him.

"Coach gave me a key to the stadium so I could practice whenever I want," Cade explained even though I hadn't asked him about that. "I don't think I've actually come in here once to practice on my own," he chuckled. "Instead, I come here when I need to think. I need to think a lot," he muttered the last part under his breath. "I especially like to come here at night, when I can look up at the stars. It makes me feel like a kid again, camping in the backyard. It reminds me of a time when things were simple and there wasn't this...this...*pressure*. When everyone was happy."

"Who's everyone?" I whispered, rolling onto my side to face him.

"My dad. My mom. My whole family," he answered after a moment. His face darkened and an immeasurable sadness reflected in his eyes. Something bad happened to Cade, I could feel it. You didn't get that kind of look in your eyes because your ice cream fell on the ground. No, Cade had suffered some sort of tragedy and that made me wonder if maybe he would understand what I'd been through—but I wasn't willing to risk telling him the truth.

I saw that he didn't want to elaborate, and since he hadn't pushed me to reveal my secrets I would respect his boundaries.

"I like it out here," I said instead, changing the subject.

He chuckled. "You do?"

"Mhmm," I hummed. "I can see why you come here to think."

I shivered from the cold and he murmured, "Come here," as he pulled me into his arms. I laid my head on his chest, cradled below his neck. It didn't feel stiff or awkward being in his arms. It felt *right*. More right than anything ever had before and that scared me. I didn't try to move though.

He rubbed a hand up and down my arm, trying to create friction.

It didn't take long for the whole sky to grow dark and for the stars to twinkle above us.

If I was honest with myself, I didn't care about the stars or the moon or any of that.

I was here for one reason and one reason only—because Cade asked me to stay.

chapter thirteen

"WHAT THE HELL IS GOING ON HERE?" A gruff voice invaded my sleep.

I blinked my eyes open and the world came into focus—and the world, was not my dorm room like it should've been.

Instead, I was curled against Cade asleep on the football field.

And the man looming above us had to be the coach.

I looked beyond him and sighed in relief when I saw that it was only him. I'd been afraid the whole team might be looming behind him.

Cade sat up and rubbed his eyes. "Hey, coach."

"Don't 'hey, coach' me, Montgomery," he scolded. "What the hell do you think you're doing out here? And with a girlfriend no less?" The man plucked a toothpick from between his teeth.

"Sorry, coach," Cade shrugged, seeming unaffected at being caught, "we were looking at the stars and fell asleep."

"Well how romantic," the coach droned. "That key is for practice use only. Not wooing this little lady here." He waved a hand in my direction.

"It won't happen again, coach," Cade chuckled. I thought he should be more worried about us being caught, but he was completely at ease. I felt like running away.

"Like I believe that one, Montgomery." The coach turned to walk away. "Walk that one back to her dorm and get ready for practice."

"Yes, sir," Cade called.

"Oh my God," I clutched at my shirt, because I needed something to hold on to, "I can't believe that just happened."

Cade chuckled. "It's okay. Coach was cool."

"Cool? *Cool?* He did not seem cool with this to me," I babbled, pushing my sleep mused hair off my forehead.

"Trust me, he was fine, and he didn't really care. Coach likes to act tough but he's really a softy." Cade stood and stretched his arms above his head.

"I am mortified," I continued, still sitting on the ground. At this point I wasn't sure if I could even walk. "This is the most embarrassing thing to ever happen to me."

"Oh, I doubt that sweetheart," he chuckled.

I leveled him with a glare, which only made him laugh harder.

I slowly picked myself up off the ground and together we headed back to the tunnel and through the locker rooms. I silently thanked whichever god was listening that the room had been empty. I didn't think I could handle any more humiliation.

The campus was clear of students as Cade walked me to the dorm. It was still early in the morning and people hadn't started roaming around yet. I was glad that no one was around to witness the two of us together at this time of the morning. If someone caught us the rumor mill would start up.

Cade stopped beside the doors of my dorm and glided his fingers over my cheek. He did that a lot. "Thank you for last night," his voice was low. Leaning forward, he whispered, "For the record, I really wanted to kiss you."

The dorm room was dark and I eased inside, making sure the door closed silently. I was still reeling from Cade's admission and I didn't know what to make of my feelings. They were all over the place. A raging storm.

"Where have you been all night?"

Fuck.

I'd never imagined I'd have to worry about waking Thea since she usually slept like the dead until her alarm went off.

"Tell me everything." She clapped giddily with a grin. Suddenly she frowned. "On second thought, maybe you shouldn't tell me. You were probably with my brother and that would be gross."

I leaned against the door and sighed. I knew there was no way I was getting out of this. "Yes, I was with your brother."

"And did anything happen?" She prompted.

I frowned, thinking of the almost kiss. "No."

"Did you want something to happen?"

"Thea," I snapped, "would you please stop prying? I have no idea what all these feelings inside me mean and talking about them with you only makes them get even more jumbled." I started to pant from lack of oxygen.

"Oh." Her eyes widened in surprise. "I'm sorry I asked."

"Please, don't be mad," I pleaded, "but I hardly understand what I feel and when you ask me questions it only makes it more confusing." I pressed a hand to my head, feeling a headache coming on. "God, this is confusing."

"Have you ever been in love before? Sorry," she slapped a hand over her mouth, "that was another question."

I sat down on my bed and decided to open up and share a little bit of myself with Thea. "Yes, I've been in love. I thought he was my forever."

"So...what happened? Did he turn out to be a jerk?"

I closed my eyes and swallowed thickly, tears pricking my eyes. "He died." *And it was my fault.*

"Oh," her mouth parted, "Rae, I'm so sorry."

I looked away, not wanting to see the pity in her eyes. The people that didn't know the whole story were always so sympathetic. I didn't deserve it. Not when I was the one responsible. Sometimes, I felt like the hate was easier to deal with than the pity. At least the hate I could understand. I felt it too, because I hated myself. That didn't mean I wanted to surround myself by those people, though.

"Some things just aren't meant to be," I shrugged like it was no big deal. I didn't want her to know how much I was still affected by Brett's death. Forcing my eyes to hers, I pleaded, "Could you do me a favor and not tell your brother about this?" It had been hard enough telling Thea, I didn't want Cade to know too. I didn't want to become that girl, the one where whispers were heard behind her back as people pointed and speculated. I'd gotten enough of that back home and the last thing I wanted was Cade asking questions, because he would.

Thea nodded slowly. "If you don't want me to, I won't, but I don't see what difference it makes if he knows or not."

"You wouldn't understand," I muttered.

She sighed. "Maybe I would if you'd actually trust me." With a sigh, she lay back down and rolled over with her back to me, effectively ending the conversation.

I pinched the bridge of my nose.

I could see now that if I didn't open up to Thea, and Cade too, about everything I would inevitably lose them.

I wasn't sure which pain would be worse—having them know the truth or not having them in my life?

chapter fourteen

"WHAT THE HELL SHOULD I WEAR?" I asked Thea, as she primped in front of the mirror in the bathroom. "I don't think I've ever been to a club before."

She peeked around the doorway of the bathroom. "I can tell you right now that I know for a fact there is nothing remotely club related in your closet."

"I don't even want to go to a club," I whined.

I'd been talked into going, because Thea was desperate to go to this new club and I refused to let her go by herself. Stranger danger and all that jazz.

"Then you don't have to go," she countered, putting on a necklace.

I sighed. "And let you go by yourself? I don't think so."

"Then stop complaining," she chided, heading to her closet.

She grabbed a slinky black dress and threw it at me. "Wear that."

I eyed the short dress with strategic cutouts. "I think a nipple might pop out."

She snorted. "Rae, you'll be fine. Have I ever steered you wrong?"

So far she hadn't but there was a first time for everything.

I slipped into the dress and felt extremely naked in it. "I'm going to freeze to death."

"Oh, please," she rolled her eyes, "you're such a baby. I know you have that super cool leather jacket with the studs on it in your closet somewhere. That'll work just fine and keep you warm."

"That might keep the top half warm, but what about all of this," I waved a hand at my bare legs.

"Sometimes you have to suffer for fashion. It's a fact of life."

I didn't really think one should have to suffer, but I knew there was no arguing with Thea.

I pulled a pair of combat boots on and said, "Okay, I'm ready."

"You're not going to do anything with your hair?" She asked.

I tugged on a curly strand. "Nope. I'm leaving it down."

She smiled and grabbed her clutch. "Well, if you're ready, let's get out of here."

I followed her out the door feeling like this had been a very bad idea.

⁓

"It's so nice to get out on the weekends!" Thea yelled over the music, taking a sip from some fruity concoction.

"It is," I agreed, because it seemed like the right thing to say. I would've rather been at the dorm editing photos but I knew Thea wouldn't understand.

"Ah!" Thea sat her glass down on the bar roughly, so that some of her drink sloshed over the sides. "I *love* this song! Let's dance!"

I wrinkled my nose. Dance? Um, no thanks.

But the girl would not take no for an answer and whatever she was drinking must've been strong because she was definitely not in control of herself.

She dragged me onto the dance floor and started dancing in a way that would make other clubbers think we were lesbian lovers. Not cool. Not that there was anything wrong with lesbians, but I didn't want anyone getting the wrong idea or to think we were going to put on a show.

"Thea, stop," I groaned, when she started getting touchy feely. "This is weird."

"You're no fun, Rae," She pouted. "I need fun!"

I groaned. We'd barely been here thirty minutes and I could already tell I was going to have to drag my drunk roommate home, which was going to be so much fun. We'd taken a cab here, so I'd have to call one to come get us and I was sure they'd be thrilled if she threw up in there.

But I didn't need to be thinking about that. Instead I needed to focus on what she was doing now, which was—

"Thea! Did you just grab my ass?!" I gasped.

She giggled and hiccupped, before sashaying her hips. "Maybe! You need to lighten up!"

"Thea," I groaned, when she put her hands on my hips trying to get me to move to the beat of the song, "stop it."

"Fine," she pouted. "You're no fun."

"Thea!" I called when she melted into the crowd of dancers and disappeared.

I should've just kept my mouth shut, because now I'd lost a drunk girl in the middle of an insanely large crowd. Not good.

"Thea!" I called again, pushing my way around people. I even elbowed some dude in the gut when he tried to grope me. Honestly, couldn't people keep their hands to themselves?

I looked and looked, moving through the crowd but Thea was gone.

Fabulous.

I made my way back the bar, figuring it would give me the best vantage point to try to find her.

I grabbed an empty stool and sat down, craning my neck.

"Looking for someone?"

I jumped at the male voice.

I turned around to face the man. He wasn't much older than me, maybe twenty-two. He had light gray eyes—they almost seemed white, like they were leached of color. His brown hair fell in messy waves over his forehead. "Uh, yeah," I muttered, feeling a bit creeped out. I scooted the stool a smidge away and prayed he didn't notice. "My boyfriend." The lie slipped out of my mouth easily. Something about the guy was just...off. I hoped that if he thought a guy was going to appear any second he'd stop looking at me like...like he wanted to lick me.

"A boyfriend? Really?" He raised the glass of whatever he was drinking to his lips. "You came in with another girl and I haven't seen you with a guy."

My pulse jumped and a sweat broke out across my skin.

This was not good and my gut told me I needed to get away.

"He's meeting me here," I mumbled. "Excuse me." I slid off the stool, scurrying away from Icky Guy.

I was going to find Thea and we were getting the fuck out of here whether she liked it or not. I was also never ever letting her talk me into this ever again.

When I still couldn't find her I headed to the back where the bathrooms were, figuring she had gone there.

I hadn't made it far when my body was slammed roughly into the wall, causing my teeth to clank together and blood to blossom on my tongue.

Before I could scream a hand slammed against my mouth.

My eyes connected with Icky Guy's. I was so screwed.

Panic began to choke me, but I tried to talk myself down. If I panicked I wouldn't be able to think straight and since I couldn't count on someone coming along and helping I had to rely on myself.

His other hand groped my side where there was one of the cutouts. "You have beautiful skin," he whispered, lowering his head to mine. "It's soft. Like velvet."

I whimpered when his nose grazed mine. I didn't want any part of him touching me.

"I love your hair," his fingers went to grasp one of the long curly strands. "There's something exotic and hypnotizing about your eyes," his voice lowered. "They tell a story."

I wondered if they told the story of how I was going to kick his ass, because if he thought he was taking advantage of me then he was insane. I was not going down without a fight. He wasn't the biggest guy on the planet and I was fairly certain I could get him off me and have time to run away.

The question was, how far would this go before I found the opportunity to get away?

He lowered his hand from my mouth but before I could suck in oxygen to scream his mouth was on mine in a bruising kiss. I bit down on his lip and the fucker bit me back like he enjoyed it.

Stay calm, Rae. Stay calm and think.

Brushing off my rising panic, I tried to relax my body. Maybe if he thought I was giving in he wouldn't hold me so tight. With the way he held me now I knew I'd have bruises on my arm and hip from his hold.

I hated the taste of his lips on mine—ashy like cigarettes mixed with alcohol. It was enough to stir my stomach. I was sure he wouldn't be thrilled if I threw up in his mouth, but it would be sure to get him away.

I felt tears prick my eyes and about that time, his hold lessened.

Now was my chance.

I maneuvered my legs so that one was between his.

And then I kicked.

With a yelp he fell to the ground.

I stood for a few seconds, stunned that it had actually worked.

Then my mind screamed at me to run, so I did.

My legs couldn't carry me away fast enough. Panic still choked me and I was terrified that at any second he would grab ahold of me and drag me back to that dark corner.

My hands slammed into the exit doors and I ran outside.

Breathless, I sat down on the sidewalk, trying to calm my racing heart.

I was in shock and my body shook uncontrollably.

Did that really just happen?

The tracks of my tears on my cheeks told me that it did.

I expected the guy to bust out the door any second and I wished I had driven here instead of taking a taxi, because now I was stranded here.

I heard footsteps and jumped up, ready to run, but when I turned it was Thea.

Seeing Thea did nothing to calm me, though.

"Rae!" She cried, all but falling in her heels. "I saw what happened! Oh my God, I couldn't believe that! Are you okay?!"

I backed away from her with my hands held up and my lower lip trembling. "Stay away from me," my voice cracked. I was livid with Thea. This had been her idea. Then she'd run away and because of her I'd end up having Icky Guy try to...I wasn't going to let my thoughts go there.

"Rae?" She stopped, looking at me with a hurt expression.

"This is your fault," I accused. "Stay away from me." I crossed my arms over my chest and started to walk away.

"Rae! You can't just leave!"

"Watch me," I growled.

"Rae! I called Cade, he'll be here any minute!"

I whipped around and screamed, "I don't care! He can pick you up then, which is great since I really don't even want to look at you right now!"

I felt like if I was stuck in her presence for a minute longer I might end up strangling her.

"Rae, please be sensible," she pleaded.

Oh, she'd gone and done it now.

"Sensible?!" I screamed. "Sensible would've been staying in the fucking dorm like we're supposed to! Not going to a fucking club in the middle of fucking nowhere!"

"You didn't have to come with me," she defended.

"Yeah, well guess what, Thea? I came because I was scared something like *that*," I pointed towards the building, "would happen to *you*! I was looking out for you, but where were you when I needed you? Huh? He could've hurt me, Thea!"

She started to cry. "You're right. I'm so, so sorry. This is all my fault," she buried her face in her hands.

Wrapping my arms around my body I sat down on the sidewalk once more. When I heard her heels clack towards me, I snapped, "Thea, seriously back off." She cried harder, but my own tears seemed to have dried up. Now I was angry and I was taking it out on her. At least this time the person I was angry at actually deserved my wrath.

A few minutes later headlights lit up the parking lot and Cade's black Jeep screeched to a halt in front of us. He got out of the car and slammed the door shut, making me flinch.

"What the fuck were you two thinking?" He shouted.

"I'm sorry," Thea sniffled, "I'm so sorry."

Cade stormed over to her and spoke in a hushed voice. Thea's head lowered and she nodded, muttering something back.

He opened the back passenger door and helped her into the Jeep like she was a small child.

Then he stalked over to me. His body towered above me and for the first time in a long time I felt small. Fragile. Like I could break apart into a million pieces too small to be put back together.

"Rae," he crouched in front of me and reached a tentative hand out to my face. I recoiled against his touch, but he was unfazed. "Rae, please let me take you home."

Home. What was home? Certainly not the place I'd grown up and not where I was now. I didn't have a home. I belonged nowhere.

Now that my anger was fading, sadness was taking its place.

I slowly brought my head up and my eyes connected with Cade's. He looked worried, his brows drawn tight.

A million different emotions swam through my body and I wasn't sure if I could wade through them.

"Take my hand, Rae," he held his hand out for me, "take my hand, and let me get you away from here. Please."

With my fingers trembling I placed my hand in his. It closed around mine and he hauled me up into his sturdy arms.

Suddenly my tears came back in full force and I was helpless to stop them.

He wrapped his large arms around me and I cried against his solid chest. If it wasn't for him I was pretty sure I would've crumbled to the ground.

"Shh," he hushed, rubbing his hand up and down my back. "I'm here now. You're safe."

I clung to him, my hands grasping the fabric of his sweatshirt so tightly in my fist I was sure it would be wrinkled later.

"Let it out, Rae," he cooed, laying his head on top of mine. "I've got you." I felt his warm lips press against my cool forehead. My eyes closed and I inhaled his scent—clean, woodsy, Cade.

"I'm so sorry this happened to you," he continued, "but it's over and I'm here, and I'm not going to let anything hurt you ever again."

It was a promise he couldn't keep, but I appreciated the gesture nonetheless.

He pulled back a little, holding onto my arms with his hands, and lowered his head so he could peer into my eyes. "Are you okay now?"

I nodded slowly. "I'm okay," I echoed. *Now that you're here.*

"Come on," he wrapped an arm around my shoulders and guided me to the Jeep. My body still seemed numb and when he saw that I didn't possess the energy to climb into the vehicle he helped me inside.

I felt like I was disconnected from my body. Here, but not. I kept replaying what had happened over and over in my mind—but the outcome was always different as I imagined the various ways Icky Guy could've hurt me. Things could've been so much worse than they were. I could've become one of those stories you hear about on the news.

Once in the vehicle Cade cranked up the heat and reached over, giving my knee a reassuring squeeze.

"I'll deal with you later," he hissed at Thea. He sounded like a father scolding his child and disappointment laced his tone.

Thea didn't reply. I was glad. I didn't want to hear her voice.

Cade started to pull out of the parking lot, but his headlights flashed over a man leaning against the side of the building smoking a cigarette. It was him. My body stiffened and I whimpered. Cade noticed and slammed his foot on the brake, which shoved all of us forward.

"Is that him?" He asked. "That's him, isn't it?"

He didn't wait for me or Thea to reply. He was out of the vehicle in one lightning fast move. I watched, frozen, as he ran up to the guy. He must've yelled something, because Icky Guy looked up and then Cade's fist slammed into the side of his face.

The guy fell to the ground, his cigarette forgotten, as he clutched the side of his face.

Cade bore down on him and hit him again and again.

"Oh my God," Thea gasped from the backseat, "he's going to kill him." I heard the seatbelt click undone and then she slipped out of the car after Cade.

She grasped her brother's arm, pulling as hard as she could. She finally got his attention and pointed at the vehicle. No, not at the vehicle, at me.

Cade shoved his fingers through his hair and nodded.

They got back in the car and Cade sped out of the parking lot, his jaw clenched tightly.

I leaned my head against the cool glass of the window and closed my eyes.

I wanted to pretend that tonight didn't happen—to erase it from my memory with one swipe of my fingers over the delete button.

I'd tried that once before, but memories have a way of haunting you for the rest of your life. They don't just go away. They become a part of you—an essential element of your make up.

chapter fifteen

I CRACKED MY EYES OPEN on Sunday morning to find Thea standing above me with a tray of breakfast food. After last night I hadn't bothered to get up and run this morning. When I woke up at five I promptly went back to sleep, muttering, "Screw it."

"What are you doing?" I rubbed my eyes free of sleep and glared at Thea.

"Well," she frowned, "I'm trying to apologize for last night."

"I think you did that with the thousand and one times you told me you were sorry." I sat up, stretching my arms above my head.

Thea sat the tray in my lap and then proceeded to perch on the end of my bed.

"Yeah," she frowned, looking forlorn, "but I didn't think you forgave me."

She had that right. "No, I didn't."

Tears pricked her eyes. "You have no idea how sorry I am, Rae. I was selfish by running off and leaving you alone. It was stupid of me. I can't take back what I did, but I want you to know that I feel awful." She swiped at a tear coursing down her cheek.

I swallowed thickly. I didn't want to fight with Thea. "You're forgiven." She brightened at my words. "But don't you dare try to get me to go out some place like that ever again."

"Deal," she agreed, reaching forward to hug me.

I stiffened at first, but then returned the gesture.

Thea was sweet and she had good intentions. I also felt that Thea could be a bit naïve to the ways of the world. She had an almost childlike innocence that I was envious of. I'd walked face first into the harsher facts of life and there was no coming back from it.

I finally looked down at the tray of food. She'd gotten three to-go boxes full of food from the diner. "Do you really think I'm going to eat all this?" I laughed.

"Well," she smiled, "I was kinda hoping you'd forgive me and we could share."

This time it was my turn to say, "Deal."

While we ate Thea did a good job of getting my mind off last night. She told me stories about being a kid and all the trouble Cade, Xander, and she used to get into. Apparently they were quite the troublemakers. Especially the boys.

Hearing Thea talk about her childhood made memories of mine spring to mine. I missed my friends. I missed Brett. I missed the future I could've had.

Brett and I were always close. We'd known each other since we were in diapers, thanks to our parents being friends. Not having him in my life anymore...at times his loss was crippling. I'd loved him.

I startled.

I'd *loved* him.

I was thinking of him in the past tense. *Loved.* I loved him once. No more. Well, that wasn't exactly true. A part of me would always belong to Brett, but I was...I was no longer tied down by my feelings. And that...yeah, that was sort of freeing.

After we finished eating I got dressed for the day. Nova and I had plans to meet up around lunchtime to work on our project some more. It was coming together nicely and I could even see myself becoming friends with the purple-haired girl.

"What are your plans for the day?" I asked Thea, as I wiggled into a pair of jeans.

She sat cross-legged on her bed with a magazine in her lap. "Don't know. I might go get my nails done. They're looking shitty." She held her hands out and wrinkled her nose at the chipping polish. I couldn't help but look down at my own nails and the purple polish that adorned them. "Yeah, nails it is," she nodded her head. "You're welcome to come if you want."

"Uh..." Rachael had loved getting her nails done. Rae, not so much. Rae did her own nails and a crappy job at that. "I'm supposed to meet up with Novalee to work on our project."

"Invite her!" Thea chirped. "We can make it a girl's day! Go to the mall! Come on! It'll be fun!" She pleaded.

Sometimes I felt bad for Thea. In instances like this I could tell just how lonely she really was.

"I can ask her," I shrugged, "but I doubt it's really her thing."

"You can let me know then," Thea smiled, but I didn't miss how her shoulders sagged.

I sighed, guilt eating away at me. "I'll text her and if she's not into it I'll ask her if we can reschedule."

"Really?" Thea brightened, her eyes wide and happy like a puppy's.

"Yeah," I nodded. "Plus, I think you owe me after last night's disaster," I teased.

She frowned. "I really do."

"I was only kidding, Thea," I told her, grabbing my phone off the bed.

"I know, but you're right. I don't know how I'll ever make it up to you." She looked at me forlornly.

"You don't need to make it up to me." I wished now I hadn't said anything, even if I had only been joking.

She gave me a look that said she clearly did. I ignored it and texted Nova.

Not even a minute had passed when she responded.

I looked up at Thea and grinned. "She's in."

~es

"Thea," I groaned, "so help me God if you put that hot pink polish on your nails I will beat you within an inch of your life."

She giggled and placed the bottle back on the shelf. "What would you suggest then?"

"Black," Nova spoke up.

Thea wrinkled her nose. "Um, no."

"Do you really like pink that much?" I asked, suddenly feeling bad for what I'd said.

"Not really." She admitted.

"What's your favorite color?" I asked.

"Green," she answered immediately.

"Then go with green." I picked up a deep hunter green color. "Try this one."

She grabbed the bottle from my hand and looked at it. "Okay. I'm going to do it."

Something told me this was a big step for Thea. The color of nail polish probably seemed like such a little thing, but from the little Cade had said I got the impression their mom was controlling when it came to Thea. She wanted her daughter to be a pink glamour princess.

Thea handed her nail polish over to one of the ladies working there. Now that Thea was taken care of it was my turn to pick something. I settled on a dark purple with glitter that appeared nearly black unless the light was shining on it. Nova chose a deep red.

They seated us so the three of us were in a row and could talk.

We were all quiet at first. I think Nova and Thea didn't quite know what to make of each other.

Nova was the first to break the silence. "If you like green, why were you choosing pink?"

Thea shrugged and the nail lady scolded her for moving. "My mom," I knew it, "likes me to look a certain way."

Nova eyed the designer jeans and pale yellow blouse Thea wore. "So I'm guessing this uppity nun garb you're wearing isn't quite your style."

I snorted. Nova was blunt, and I kind of liked that about her.

"No," Thea laughed. "It's not."

Nova nodded and seemed to be pondering something. Finally she said, "I find that pleasing other people in turn makes ourselves miserable." Pain flashed in her eyes and she hastily looked away. I studied the side of her face wondering what that look meant.

"Yeah," Thea sighed, "I feel pretty miserable a lot of times."

My spine straightened. What? I didn't know that? Thea...she was always so *happy*. I would never guess that she felt that way. I was shocked to say the least. I guess it showed that I didn't know as much about her as I thought I did. Just like she didn't know the truth about me.

Some friends we were.

Nova turned back to Thea. "I think after we're done here, we should go shopping and get some clothes that *you* like."

Thea pondered her words. "I'm not even sure I know what I like."

Nova smiled sympathetically. "We'll figure it out."

Right then, my gut clenched. This was so familiar. I used to do things like this with my best friends, Sarah and Hannah, but they we were gone now and I was...I was here. I was here with Nova and Thea, and I felt like, maybe, the three of us could be best friends—if I found it in my heart to let them in.

When our nails were done we strolled through the mall, going in to practically every store we came across. I was glad I'd worn my Converse, otherwise my feet would've been killing me.

Nova and Thea seemed to have instantly bonded which I found funny, since they seemed so opposite. Thea was obsessed with Nova's purple hair and I wouldn't have been surprised if in a few days hers was purple.

Exhausted, we stopped to eat at one of the restaurants in the mall.

We'd just placed our order when two guys I recognized strolled in. Nova and Thea were sitting on the opposite side of the booth so they didn't see them.

Cade smiled when he saw me watching him and sauntered over with Xander close on his heels.

"Hello, ladies," Cade slid into the booth beside me. Xander squeezed in next to Thea and lowered his head to quickly whisper something in her ear.

"What are you doing here?" I asked.

Cade held up a shopping bag from the sporting goods store. "Shopping." After giving the bag a shake he dropped it on the floor. "I hope you don't mind if we join you."

"Not at all," I smiled. I shouldn't have been happy to see Cade, but I was. My body hummed pleasantly anytime he was near and I'd become addicted to the feeling.

Cade finally swiveled his gaze to Thea and glared at her.

I may have forgiven her for last night, but it was clear Cade hadn't. "I can't believe you dragged her out again."

Thea frowned and seemed to close in on herself at his words. "I thought it would be nice to get out. She didn't have to come. I would've come by myself," she defended.

"Cade," I put a hand on his forearm, "I wanted to come. It's okay."

"No, it's not okay." His muscles flexed beneath my touch. "Last night could've been a whole lot worse and I don't think Thea grasps that."

Thea's face grew red and she slammed a hand on the table. "I do understand that and I feel *awful*. I don't need my douchebag brother making me feel worse."

Whoa. I thought that was the first time I'd ever seen the siblings argue. It was weird. And...and they were arguing because of me.

"As long as you understand I might forgive you...one day." Cade muttered. He picked up my glass of Sprite. He took a sip and slid it back my way. At my look he shrugged. "I was thirsty."

Of course he was.

The waitress came by and startled at our new guests. "I'll get you guys a menu," she muttered before walking off.

She returned a moment later with the menus and got their drink order. Cade insisted that we would share. "Rae doesn't mind," he winked at me.

The waitress nodded and walked away.

"You should've gotten your own," I muttered, feeling Thea's eyes on us.

He shrugged. "And miss the chance to share straws with you, I think not. Especially since," his voice lowered and he whispered in my ear, "I haven't kissed you yet. And trust me, Rae, when you're ready I'm going to kiss you like you've never been kissed before."

My breath caught and something told me he was right. Kissing Cade would be unlike anything else I had ever experienced. Even with Brett. Cade was different. I saw that clearly now and it scared me. I wanted to run, but I wanted to stay even more.

When the waitress returned with Xander's glass of water the two guys placed their order.

I realized then that poor Nova was completely out of the loop.

"Nova, this is Cade. Cade, this is Nova. We have class together. She's a photographer too. Cade is also Thea's brother," I added.

"Nice to meet you," Nova smiled.

"Likewise." Cade reached for my drink again. I was about to ask the waitress to just bring me my own, but I knew Cade would only drink from that one too.

"And this is Xander, Cade's best friend." I pointed to the guy seated beside Thea.

Nova had to lean forward to see him. "Hi." She gave a small wave and he returned it. I didn't miss the way his hand grazed lightly over Thea's shoulder before dropping below the table.

Thea caught my gaze and hastily looked away. Clearing her throat, Thea turned back to me. "What are you doing for Thanksgiving?"

I shrugged, taking my Sprite from Cade before he drank it all. "Just staying on campus."

Cade swiveled in the booth to look at me while Thea's jaw dropped. "You can't spend Thanksgiving by yourself! That's just...wrong!"

"I don't want to go home," I muttered. I felt bad because I knew my parents wanted to see me, but I couldn't do it. I wouldn't subject myself to that town's ridicule anymore. I couldn't bear to run into Brett's parent's—and they were nearly impossible to avoid since they lived next door.

"Why don't you spend Thanksgiving with us?" Thea pleaded. "I'll ask my mom, but I know they won't care. She always makes too much food anyway. Please, Rae?" She begged. "You can't be alone on Thanksgiving."

"It'll be fun." Cade waggled his eyebrows with a grin. "We can have a Harry Potter marathon."

I felt unsure of what to do. A part of me was ecstatic that they'd offer, but I was also scared. A whole four days at their house—sleeping near Cade? Something told me this could be dangerous. But I found myself saying, "If it's okay with your parents then I'm in."

"Yay!" Thea clapped her hands together. "This is going to be so much fun!"

Fun? Or a disaster?

chapter sixteen

THE HOUSE WAS MODEST IN SIZE, smaller than I had expected. The front was gray stone with large windows. The wood front door had orange and yellow leaves hanging around it with a wreath in the center. It had a cozy, lived-in look to it.

"Home sweet home," Cade mumbled, sliding out of the Jeep. He didn't sound all that thrilled to be home.

I'd stepped onto the driveway when the front door opened and a short woman with hair the same color as Thea's came running towards us. "You're home! You're home!" She chanted. She acted as if she hadn't seen them since they left for school, which I found odd since it had only taken us thirty minutes to get here. Surely she'd come to one of Cade's football games.

She hugged Cade and then Thea. She didn't appear to want to let either of them go.

"I've missed you." She held Thea at arm's length as her eyes narrowed. "What are you wearing?"

Thea looked down at the leggings, brown boots, and jean shirt she wore with a coat. "Um...clothes."

"You look like you're homeless." With that her mom turned to me. "You must be Rae." She enveloped me in a motherly hug. She seemed nice enough but her previous words to Thea had been rather rude.

"I made lunch. I thought you guys might be hungry. Get your bags, eat, and then you can get settled." She patted my cheek. "You're a pretty girl."

I wasn't sure if I should say thank you, so instead I stood there. She seemed to take that as an answer.

Once she was gone, I said, "Your mom seems...nice."

Cade laughed, getting all of our bags from the trunk. "Yeah, if nice is a code word for crazy."

"Hey," Thea slapped his arm lightly, "she's our mom. Be nice."

Cade sighed and looked at me. "She tries, but she can be very judgmental. Our mom, I mean," he added as if I hadn't figured out who he was talking about. "Like I told you before, she's zany."

"But we love her," Thea added, like it needed to be said.

"Where's your dad?" I asked, looking around like he might pop out from behind a bush.

"Probably inside spying on us," Cade grumbled.

Thea picked up her duffel bag. "I'm starving." She headed towards the house, leaving Cade and I alone.

"Wish you'd stayed on campus yet?" He asked, peering down at me with a sad look on his eyes.

"No."

With a sigh, he turned his face towards the sky. "There's still time."

∼∽∼

After we ate, their mom, who's name was Lauren, led me to the guest room. It was across from Thea's room and down the hall from Cade's. I was thankful that they were near.

The room was decorated in soft blues and purples. It was peaceful and nicer than most hotels. It even had a bathroom attached.

I sat my duffel bag on the chair in the corner and looked around.

I was startled when there was a knock on the door.

I went and opened it and found Cade standing there. He pushed his way inside and sat on the bed. I closed the door once more, wondering why he was here, since I'd literally just been with him.

"Is everything okay?" I asked quizzically and sat down beside him.

He sighed and lay back on the bed, looking up at the ceiling. "Nothing is okay when I'm here."

"What do you mean?" I lay beside him.

He turned his head away from the ceiling to face me. "You'll see soon enough," he muttered. "I hated the thought of you staying on campus by yourself," he added, "but now that you're here...I'm sorry. I'm going to try to make this weekend good for you, but..." He trailed off.

I wondered what had happened to the Cade who had joked about a Harry Potter marathon. He clearly didn't want to be here.

"Don't worry about me," I assured him. "This weekend will be fine."

"I hope so," he sighed. "My dad called me before we left campus—" I figured that was where this sudden mood of his had come from. "—and he was being an asshole. I almost told you to stay behind so that you wouldn't have to deal with this shit." He reached up and swiped his fingers over my cheek and into my hair. "But then, because I'm a selfish prick, I decided that I could get through the next four days so much easier if you were by my side."

"Cade," I sat up and my long hair fell forward, tickling his chest, "I'm glad I'm here. Especially if I can make things easier for you."

"You're too good for me." His voice was soft and his fingers brushed over my lips. That familiar hum invaded my body.

I laughed self-deprecatingly. "Cade, I think it's *you* that's too good for *me*." It was the truth too. He was...he was real. Genuine. He was one of the few guys in the world that wasn't afraid to express who he was. There were no false pretenses with Cade. It was surprising really, considering his 'type'. I'd stereotyped him at first, Thea too, so shame on me. They were two of the most kind and giving people I'd ever met.

He sat up, leaning over me. The movement caused his long-sleeved black t-shirt to pull taut over his chest. "I guess we'll have to agree to disagree." His head lowered and my heart stopped.

He was going to kiss me.

This time it was really going to happen.

I closed my eyes, startling when I felt the lightest of touches and my heart thumped madly, but when I opened my eyes it was his fingers I'd felt.

Without a word he eased off the bed and slipped out the door, leaving me alone to sort out my now muddled thoughts.

~es~

Hours later I was seated in the family room of the house with Thea and Cade. I had yet to meet their dad and their mom was in the kitchen making dinner—as well as getting a head start on making dishes for tomorrow's Thanksgiving dinner.

I'd offered to help, but she'd insisted that the three of us relax. I felt bad watching her bustle around her kitchen alone, muttering under her breath about this and that.

Cade turned the TV on and flipped through the channels. He didn't appear to be paying attention and I had the feeling he wanted to fill the silent space with noise as well as occupy his restless fingers.

I kept eyeing the large framed photo of the family hanging above the mantle of the fireplace.

Mom. Dad. Three children.

Three.

But I only knew of two.

Cade sat beside me on the couch with a modest amount of space between us. Thea sat in the leather armchair with her legs thrown over the arm, flipping through the pages of a magazine.

"Cade?" I questioned, my voice hushed.

"Yeah." He didn't look at me.

I was seeing a whole new side of Cade today—one who was distant and unhappy, except when he'd come into the guestroom earlier. I didn't like seeing him like this, but it gave me an idea of what he dealt with from me. It made me wonder why he bothered with me at all.

"That picture—"

"What about it?" He growled, brows drawn tight.

I was tempted to let it drop, because he clearly didn't want to talk about it, but something made me persist.

"Who's the little boy?" I asked, bracing myself for his reaction. I knew how much I hated it when people pried into my business, so I was prepared for him to tell me to fuck off. I wouldn't be angry if he did. I'd understand.

His eyes closed and his face screwed up as if he was in pain.

"Come with me." When he looked at me my throat closed up at the sadness I saw in his eyes.

He took my hand and dragged me upstairs, down the hall, and into the room I knew was his.

I took a moment to look around at the décor—trying to get to know Cade a little more.

The walls were painted green and the furniture was a dark cherry color. Bookcases lined one wall, and they were indeed covered in books with the odd trophy sitting on a shelf here and there. A desk sat in the corner with a Macbook. It was clean. Sparse. Almost like Cade had cleared most of his possessions out—at least the ones he could easily take to college.

"I should've explained to you about Gabe sooner, but...it's not something I like to talk about." He sat down on the end of his bed, scrubbing the palms of his hands on his jeans.

"I'm sorry, you don't have to tell me." I started to back out of the room, my hand on the knob of the closed door.

He shook his head. "No, you deserve to know. It's why my mom's so...well, you know and why my dad's an ass. Sit," he nodded his head towards a chair in the corner. "Get comfortable."

It didn't escape my notice that he was putting space between us.

He ran his fingers through his hair, making it stick up in random directions.

He looked to the ceiling and let out a breath. "We were on vacation and Thea wanted all of us to go horseback riding. I was fifteen, Thea was eleven, and Gabe was eight. My parent's arranged for us to go on this trail ride, all five of us. My dad and I were up front with the guide, while the others hung back. Gabe was nervous and didn't really like it so my mom had to keep coaxing him along." Cade paused, clenching his jaw. "The horse got spooked, reared back, and sent Gabe flying." I watched with shock on my face as a tear coursed down Cade's cheek, getting lost in the stubble. "When he landed he broke his neck and fractured his skull on a rock. He was paralyzed instantly and then bled out." He swallowed thickly. "He was just...gone."

Cade looked away and out the window. His shoulders were slumped, like the burden of his memories was too much to bear.

"Nothing was ever the same after that," he whispered, his voice gruff with barely contained tears.

My eyes closed and my body shuddered. How often had I said the exact same thing?

I knew all about how one moment could haunt you for the rest of your life. How it consumed you and every facet of your life.

Cade wasn't paying attention as I eased from the chair and came to sit down beside him. I placed my shaking hand on his forearm and felt how taut the muscle was pulled. For once I was more concerned about someone else's pain than my own.

He slowly moved his gaze from the window to me. Strands of hair fell forward to hide his eyes. As if it was second nature to me I reached up and pushed the hair away, but left my fingers tangled in it.

"I know exactly how you feel," I whispered, the confession falling off my lips easily.

"Do you?" He didn't say the words harshly like someone else might would. His voice was soft, curious.

"Yes," I nodded, my body shuddering with a breath.

"Tell me," he pleaded. His voice lowered as his hand sought mine.

"I...I don't know if I can." I squished my eyes closed from the onslaught of memories. The squeal of tires. The blood. It was all so horrible.

"Please, Rae." He reached up, cupping my neck in one hand. My breath faltered at his touch. It shouldn't have felt so good to have him touching me. It should've been wrong, but it was so undeniably right. "Tell me." His lips grazed my chin. "Let me in. You can trust me."

I pulled away from his touch like it had burned me. I paced his room restlessly, my hands wringing together. Could I do this? Could I really tell him the truth? My stomach rolled at the thought. I was terrified of what the truth might do to us—as if there was actually an *us*.

He sat quietly, waiting for me to sort out my racing thoughts.

My hands fisted at my sides. "I don't know if I can." I wiped a hand over my forehead.

Cade didn't reply. He just sat watching me. Waiting.

Finally, I sat down once more in the chair I had previously occupied.

If Cade could tell me about his brother—and I'd witnessed how painful that was for him—then I could do this. I wasn't going to tell him because I felt like I *owed* him. No, I was telling him because he deserved to know the truth. I couldn't keep dragging out this strange, twisted relationship between us if he didn't know the truth about me.

I took a deep breath and braced myself. "It happened last summer, a few days before my senior year of high school started..." I tapped my fingers against my jean-clad knees. The words were hard to push out of my throat. I knew Cade wouldn't want anything to do with me after I told him. Hell, *I* didn't want anything to do with me. But it's kind of hard to abandon yourself.

"The top was down on my car and the breeze tickled my face." I closed my eyes and it was like I was back there in that car with Brett, Hannah, and Sarah. "The sun was warm and we were laughing. We were on our way home from the mall. Brett was grumbling about all the time us girls had wasted at the mall when we could've been at the lake. But I knew he was only joking. Brett loved me and he was more than happy to tagalong." I wrung my hands together. "I remember hearing Sarah say she loved the song playing on the radio, so I turned it up and we all started singing along. We were just...having fun."

Tears coursed down my cheeks now as I got to the bad part. The part where I made one decision that forever changed my life and took the lives of three others.

"I got a text message and like a fucking idiot I picked up my phone to read it. You know what it said?" I didn't bother to wait for his response. "It said, 'Hey, is this Bill?'" I laughed humorlessly. "They had the wrong fucking number. It was nothing important. Although, no text is important enough to take your eyes off the road, because a second...that's all it took for me to lose control of the car. I was going around a turn and the car flipped twice before hitting a tree."

I shuddered at my re-telling. I'd never told anyone everything. I didn't want to talk about it. But I wanted Cade to know. He deserved to know the truth. That I was a monster.

I squeezed my eyes shut as I was transported back to that day in the car.

I looked down at the text message on my phone. It was clearly a wrong number and not worth my time.

I went to put it back in the cup holder where it had been sitting before, when I heard Sarah scream, "Rachael! Look out!"

I looked up to see that I'd drifted off the road. I jerked the wheel, trying to get back in my lane. But I turned the wheel too hard and lost control.

Everything happened so fast.

Screaming.

The tearing of metal.

The burnt oily smell of tires.

My body jolted roughly and something slammed into my abdomen. I tasted blood on my tongue like old pennies.

I tried to move, but everything hurt.

"B-Brett?" I choked on the blood coating my mouth.

Nothing.

I closed my eyes, wiggling my fingers and toes just to see if I could. When they moved I breathed a sigh of relief.

Despite the pain I forced myself to turn and look.

"Brett?" My voice caught on a scream. "Oh my God!" Blood coated his face and his body was dotted with shards of glass from the windshield. His eyes stared blankly at me.

I was going to be sick.

"Brett," I sobbed, praying that he'd blink or move his fingers. Something. But there was nothing. He was gone.

"S-Sarah? Hannah?" I couldn't turn around to see them and I was starting to panic. I looked into the rearview mirror, hoping I would find them alive.

I saw Hannah slumped over and bloody. She wasn't moving.

And Sarah...it was like she wasn't in the car at all.

Despite the searing pain in my abdomen I leaned over the door and looked out towards the road. Maybe I'd passed out and she was okay. Maybe she'd gotten out to get help. Maybe, maybe, maybe.

I couldn't see her anywhere, but I saw something behind the car lying on the ground. I squinted my eyes, hoping to see more clearly.

My hand shot to my mouth as I sobbed.

Sarah lay on the road behind the car, broken, mangled, and bloody. Her neck lay at an unnatural angle—as did her arms and legs. She reminded me of a broken doll. So...shattered.

"Oh God," I choked, trying to force air into my lungs. She must not have worn her seatbelt and I hadn't noticed.

Tears coursed down my cheeks.

I'd done this.

I'd killed them.

I glanced down then and noticed the chunk of glass lodged into my abdomen. Blood coated my shirt and legs. I'd never seen so much blood before.

My adrenaline was fading and my eyes drifted closed.

I knew I wasn't strong enough to live through this.

Sirens rang in the distance, but I knew—I hoped—they'd be too late.

My body shuddered all over as I relived those horrible moments in the car.

"I-I never told my mom and dad, but I woke up in the car. When I realized what had happened I tried to check on the others. Brett...oh God," I sobbed, "there was so much blood and his eyes were blank and I knew he was gone. I tried to check on Hannah and Sarah. I saw Sarah lying on the side of the road. Her body...it was so mangled. It was horrible. And Hannah...she was gone too. I passed out at that point, from blood loss." My hand absentmindedly stroked the gash on my abdomen. "They said I was lucky, but there's nothing lucky about living when you kill your friends."

"You didn't kill them, Rae." He spoke softly, like he was afraid if he raised his voice to a normal level I'd be scared away.

I snorted. "Um, I'm pretty sure they're dead and I was driving so that makes it my fault. I killed them just as surely as if I held a knife to their throat. They're never going to graduate high school, college, get married, have kids. Their lives are over." I slashed my hands through the air. "And I'm still living mine. It isn't right."

Cade stood and stalked towards me slowly.

He reached up and cupped my cheek. I flinched, ready to back away, but he grasped my neck to hold me in place.

"Don't you dare try to run from me," he growled lowly.

"I'm a monster."

I tried to hide my face from him, but then the fingers of his free hand were on my chin forcing my head up.

"You're not a monster, Rachael."

I swallowed thickly. Rachael. He called me Rachael. It was the first time he'd ever said my whole name.

"Things like that happen. It's awful and it was wrong, I'm not denying that, but you can't beat yourself up for the rest of your life." The hand at the nape of my neck curled into my long hair. His forehead lowered so that it was pressed against mine. "You have to move on and live your life for the people that can't. Your friends would want that for you."

"Why would they?" I countered.

"If you were the one that had died, would you want one of them or all of them to feel as guilty as you do? To weigh themselves down with this unnecessary burden?"

No one had ever asked me that before. I pondered over his words. "No, I wouldn't want that."

"See, that wasn't so hard to admit now was it?" He smiled and butterflies assaulted my stomach. I used to think that Brett's smile left me breathless. But Cade's? It twisted my world around so that I wasn't sure which way was right side up. "Thank you for sharing that with me, Rae," his eyes flicked to my lips and back up, "I know that was hard for you."

It had been. In fact, I was sort of still in a daze that I'd actually told him—that he knew, and...and he wasn't looking at me differently.

"It was," I confirmed, my pulse jumping in my throat.

"And Rae?" He lowered his head so his lips grazed my ear. My breath faltered and he chuckled. "This   changes   nothing."

chapter seventeen

IT WASN'T UNTIL THE NEXT EVENING when we sat down for dinner that I finally met Cade's father.

He'd stayed mysteriously hidden.

Sitting at the head of the table he glowered at all of us.

I kept my head ducked to avoid his searing gaze. His eyes were blue like Cade's, but lighter like they were leached of color. Of happiness. Something about him reminded me of the creep who'd cornered me at the club. I knew, without this man saying a word, that I didn't like him.

One word kept echoing through my skull whenever I spared a glance in the man's direction.

Danger.

Malcolm Montgomery was not a nice man. That much was obvious.

I wondered now if the siblings had truly wanted me to spend Thanksgiving with them because they didn't want me to be alone, or if they'd invited me along as a buffer.

As things were now it was tense.

Food was passed around, but no one spoke.

This was nothing like the warm and happy home I'd grown up in.

The silence continued as we ate. I was the one to break it, unable to stand it for a moment longer.

"Lauren, the meal is delicious." I smiled pleasantly.

"Thank you," she replied.

Forks clanked against the glass plates.

"Have you been to one of Cade's games?" I asked her.

"No," she wiped her mouth daintily with the fabric napkin. "I'm very busy."

I wanted to ask what she was so busy doing, but I didn't want to sound rude so I kept my mouth shut.

"Cade's been playing very poorly this year," Malcolm piped in. "So you haven't missed anything."

Cade sighed and his head lowered. He used his fork to shuffle his food around the plate, not eating.

I didn't want to look at Malcolm, but I forced my gaze in his direction. "Really? I thought he'd been playing very well. Granted, I've only been to a few games."

"Believe me," Malcolm smiled and there was nothing friendly about the expression, "he's been a shitty player this year."

Cade stiffened at my side, his hands balling into fists.

I don't know what made me do it, but I reached over and placed my hand on top of his. Instantly his body relaxed, as if my touch soothed him.

"You know it's true," Malcolm sneered at his son.

Cade said nothing in response.

On and on Malcolm droned through the rest of our very unpleasant Thanksgiving dinner. I felt horrible that I'd brought up the subject. I should've kept quiet, but I had no idea it would lead to that.

Once dinner was finished Thea and I were told to wash the dishes. I didn't mind. I was happy to have something to do. I hated standing around feeling as if I was in the way.

"I'm sorry," I told Thea, since I hadn't had a chance to apologize to Cade yet. "I didn't know bringing up football would lead to that."

She sighed. "It's okay. That's...that's just my dad. He expects a lot from Cade."

"I can tell," I snorted.

"He's still a good dad," she mumbled, more like it was something she was *supposed* to say rather than the actual truth. "My dad always wished he'd done more with football, so he's been pushing Cade to do it professionally for years."

I eyed her and she looked away, wiping the plate dry. My parents had never forced me to do anything I didn't like and I couldn't imagine being in Cade's situation. I'm sure a part of him wanted to please his dad, and that had to be difficult when he knew football wasn't what he wanted for the rest of his life.

Once we were done I went in search of Cade. I didn't find him in his room, so I was left to explore the house as I looked for him.

When I couldn't find him anywhere, I stepped out onto the deck for some fresh air.

It was cold and I wished I would've thought to put shoes on and grab a jacket.

I was about to head inside to get them when I heard voices coming from below the deck.

I crept over to the railing and saw Cade arguing with his dad.

Half of what was said made no sense to me. It was all football garble—a language I was not fluent in.

I knew if I was smart I'd turn around and go back in the house.

But something compelled me to stay.

"I don't want to go pro!" Cade yelled, gesturing wildly with his hands, his back against the siding of the house.

"This is all you've wanted since you were a kid! Why would you throw that all away?!" Malcolm poked him harshly in chest.

Cade shook his head vehemently. "No, dad. This is what *you* want. Not me. I've never wanted this. Do I love football? Yes, but it's not my life."

"This is about that girl, isn't it? She's got you all messed up in the head and now you're off track!" His dad yelled and I saw spittle fly from his mouth, landing on Cade's jacket.

"Dad!" Cade roared, his teeth clenching. He reached up and tugged on his hair, like he was loosing patience. "She has absolutely nothing to do with this! I've told you for years that this isn't for me, but you refuse to listen!"

Malcolm's fist cocked back, connecting with Cade's cheek.

Cade's head swiveled to the side. He spat out blood and glared at his father. Both of the men's chests rose and fell sharply.

Something told me this was a common occurrence for Cade. He could've moved and avoided his father's fist, but instead he'd let him hit him.

"Think about what you're throwing away." Malcolm hissed before starting for the deck steps.

I scurried back inside and closed the door as quickly and quietly as I could.

I sat down on the couch and pretended to have been watching TV when Malcolm stepped inside.

He didn't look at me or acknowledge my presence in any way as he headed down to the basement.

Cade didn't return immediately and I didn't want to go look for him if he needed a moment to compose himself.

I padded into the kitchen and looked in the freezer for an icepack. When I saw none I grabbed a bag of frozen peas instead.

I jumped when I heard the glass door onto the deck slide open.

Cade saw me and kept his face turned, so that I wouldn't see where his dad hit him.

"I saw, Cade," I whispered, my voice soft. "I know."

He didn't move his head, but his shoulders sagged—from relief or despair, I didn't know.

"Come here," I coaxed.

Head downcast, he slowly made his way over to me.

I pointed to one of the stools in front of the bar. "Sit," I commanded.

His lips tipped up. "I didn't know you could be so bossy."

"I don't like seeing you hurt." My hand shook as I lifted the bag to press it to the tender skin beneath his eye. His hand clasped around my wrist, steadying it.

"Why don't you like seeing me hurt?" His eyes were dark and his voice became husky. In the dim kitchen his face was etched in shadow.

My lips parted with a breath. "Why do you think?"

"Say it, Rachael."

My eyes closed.

Rachael. He called me Rachael again. After the accident, I hated being called Rachael, but hearing Cade say my name...yeah, I liked that.

"Say it." He prodded when I didn't immediately speak up.

"Because I care about you," I snapped. "I care about you more than I should and I don't want you hurt."

"You care about me?" He smiled. The hand on my wrist dropped to my waist and I squeaked when he pulled me into the space between his legs. "That's good to hear, because I care about you a lot." His other hand tangled in my hair.

"How can you still like me after what I did?" I asked, and the tears threatened to fall once more. After our confessions yesterday neither of us had discussed it again—which left my mind free to run wildly with thoughts of how disgusted he was by me.

"You didn't do anything, not on purpose anyway. I'm not saying what you did was right, you shouldn't have looked at your phone, but you didn't set out to kill them, Rae. There was no intent there. You're not a murderer like you think."

"How'd you know I think that?" I bit my lip to stifle a sob.

His eyes softened and he rubbed his thumb against my cheek. "Because I see more than you give me credit for."

I backed away and grabbed the other stool. Being that close to Cade was making my brain fuzzy. Once I was seated I held the frozen peas against his cheek again.

"You know, you're nothing like the guy I thought you were during our first few encounters." I admitted with a soft laugh.

He chuckled with a small smile. "And what did you think of me, Sunshine?"

"Well, I thought you were hot," he grinned at that, "but an arrogant, egotistical, jerk."

He laughed. "A jerk, huh?"

"Well, you were really laying it on thick and you did drink my coffee. That was rude."

"Hey, I gave you mouth to mouth, sharing a drink was no big deal," he countered, grinning so his dimple showed.

"I actually hated how much I was attracted to you. I didn't want to like you," I admitted. "I didn't want to like anyone."

"But you do."

"But I do," I confirmed, even though it hadn't been a question.

"How much do you like me?" He asked with a boyish smile.

I snorted. "What is this, kindergarten?"

"Hey, I'm just trying to gauge my chances here." He chuckled warmly. "I don't want to push you too far, too fast. Something tells me *you* might punch me in the face."

I frowned. This brought us back to the reason we were sitting here in the first place.

"How long has he hit you?" I asked hesitantly, afraid to pry too deeply. After all, he hadn't told me about this. I'd found out by accident—which made me wonder, if I hadn't walked out there would Cade have told me on his own?

"Since Gabe died." He answered immediately. "Neither of my parents has handled their grief well...or at all. I'm actually surprised they didn't end up divorcing. For a long time my mom just cried all the time, then she started putting Thea in pageants again, because that stopped for a while after the accident, and she got a little better. But she was very controlling. She wanted us all to appear as the perfect family. My dad turned to alcohol, and when he drinks, which is all the time, he gets angry." Cade's hand came up to mine, pulling the bag away from his face. He laid it on the counter and wrapped his hands around mine. "Regardless of all the shitty things that have happened in my life, I still think I turned out okay. The bad things don't define us, it's what we make of them that does. Turn a negative into a positive, that kind of thing," he winked. "You know," he reached up and cupped my cheek, then tucked my hair behind my ear so he could see my face, "I think you turned out okay too."

I laughed. "Okay? If this is what you call okay I don't want to know what you think is bad."

"You're too hard on yourself, Rae." He stood and put the bag of peas back in the freezer. He leaned against the refrigerator's stainless steel surface and crossed his arms over his chest. "You're a good person that had to deal with a tragedy."

"A tragedy that I caused," I countered. I wanted to shout, but I couldn't risk his parents or Thea overhearing our conversation. "Everyone back home blames me for what happened, and they're right to. It was my fault."

His jaw tensed and his eyes narrowed. "Did I ask my dad to punch me?"

"No," I answered immediately, wondering where he was going with this.

"You didn't ask to kill your friends." He stared at me, waiting for me to react to his words.

I sighed heavily, like the weight of the world was on my shoulders. "That's different and you know it."

"It was a fucking accident, Rae. An *accident*," he repeated, like he was trying to drill the word into my head. "It shouldn't have happened, but it did, and now you have to find a way to stop blaming yourself."

I looked away. He was right. But how did you stop blaming yourself for something that you did?

"You said earlier that you wouldn't want them feeling guilty if the situation had been reversed. It's good that you could acknowledge that, it's part of healing," he continued. "And I'm not going to lie, healing is hard. It's painful. It isn't the easiest thing in the world, but you have to do it. I couldn't have prevented Gabe's death anymore than you could have stopped theirs."

"I didn't have to look at my fucking phone!" I screamed and slapped a hand over my mouth.

Cade's face softened as I began to cry. He stepped forward, pulled me off the stool, and wrapped his arms around me.

I cried into the wall of his chest. "Some things...they just happen. There's no explanation and no justice in them, but it happens anyway, because sometimes it's just a person's time. Gabe, he was only a little boy, but he died because it was his time. I had to get older before I saw that, but it's the truth."

"You're saying that it was their time to die?" I cried, clinging to the fabric of his shirt. "I don't know if I can believe that."

"I believe it for you." His lips brushed against the top of my head.

He pulled my face away from his chest and used his thumb to wipe away the wetness clinging to my cheeks. "Despite what you believe you are a Rae of Sunshine and I'm going to make you see that. I swear it."

chapter eighteen

I LAY AWAKE IN BED, staring at the ceiling of the Montgomery's guest bedroom.

After our talk in the kitchen Cade and I sat down on the couch and indulged in that Harry Potter marathon he'd talked about.

It had been nice...something a normal couple would do—although, we were far from normal and definitely not a couple. I'd enjoyed myself nonetheless.

I'd fallen asleep against his shoulder and when I woke his head was on top of mine. It had been sweet and I'd liked it more than I should have.

Now that I was alone in bed my thoughts were free to run wild.

Was Cade right? Was it their time to die and nothing could've prevented the accident?

I *wanted* to believe that, but I couldn't.

I was a logical thinking person and the facts were glaringly obvious.

If I hadn't looked down at my phone they'd still be alive.

Just like if Cade's family hadn't gone horseback riding Gabe would still be alive.

But 'if' doesn't matter. There is no such thing as a do over. And we can't allow ourselves to question every single little detail, but that's exactly what I had done for the last fifteen months. Cade was right, I had to stop beating myself up over this. It was going to take time for me to get beyond this, though. I couldn't snap my fingers and magically become Rachael again.

I jumped when the door to my room creaked open.

I sat up as a tall dark figure stepped inside.

"Cade," I hissed, "what are you doing?"

"I couldn't sleep." He tiptoed across the room, and let me tell you it was funny watching a guy as burly as him try to be quiet. "I thought maybe you couldn't either."

Without asking for permission, because let's face it this was Cade, he pulled back the covers and slid into bed beside me.

"So...you thought you'd sleep in here?" I whispered into the dark room.

His chest was bare. I could tell because he wrapped his arms around me and pulled my body against his.

"Well, I think that's pretty obvious. Should I tell you a bedtime story?" He smoothed the hair away from my neck and kissed the spot where my pulse raced.

"Um...no." I wiggled around, trying to get comfortable.

"If you keep that up we'll have a problem," he warned in a low voice. "Now, it's story time."

"I didn't ask for a—"

"Once upon a time, there was a girl. She was beautiful, like a ray of light, but when she looked in the mirror she saw nothing but darkness."

I squished my eyes closed, wishing I could block out his words.

"She thought she was an evil, soul-sucking creature...like a vampire," he chuckled. "But to everyone else, she was an angel. A beautiful soul. But she was sad and that made her prince sad."

"Her prince?" I asked, my voice sounding squeaky.

"Yeah, her prince. He was a nice guy. And very handsome."

"Of course," I snorted.

"He saw how beautiful, smart, amazing, and kind she was. He wanted to banish the darkness she clung to so desperately—the darkness that didn't even exist. But he knew that the only way to do that was to win her heart..." He trailed off.

Minutes passed in silence. Finally, I spoke. "Did he?"

"Hmm? Did he what?" He asked, his voice sounding sleepy now.

"Did he win her heart?" I whispered, afraid to push the words passed my lips.

"Not yet," he rubbed his thumb lazily against my stomach, "but he will."

And I believed him.

꧁꧂

"Do you really have to go back?" Lauren cried, hugging her daughter goodbye.

I stood by Cade's Jeep, feeling like an awkward bystander. Our four day break had been anything but a break. The secrets revealed between Cade and I had been enough to rid me of all energy. And while his mom was nice enough, his dad gave me the creeps, even more so after I saw him hit his own son. The man was just...odd. Even now, he wasn't present to say goodbye to his kids...and yet, I could see him lurking by the front windows. Watching. Always watching.

"Mom," Cade groaned, "let her go, we need to leave."

Lauren released her daughter and leveled her son with a glare. "The University is only thirty minutes away. It's just silly to leave before you've even eaten breakfast."

Cade looked at me and I saw his eyes flick to the window where his father lurked like a ghost. "I think it's time for us to leave, don't you?" He asked his mom.

She sighed, seeming to know what he was talking about.

Could she know that her husband hit her son and let it happen? My God.

She hugged Cade, stretching up on her toes to reach his shoulders. "I love you."

"Love you too, mom." He closed his eyes, squeezing her tight.

I turned away and climbed in the vehicle. Thea was already seated in the back.

"I don't know about you, but I'm ready to get back to campus...man, I never thought I'd say that." Thea laughed and I heard her rummaging through her purse. A moment later I could hear her chewing on gum. I wondered if Thea knew about her dad hitting Cade. I got the impression that she didn't. But watching their mom, and the way she now kept looking over her shoulder at the house, she knew. Yep, she definitely knew.

I couldn't help thinking of a fifteen year old Cade, dealing with the grief of losing his little brother, and having his father smack him around.

And now he was twenty-two and it was still happening.

It was awful—but sadly, stuff like this happened all the time. People either didn't notice or looked the other way.

I began to think of how painful the last year of my life had been and how Cade had been dealing with this for seven years. I suddenly felt selfish for how I had dealt with things. Yes, what I did was wrong, there was no denying that and I knew it would *always* haunt me. But there were other people out there suffering, it wasn't just me. I'd overlooked everyone else's pain, because I'd selfishly believed that my pain was greater than others—as if suffering was some kind of competition to be won.

Cade slipped into the vehicle and reached over to squeeze my knee. I couldn't help the small smile that graced my lips in response.

"Ready?" He asked, glancing back at Thea.

"Yep," she nodded.

"Let's get out of here," he sighed, and his words were heavy with meaning.

He looked at the house one last time, and then backed out of the driveway.

Instead of going straight to the dorms the three of us stopped at the diner for breakfast.

Cade sat beside me, his hand resting on my leg where Thea couldn't see. I felt like this weekend had changed something. There were no more secrets between us. It felt good having him know. I'd thought once he knew he would hate me, or look at me like everyone else did—with disgust and pity—but he didn't. Cade never ceased to amaze me.

I knew I still had a long way to go until I was healed and ready to truly move on with my life, but I felt like with Cade's help I was going to get there. It didn't seem like this insurmountable feat anymore.

Thea stretched out in the booth and looked over at the two of us. She seemed to be trying to figure out exactly what was going on. I knew once we were alone in our dorm I would end up assaulted with a billion questions—none of which I'd have any answers for. I was clueless as to exactly what Cade and I were to each other, and that was fine. I didn't see the point in rushing things.

Cade looked down at his phone and then at us. "Hey, I got a text from Jace. He's playing a bar tonight. You want to go?" He looked at me when he asked the question.

"Sure. Sounds good." I smiled. It was better than staying in the dorm all evening—which was funny since when I arrived on campus my plan had been to lie low all year. So much for that.

"I'm in," Thea shrugged, taking a sip of water.

The waitress brought our food and my stomach rumbled. I hadn't realized how hungry I was.

"So, Jace is a musician?" I asked.

Cade shrugged. "He plays guitar and sings, but he's really an artist."

"Really?" My eyes widened in surprise as I thought of the blond haired, tattooed guy. "An artist?"

"Yeah," Thea piped in, "he does these amazing pen and ink drawings. He's really talented. He even does sculptures."

"Wow," I gasped in awe. "I had no idea."

"He does tattoos too—draws them, I mean," she added. "All the ones he has he designed himself."

"That's really cool." I meant it too. While I was into photography—which was obviously creative—I'd never known someone that was an artist the way Jace was.

"Yeah," she agreed. "I'm thinking of having him design a tattoo for me. I haven't decided what I want yet, though."

"It should be something important."

"Do you have any?" She asked me.

"No," I laughed, shaking my head.

"Cade does," she grinned. "Jace designed that one too and our parent's were livid when they saw it."

"You have a tattoo?" I gasped. "Can I see it?" The words tumbled from my mouth and my cheeks colored when I realized what I'd asked.

He appeared sheepish. "It's not that big of a deal. And," his voice lowered, "I'd have to take my shirt off for you to see it."

"I've seen you shirtless before and I never noticed a tattoo."

Shit. I'd said that in front of Thea. Now she was really going to ask me questions.

Cade chuckled, ducking his head so strands of dark hair fell forward to hide his face. "It's on my shoulder."

"Oh." That explained it.

Leaning towards me, he whispered in my ear, "It's a sun. Ironic, huh?"

"A sun?" I choked.

He nodded, nuzzling his head closer to the crook of my neck. My pulse jumped. "Yeah, because I always wanted to carry a little ray of light with me—so even when things got bad I'd be reminded that the sun will always shine again."

I swallowed thickly. I didn't know what to say.

He brushed his lips against my ear and my body jumped in response, which made him chuckle. "So jumpy," he murmured and pulled away.

I relaxed, but instantly missed the warmth of his body.

Cade started talking to Thea about something, but I wasn't paying attention. I was lost in my thoughts and still reeling from the fact that his tattoo was of a sun. What were the odds?

We finished our meal and Cade dropped us off at our dorm before departing.

"Did you enjoy your weekend?" Thea asked while unpacking her bag.

I nodded. "Yeah, I did." Despite the weirdness with their mom and dad I did enjoy myself. Even more important was the fact that I'd shared my secret with Cade and he was okay with it. I'd never expected that reaction from him—or anyone. I hated myself for what happened, so naturally I assumed that everyone else would too. Telling Cade the truth had been freeing. I wondered if I should consider seeing a therapist again. Maybe now would be a better time, because the last one hadn't been able to do much good.

I knew in my heart that I was finally ready to heal and restore myself to the Rachael I once was. She didn't have to die because her friends did. Instead, she had to live because they couldn't.

chapter nineteen

I BUBBLED WITH EXCITEMENT—and I wasn't sure if it was because we were going out, or because I was going to see Cade again. Probably because I was going to see him. We'd only parted this morning and I was already desperate to see him. That was scary and exciting all at the same time.

I changed into a ratty pair of jeans and a loose cream-colored sweater that draped over one shoulder. My long brown hair hung in curls down my back. Thea had opted to leave her hair curly as well. I smiled when I saw she wore some of her new clothes from our shopping excursion with Nova. She looked killer in a leather skirt, black boots, a white shirt, and studded leather jacket. Yeah, I could totally get used to this new badass Thea. The pink had been overwhelming.

"Are you ready?" She asked, twirling in front of the mirror. She smiled at her reflection. I got the impression she was glad to be rid of the pink too—although her pink bedspread stayed.

"Yeah," I told her, grabbing my own army green jacket.

She looked me up and down and grinned. "It's like we did a role reversal."

I had to laugh. It was kind of true. I was wearing less black and Thea was wearing more.

"It is," I agreed.

"You know," she sobered, "I think we needed each other."

I mulled over her words. In a way, I had needed Thea. She had managed to start breaking down my walls and weaseled her way into my heart—becoming my best friend. "Yeah, you're right. We did." I paused, unsure if I should continue. "Thank you."

"Thank you?" She repeated with a mystified look on her face. "What are you thanking me for?"

"For being my friend."

"Oh." Her face softened. "You don't need to thank me for that. Besides, I feel like I've been a pretty shitty friend. I'm still sorry for that night at the club."

I laughed. "Thea, I forgave you and I meant it."

She shrugged, a sad look on her face. "I haven't forgiven myself."

"Well, you should." I pulled my hair over one shoulder. "We should go. Cade said he was here like five minutes ago."

Thea giggled. "Yeah, if we take much longer he'll bat his eyes and sweet talk some poor defenseless girl into letting him into the dorm."

"He definitely could..." I paused and tilted my head. "Has Cade ever had a girlfriend?" I couldn't imagine a twenty-two year old guy never having a girlfriend, but stranger things had happened.

Thea's face screwed up. "That's not my story to tell. You'll have to ask him."

"Did he get screwed over?"

She pursed her lips. "Something like that."

I let it drop, because I knew Thea wouldn't say anything else. She might've been the younger sibling, but she was as protective of Cade as he was of her.

When we reached the stairway to head down to lobby I wasn't surprised to see Cade coming up the steps. I started laughing and couldn't seem to stop.

"What's so funny?" He asked his sister.

She shrugged. "We just had a conversation about how we were taking too long and you'd find a way into the building."

He smirked. "I'm glad you both know me so well."

My eyes slithered up and down his body. Jeans hung low on his hips and he wore a dark green sweater. His hair was still damp from a shower, making it appear nearly black instead of its normal brown. Stubble dotted his cheeks and his eyes were bright and happy.

"Like what you see?" He smirked.

I blushed at having been caught staring. "Only a little."

He chuckled at my reply. "Only a little? Should I take my shirt off to bump that statement up to a lot?"

Several girls stopped on the stairs at his words and swiveled to look at him.

"Keep your shirt on," I warned. There was no reason to give the whole dorm a show.

"I'm thinking I should." He smiled playfully and began to ease up his shirt, exposing his toned stomach with those drool-worthy indents that disappeared into his jeans. A trail of hair started beneath his belly button and disappeared just like the indents. Before he raised it anymore he shrugged and let it drop back into place. "Never mind. It's cold. I might get frostbite."

I'm pretty sure one of the girls behind me whimpered.

I quirked a brow. "I don't think you can get frostbite in a dorm."

"Hey, you never know, and I like to err on the side of caution." He looked around at the leering girls still occupying the steps. "On second thought it looks like being eaten is more likely than frostbite. It's like I'm man-meat or something." Taking a dramatic bow he jogged down the steps. "Have a wonderful evening, ladies!" When neither Thea or I moved, Cade huffed, "Don't make me show my abs again. We're going to be late."

Thea and I rushed down the stairs.

Cade grinned proudly. "Now I know how to get you guys to do what I want."

"Oh, shut up." Thea pushed his shoulder.

Cade bowed his head, laughing. I loved watching the two of them interact. Cade slung his arm over her shoulder and they started for the door. Suddenly, he looked back and his eyes connected with mine. He grinned slowly. "Are you coming, Sunshine?"

Always.

The bar was packed when we arrived, but Xander and Jace had snagged a booth for all of us. Cade slid in first across the black vinyl, beside Xander, and grabbed my hand so that I was forced to sit beside him—as if it was such a burden to be close to Cade.

"Hey, guys," I said to the other two.

Xander smiled and Jace gave me a head nod. They both seemed like guys of few words.

"I didn't know you were a musician, Jace."

He looked up at my words and shrugged. "I'm not."

Thea rolled her eyes. "He's amazing."

"No, I'm not," he mumbled, looking around the bar broodily. "I'm going to smoke."

He slipped out of the booth and disappeared.

Thea sighed and looked at me sympathetically. "That's just Jacen. Don't take it personally."

Cade nudged my shoulder. "He's kind of like you. Bristly like a porcupine but once you get to know him he's a fluffy teddy bear on the inside."

I snorted. "I doubt that, and are you comparing me to a porcupine and teddy bear?"

He grinned, squeezing my knee. "You know it's true."

It was true. I was feeling less and less like that prickly porcupine and more like the squishy teddy bear. I didn't have to hate myself. I didn't have to hate the fact that I was alive. I'd been punishing myself for too long and it couldn't continue. It didn't mean I had to forget my friends, just that I had to forgive myself. And forgiving? That was hard.

"You guys!" We all looked up to see a winded Jace sliding back into the booth. I'd never seen him so exuberant before. His green eyes were bright with excitement. "I just saw the hottest chick I've ever seen in my fucking life. Like...damn." He whistled. "She was driving a fucking motorcycle. It was the sexiest thing ever."

Could it be...?

"Did she have purple hair?" I piped in.

Jace turned to look at me, his mouth falling open in surprise. "Yeah, do you know her?"

"She's my friend. We have some classes together."

Jace grinned. I was pretty sure it was the first time I'd ever seen him smile. He had a nice smile. It transformed his whole face. "Would you introduce me?"

"Sure," I shrugged. I didn't see the harm in that.

I looked around and when I saw her step inside I waved her over. She smiled and pushed her way through the crowd around the bar.

"Hey," she stopped at the table. "This place is packed. I didn't think I was going to get a seat at the bar. You're a life saver."

I slid closer to Cade and Thea slid closer to me so we could make room for the new addition.

"Nova, this is Jace. You didn't get to meet him the other day. He's another friend of Cade's."

"Jace," she seemed to be mulling over the name. "You wouldn't happen to be Jacen Andrews would you?"

"Yeah." Jace's eyes widened in surprise and he sat up straighter.

"Oh my God," Nova gushed, "I've seen some of your drawings. You're amazing." She suddenly blushed. "Sorry, I sound like a gushing fangirl, but I've always wanted to draw like that."

Jace cracked a half smile and smoothed his hair out of his eyes. The look he gave her could only be described as a smolder. Oh yeah, Jace was putting the moves on Nova. This was funny to watch. I kind of wanted to lean back and munch on popcorn while it all played out.

"Really?" He leaned forward, like he was trying to bridge the gap the table provided. "Maybe I could give you lessons sometime?"

"That would be awesome," Nova chimed.

"Excellent," Jace grinned, and slipped from the booth. "If you'll excuse me, it's time for me to play."

"Play?" Nova asked, looking around at the four of us as Jace disappeared.

"You'll see," Cade chuckled, reaching over to play with a strand of my hair. Leaning into me, he rubbed his nose against my cheek. "You have the softest hair."

"And you seem to like playing with it," I commented.

He grinned, tucking the piece behind my ear. He made sure to sweep his thumb over my cheek. "I like to see your face. That's why I play with your hair. You tend to hide behind it." Brushing his lips against my ear, his voice lowered so no one could hear. "You don't need to hide, Rachael. Not ever. And definitely not from me."

When he said stuff like that it did make me want to hide, because I didn't want him to see just how much those words meant to me.

His hand fell away and he returned to his previous position, as if none of that had happened.

I took several deep, steadying breaths.

One person should not turn your whole body into a fluttering mass of butterflies, but Cade did that. It was a good feeling too. One I could get used to. I could get used to *him*—having him in my life as more than a friend.

Cade glanced down at me and grinned, his dimples popping out. "What?" He asked. "Why are you looking at me like that?"

"Sorry," I shook my head, "I didn't know I was."

His smile softened and his eyes twinkled. "It's okay, I like that you were looking."

"Why?" I asked, not caring that Thea was beside me, listening to every word we spoke.

"Because it gives me hope that you have feelings for me too."

"I do have feelings for you," I admitted, the words falling from my mouth before I could stop them. A part of me wished that I could bend down and pick them up and pretend I'd never said it—but word vomit was mess that couldn't be wiped away.

Despite my embarrassment, my words were true. I did have feelings for Cade. Strong feelings. I wasn't sure when they first surfaced, but they were there, and growing stronger every day. The fact that I'd spent the afternoon missing him proved that. And now that he knew what I'd done, there really was nothing holding me back except my own hang-ups—that I might cause someone else I cared about to die, like I was some kind of grim reaper or something.

"These feelings you have, are they good feelings?"

I laughed. Only Cade. "Yes, very good." There was no point in lying now. Besides, I was sick and tired of denying my feelings to him and myself. I didn't have to be ashamed. Not anymore.

He grinned like a little boy who'd just been given the best Christmas present ever.

He was cut off from saying anything further as Jace's voice rang out around us.

Jace didn't bother to introduce himself to the patrons. His voice was soft, almost hesitant as he started, but as the song picked up so did his voice. He closed his eyes and I knew he *felt* the words he was singing.

"Holy shit," Nova muttered. "I think I just fell in love."

I snorted at that. Cade turned to me at the sound, the same grin still on his face. I loved his smile, and maybe if given a little more time, I could fall in love with him.

Then again, maybe I was already there and too stupid to see it.

Jace's voice might've been incredible, but I found myself unable to take my eyes off the man beside me.

"You want to get out of here?" Cade asked, his eyes heated.

"Yes," I breathed. I wanted that more than I wanted anything else in the world.

Cade turned to Xander and said, "Excuse us."

Xander smiled knowingly and slid out of the booth so we could follow.

"Can you take Thea back to the dorms?" Cade asked him, grabbing ahold of his arm before he could sit back down.

"Yeah," Xander shrugged, "that's not a problem."

Cade released him and Xander sat down.

We shrugged into our coats and he reached for my hand, entwining our fingers together. His eyes crinkled as he smiled. "Let's go."

The chaos of the bar melted away along with the soulful sound of Jace's voice.

Cade pushed open the door and we stepped outside. In the short time we'd been inside the world had been covered in a thin sheet of white snow. It fell down around us in tiny white puffs like the feathers of an angel.

Our collective breaths fogged the air and I couldn't help smiling.

This moment it was perfect, and Cade was about to make it even more perfect.

"Rae?" He asked, his voice thick with emotion. Little flakes of snow stuck in his hair.

"Yeah?" The one word sounded like a gasp.

"I really want to kiss you right now, but I don't want to scare you."

I closed my eyes, a smile on my lips. If only he knew how many times I had wanted him to kiss me and he hadn't.

"Kissing me would be more than okay. If you don't, I might never speak to you again." I opened my eyes so he could see that I was serious.

"Really?" He smiled cockily, stepping forward. "You'd give me the silent treatment?" He cupped my cheeks in his large hands, and his touch managed to heat my whole body.

"Oh, shut up." And then I did something that completely shocked Cade.

I took charge.

Yep, that's right. I took what I wanted and that was a kiss from Cade.

I wrapped my arms around his neck, and even though I was tall he was even taller so I stood on my tiptoes, and pressed my lips to his.

Softly, at first, almost hesitant.

I'd only ever kissed one boy, and for all I knew I sucked. So I was a bit scared to try out something crazy. I figured Cade could take the lead.

His body was rigid against mine with surprise, but once he realized that I had kissed him he relaxed and his mouth moved against mine.

It was like we were dancing.

But with our lips.

A dance only the two of us knew.

He tilted my head back and deepened the kiss. I couldn't stop the moan that passed between my lips and into his. He growled in response as his teeth lightly nipped my bottom lip. Then he was soothing the spot with a flick of his tongue.

Kissing had never been this soul shattering.

It was like with one kiss Cade was tearing me apart and putting me back together.

I swore with the heat we were generating the snow had to be melting around us.

The passion with which he kissed me was intoxicating.

This was the kiss of a man staking claim. He wanted to make a point, to show me that I belonged to him. But if I dug deep enough into the recesses of my mind, I knew that he'd staked his claim the very first time we'd met.

I hadn't been looking for love.

Or friendship.

Or a lot of things.

But the things you think you don't need can turn out to be *exactly* what you didn't know you were searching for.

Cade Montgomery crashed into my life, literally, and now I never wanted him to leave.

He was my salvation.

My hands moved from around his neck to fist the fabric of his jacket.

I wanted closer to him—to sink inside him so that his light and goodness could clear away all the dark shadows around my soul.

I knew it didn't work that way, but for a moment I wanted to pretend that I was worthy of him—that I was healthy and whole, and not this fractured and splintered girl I'd become.

For a moment I wanted to be enough.

And I was.

chapter twenty

CADE PULLED AWAY and placed a light kiss on the end of my nose.

"I feel like I've been waiting forever to do that," he breathed.

"Not quite forever," I joked, "but close enough."

He grinned crookedly and entwined our hands together, heading back to his Jeep. "Wanna go to the football field?"

I waved my hand at the swirling snow. "Isn't a bit cold for that?" Not to mention his coach might bust us again.

He chuckled and lowered his head to nuzzle my neck. "Don't worry, Sunshine. I'll keep you warm."

My body hummed at his words. Oh, I had no doubt he could keep me warm, and my cheeks flamed with thoughts of just how he'd go about it.

"Sounds good," I agreed, as he opened the passenger door of the Jeep for me.

When Cade slipped into the driver's seat he took my hand once more. I couldn't help staring at how our fingers wrapped around one another's, like neither of us ever wanted to let go.

Things had been changing between us for a while, slowly at first, and now all at once. I didn't think there was any coming back from this.

"What are you thinking about?" Cade asked, rubbing his thumb in soothing circles on my hand.

I shrugged, wiggling in the seat. I pretended my restlessness came from a need to adjust the seatbelt.

"Come on, Rae, tell me," he pleaded, glancing over at me.

"It's embarrassing," I mumbled.

The glow from headlights brightened his face for a moment before he was bathed in darkness once more.

"Do you really think I'll laugh at you?" His gaze flicked in my direction. "You should know me better by now. I won't laugh. I promise."

I knew he wasn't going to leave it alone. "I was just thinking that I don't believe there's any coming back from this. Not for me anyway. It's different with you," I admitted, biting down on my bottom lip before anymore truths could come tumbling out of its depths.

He didn't say anything. Or smile. Or give me any sort of indication of what he was thinking and that scared me. I thought maybe I'd said the wrong thing and admitted too much. The only thing that kept me from completely freaking out was the fact that he still clasped my hand in his.

One heartbeat...

Two...

Three...

I waited. Counting until a full minute had passed.

"I agree completely," he finally replied. I let out the breath I hadn't realized I was holding—the sound of my exhale seeming to echo around the car. "I've never felt anything like this before." Grinning now, he added, "That's why I was so relentless in my pursuit of you."

Relaxing, I joked, "Really? I thought it was because you were a cocky jock that couldn't take no for an answer."

His smile sweetened. "Rae, you should know by now that I'm not a cocky jock."

He definitely wasn't. Cade Montgomery was unlike anyone I'd ever met before.

He parked near the stadium and we headed inside the locker room and out onto the field.

Instead of leading me onto the field, Cade surprised me by turning and jogging up the steps to the bleachers.

When he turned and saw me still standing below, he said, "Come on. I never get to experience it from up here. Let's sit here for a while." He was already making his way down one of the aisles.

"Sure," I agreed, hurrying up the steps after him.

The stadium was open on top so the snow still swirled around us, coming down more frequently now. The whole field was a sheet of white. Maybe it was a good thing we hadn't gone out there. Our tracks would show a disturbance and his coach would no doubt figure out it was us.

Cade sat down and stretched his feet out in front of him. Lifting his arm, he waved me over to curl my body against his. It was all the invitation I needed.

His warmth wrapped around me as I snuggled close.

After losing Brett and my friends I'd never though I'd have this closeness with another human being. I'd never been happier to be proven wrong in my life.

Cade looked around and chuckled softly under his breath. "You know it's funny, when this place is empty it kind of reminds me a skeleton. Just a shell of what it can be."

I looked around and shrugged. "Yeah, I can see that."

"You think I'm crazy," he chuckled, his fingers tangling in my hair.

"No, not crazy," I snuggled closer, resisting the urge to purr like a kitten at his touch, "just passionate."

"Passionate," he mused. "I don't think I've ever had anyone call me passionate before."

"Really?" I asked, sliding down and stretching out my legs on the bleachers so that I could lie down. I rested my head on his thigh and he resumed stroking my hair.

"Yeah," he nodded, looking out at the field. Smiling down at me, he added, "I think I like being called passionate." He reached out and traced the shape of my lips. "I also really like kissing you."

My cheeks warmed despite the cold. "I like kissing you too." My heart fluttered and I felt like a little girl again, falling in love for the first time, where everything was still sweet and innocent and there were no complications. Clearing my throat, I asked, "How many girlfriends have you had?"

Cade's jaw clenched and his eyes darkened.

"I'm sorry," I mumbled hastily, "I shouldn't have asked that."

"No, it's fine," he sighed, his breath fogging the air with a thick cloud. "I just didn't expect you to ask that." He looked away and seemed to be gathering his thoughts.

"You know there was only Brett for me and I just...I was curious," I rambled, feeling the need to explain myself.

He smiled down at me then. "Don't feel bad, Sunshine. Just give me a minute." He looked out towards the field and took a deep breath. "There was a girl in high school. We dated from the time we were sophomores until it was time to leave for college. That's when it all fell apart..." He trailed off. "She wasn't happy when I told her I wasn't planning to go pro. She argued that I ruining *our* lives. Throwing everything we could have away. She didn't understand that I'm not that kind of person. I'm in it for the love of the game, not the fame."

I sat up, leaning my head on his shoulder and reached for his hand. I gave it a small squeeze for reassurance.

"She said some things that were hard to swallow, and I kept trying to get her to see where I was coming from. But it became clear that she was only with me for the future I could possibly provide for her. She didn't love *me*. She loved the *idea* of me," he sighed, pinching the bridge of his nose. "I was hurt for a long time after that. She was my first love," he smiled at me, "and I was a lovesick fool. For a long time I kept hoping she would change her mind. I heard from someone that she'd moved on to a guy that was due to inherit his dad's millions. That confirmed to me that it was all about the money for her. After that, I dated here and there," he shrugged, "but most girls were just like her. And the ones that weren't didn't hold my interest. To be completely honest with you, I fucked a few of them." He mumbled, and I could see the shame etched on his face. "I hated myself for that, for using those girls for selfish needs. My dad might be an asshole, but neither of my parents raised me to act like that. So, I started keeping to myself." He began to play with my fingers. "I hated the cocky jerk I'd become, so I changed."

I lifted my head to look at him. "You changed? Just like that? I find that hard to believe and you acted very cocky with me," I jested.

He chuckled and scratched at his stubbled jaw. "Do not mistake my confidence for cockiness. Big difference. *Huge.*"

I narrowed my eyes. "That sounds suspiciously like an euphemism."

"Sunshine," he winked, "I'm not one to be coy."

I shivered and he moved to wrap his arms around me, bringing me close to his body. I inhaled the scent that was uniquely Cade and let it comfort me.

"I still don't know what you see in me," I whispered, my words carried away by the wind.

He lowered his head and tenderly kissed my forehead. "I knew from the moment I saw you that there was something different about you. I had to get to know you." He paused, seeming to contemplate his next words. "I could tell that you were sad, and I wanted to know why, and frankly I wanted to make you smile." Wrapping a strand of my hair around his finger he said, "But I really wish you could see how amazing you are, because then you'd never ask me that question. You'd know."

I closed my eyes, exhaling softly.

Me, amazing?

I wasn't amazing. Not even before the accident.

I was boring Rachael Wilder. My life was average. *I* was average.

"Do you ever think of them?" He asked suddenly, changing the subject.

"Who?" I asked, although I was sure I already knew.

"Your friends. Your boyfriend." He cleared his throat and wiggled a bit, like he was afraid the question might set me off.

I looked up at him. "I try not to, but I think of them all the time. How could I not?" I babbled. "Sometimes I swear I can feel them around me." I feared I might start crying. Talking about them was nearly unbearable. "I feel so horrible for what happened. I wish I could forget it—have some miraculous loss of memory, but I know that's never going to happen. Getting away from home was the best thing that ever happened to me, because when I was there, I definitely couldn't escape their presence. Their families made sure of that."

I didn't tell Cade, but Brett's parents were the worst of them all. Since they lived beside my parents Brett's mom made it a point to come around and let me know that she thought I was a murderer. Maybe that's when I started believing it too. Hearing someone, especially an adult, say such horrid things about you can make you crack.

He smoothed his fingers through my hair and was quiet for a moment. "You know it wasn't your fault right?"

I laughed, but there was no humor in the sound. "Cade, it was my fault. Nothing you say can make me see it differently. If I hadn't looked at my phone, three people would still be alive. But I'm learning that I can't blame myself forever," I admitted, "and that's all thanks to you."

He smiled, rubbing his hand up and down my arm to keep me warm. The snow wasn't falling as frequently now, but it still dotted our hair, and stuck to our lashes.

"You know it's not your fault that your dad hits you, right?" I mimicked his words.

He chuckled. "Yeah, I know. Didn't used to, though. For a while, he had me convinced that I was a horrible brat that needed to be punished. By the time I got old enough to see that he was just a miserable human being I..." He paused and looked at me, suddenly uncomfortable. "This is going to sound so stupid, but I pitied him."

My eyes widened in surprise. "What? Why?"

He shrugged, clasping my hands in both of his. I was thankful for the added warmth.

"He lost his son, and that would crush anybody. Once I put myself in his shoes, I felt bad. I'm not saying if I lost a kid I'd hit my other one, but...I get it, I guess. Besides," he shrugged, "hitting him back wouldn't solve the problem. It would only make more."

I looked up at Cade with awe in my eyes. In many ways, he had things worse than I did and he thought of everything so sensibly. That was rare and I wished I could be that way too.

Before I could speak I shivered again.

Cade stood up. "We should go. You're going to get sick again and I don't want it to be my fault this time," he winked.

I bowed my head, a smile on my lips as I remembered being locked in my dorm all day with Cade. I'd been so mad at first, but then I became thankful for his presence.

He led me down the bleachers and through the tunnel and locker room.

Once in his car, he turned to me. His eyes were serious. "I'm not ready for tonight to end."

"Me either," I confessed, holding my hands out where the heat could warm them.

"Not to sound presumptuous, but would you want to come back to my dorm? I'm in a single, so we don't have to worry about disturbing a roommate," he winked. "Not that I expect anything to happen," he hastened to add.

I shook my head, a smile on my lips. "You are one strange guy."

"Strange?" He repeated. "How?"

I laughed. "Most guys *would* expect something, but I know you mean it when you say you don't."

He chuckled, backing out of the parking space. "Are you saying I'm weird?"

"That's one word for it," I laughed again.

"Would you rather me be like other guys?"

"No," I answered without any hesitation, "I like you just the way you are."

"And I like you the way you are," he chuckled.

I smiled. "Even though I'm an incredibly fucked up head case?"

He laughed and reached for my hand. "We're both fucked up, Rae." His face darkened from the shadows in the parking lot. "But that doesn't have to define you."

"It doesn't?"

He shook his head. "No, it doesn't. You had no idea what I'd been through with my dad and brother. You thought I was 'normal,' didn't you?"

"Yes," I admitted reluctantly.

"Exactly," he nodded, "that's because those things don't define who I am as a person, they're one of the many pieces that make up who I am. A *piece* is not a *whole*. Remember that, Rae."

"But is there really such a thing as normal?" I countered.

He pondered my words. "I guess not, but I think we all have our own idea of what normal is." He parked his car in front of his dorm building. A grin lit his entire face. "Ready to see my room?" He waggled his brows. "The bed is small, so we'll have to snuggle."

I snorted. "Of course we will."

He grinned and it was so infectious that I couldn't help smiling back. "I'm a master snuggler."

"I'm aware," I laughed, undoing my seatbelt, "remember when I was sick?"

He chuckled. "Oh, I can snuggle way better than that. There's even a special kind of cuddling where we don't wear any clothes."

I laughed at his comment, but then it had me picturing Cade naked and that was no laughing matter. I wondered what he'd say if I told him I was a virgin. Brett and I had been serious, but I'd never been ready to make that leap.

And now my brain was picturing Cade and I rolling around in his bed.

He'd told me he wasn't going to push me for more, but then his joke had me thinking all kinds of naughty things. My hormones needed to take a hike before I did something stupid.

Cade hopped out of the Jeep and jogged around to get my door.

It was late, nearing midnight, but on a college campus that was still considered early.

The people milling about didn't bother to hide their stares as the two of us made our way to the building holding hands.

I wasn't sure I'd ever get used to the fact that Cade was considered a celebrity on campus. Hell, I didn't think Cade was even used to it and he'd been going to school here for four years.

"Ignore them," Cade whispered, releasing my hand and moving his to the small of my back. "I do."

I wished I could ignore them, but I couldn't help wondering what they saw when they looked at us. Probably the school's football star slumming it with the freak. Yeah, I was probably way off base, but ever since the accident I felt like an outsider. I think a huge part of me was convinced that everyone could know what I'd done just by looking at me—as if I'd stuck a post-it note to my forehead declaring my transgressions.

When we finally entered the building I breathed a sigh of relief.

Rachael had been fine being the center of attention, but Rae didn't like it.

Luckily the dorm was empty as Cade led me to his room. I was thankful that no one caught me going into his room. I was sure if someone had it would've been the talk around campus for the next week.

His room was dark and he fumbled around to turn on a light.

The room was a little smaller than the one I shared with Thea, but large enough not to induce claustrophobia.

He didn't have anything decorating the walls, which I thought was weird.

His bed was made and the room was clean. I wondered if Cade had some sort of issue with tidiness, since his room at home had also been impeccably neat.

I sat down on the edge of the bed and closed my eyes, letting myself pretend for a moment that I was just a normal girl unscarred by her past.

I knew telling Cade had helped me heal, but only a little bit.

It was going to take far more than a confession to a man I was falling for, for me to get better.

I felt like I'd only put a Band-Aid on the situation, and if I didn't do more to rectify this I'd be right back to where I was before.

"It's not much," Cade shrugged, "I didn't feel like decorating."

"I like it," I told him, and it was the truth. While it was sparse, it was still his. And the stacks of books in the corner, mostly fantasy, more than made up for the lack of decoration. Besides, he was a college senior, and a guy. I figured most guys with decorations hadn't put them up themselves—it was either done by a girlfriend or mom.

"You look really uncomfortable sitting like that." He waved a hand where I sat on the end of his bed. My hands were clasped in my lap and my back was ramrod straight.

With a laugh, I kicked off my shoes and removed my jacket. I stretched out on his bed, wiggling around until I was comfortable. Propping my head on my hand I eyed him. "Is this better?"

His blue eyes had turned a stormy gray as he looked at me. His tongue flicked out the tiniest bit to moisten his lips.

"Much better." His voice came out as a low throaty growl.

He removed his own shoes and jacket before fitting himself onto the empty bed space beside me. He lay down on his back and wrapped his arm around me so that I was fitted against his chest.

Cade cleared his throat and put a finger beneath my chin to raise my face to his. "I never knew it could be like this, that something as simple as lying in bed with someone could feel this good." His fingers skimmed gently up my arm, and even through the fabric of my sweater his touch was searing.

I wanted to open my mouth and tell him that I agreed. I'd loved Brett, in whatever way a seventeen year old girl could possibly love a boy—like as if at eighteen I had so much more life experience, but I guess in a way I did since life's events had changed me so much. But for whatever reason, I couldn't make myself say the words. A part of me was terrified to acknowledge the presence of something *more* between Cade and I. It felt like an insult to Brett's memory, like he didn't matter, when he always would. He might've been gone, as well as Sarah and Hannah, but that didn't mean I forgot them and the relationships we had.

Realistically I knew I wasn't replacing Brett with Cade—this was me moving on, but it didn't feel that way in my warped mind.

I startled when Cade tapped his fingers against my forehead. "What are you thinking about? I know something has you upset. Talk to me," he pleaded.

Instead of lying or saying 'nothing,' I decided to be honest. "I'm scared I'm replacing Brett with you...but I know that's wrong. And what I feel for you is so much stronger, and that..." I paused. "That scares me and makes me sad at the same time, because I worry that maybe I didn't care about Brett enough." I sat up a bit, so my hair swooped down between us.

Cade's fingers curled into my hair, his hand resting at the nape of my neck.

"You know that isn't true. If you didn't care for him so much you wouldn't be worrying about this." He moved his hand to my face, rubbing his thumb over my bottom lip. "It's okay to let go of the past," he whispered, "letting go doesn't mean forgetting."

Deep down, I knew that, but it was hard to accept.

I lowered my head once more, to burrow into the space where his head met his neck.

Protected.

That's what I felt when I was in Cade's arms.

I squeaked when he moved suddenly, causing me to sprawl on my back with him hovering above me.

He lowered his head so strands of his hair fell forward to tickle my face. "I'm thinking I should kiss you now."

I reached up, my fingers grasping his shirt. All thought of our previous conversation was gone.

With one declaration Cade had turned me into a normal girl, at least for a moment, and all I could think about was how his lips would feel against mine again.

"Don't tease me," I warned, my mind emptying of all worries. Right now, all that existed was Cade and Rachael. Yes, Rachael, because right now I felt like her again and it felt good to know she wasn't entirely lost.

He chuckled, his lips turning up into a playful smirk. "Never, sunshine, especially when kissing is involved."

And then he closed the space between us and kissed me hard and fierce. It was a burning kind of kiss, one that shattered worlds and left you striving for another breath because all of yours had been stolen.

With a brush of his tongue he had me gasping beneath him, ready to beg for more.

My legs wrapped around his waist and I pulled him down so that we were touching in the most dangerous of places.

My fingers moved from his shirt to fist his hair. His stubble scratched my skin but I didn't mind.

"Rae," he gasped between our lips.

A moan escaped me at the sound of my name.

Kissing had never been like this before.

I wanted more, so much more, and that was scary.

If I let myself think that far ahead, I saw a future with Cade, a life I had stopped letting myself imagine when I lost Brett. But now I saw it all and beyond that I *wanted* it.

His fingers skimmed beneath my sweater, ghosting along my skin like he was afraid if he truly touched me I'd run screaming.

"Cade?" I gasped, pulling away from his lips.

His hand stilled and he started to pull away, but I tightened my hold on him. "If you don't really touch me I'm going to lose my mind, and don't you dare stop kiss—" He silenced my following words by doing exactly what I wanted him to do.

With every brush of his lips to mine I felt as if the shackles binding me to my past began to weaken and crumble.

His fingers pressed more firmly against the skin of my stomach, easing my shirt up slowly. I finally grabbed the garment and ripped it off. I knew he didn't expect me to go that far, not tonight, but I needed to feel him against me.

Once my shirt was gone his lips ghosted down my neck, lingering against the spot where my pulse raced.

My body arched against his and a breathy sigh passed between my lips.

"I want you so bad," he confessed. "But I want all of you, before we go that far."

I closed my eyes, knowing what he meant. He wanted *Rachael*. The real me. The whole me. Not this shell that was grasping onto life with weak fingers.

I knew I had to change, not for him, but for me. I needed to take ahold of my life and move on. I had to get better before I lived my whole life being miserable, because let's face it, that would be no life at all.

I felt like a baby fawn, trembling on new legs—terrified at what may lie ahead of me, but knowing that I had to do it.

I *wanted* to be able to tell Cade that he did have all of me, but we would both know that was a lie.

I had to hope that by the time I was ready to give him everything he hadn't given up on me.

"Stop thinking, just feel," Cade growled, nipping my chin.

Suddenly, he pulled away, grasping me by the waist so I went with him. I ended up straddling him with my arms around his neck so we were face to face.

He stared at me for a moment. I noticed that his lips were slightly swollen from our kisses.

His fingers tangled in the curls of my hair. "I wasn't looking for anyone to care about like this, but now that I have you...I wouldn't trade this moment for anything."

And then his lips were on mine again and the night, the room, everything, ceased to exist.

chapter twenty-one

I WOKE UP, stretching my arms above my head—and promptly smacked Cade in the face.

"Oh, shit." I rolled out of his bed and onto the floor, probably bruising my ass in the process.

I'd fallen asleep in his bed. Lovely.

Cade groaned and rolled over. He lazily peeked his eyes open to spy me on the floor. "Why the fuck are you down there? That doesn't look the least bit comfortable."

"I fell," I defended.

He cracked a smile. "That's funny."

It kind of was, but then the enormity of the situation hit me. "Cade," I groaned, "we fell asleep."

"I'm aware of that." He rubbed his eyes sleepily and stifled a yawn. "Best night of sleep I've ever had...and it doesn't have to end. Get back in bed, Sunshine."

"What will Thea think?" I hissed, looking down and realizing that I was only clothed in a bra and panties. Where the hell were my pants?

Cade noticed what I was looking for and chuckled. Propping his head on his hand, he said, "You got hot in the night and kicked them off."

I groaned and used my hands to hide my face.

"I promise I had nothing to do with it," he continued.

"I believe you," I muttered, but his words did nothing to alleviate the embarrassment I felt. "How am I going to walk out of here?"

"Easy," Cade grinned. "You stand up, put your clothes on, and walk out the door." He used his fingers to mime a person walking.

"Don't be a smartass," I groaned. "You know what I mean."

"So what? There's nothing to be embarrassed about," he shrugged, then rolled onto his back. "What time is it anyway?"

I located my phone. "Seven," I answered. "And you know it isn't that simple. You're, well, *you*," I waved my hand at him, "people pay attention to what you do and I don't want to become some story for gossips."

Cade rose up once more, leveling me with a glare. "You act like we had a fucking one-night stand and that if you walk out the door everyone will think you're a slut. Maybe I didn't make my intentions clear enough, but after last night I very much thought you were my girlfriend."

My eyes widened in surprise. I hadn't expected him to say that. Not at all. In fact, I was pretty sure all the air left my lungs and the room, because I suddenly couldn't breathe.

"Girlfriend?" I repeated, my voice no more than a squeak.

"Yeah," he looked at me like I'd lost my mind. "Did you really think I would fuck you and kick you out? And might I add, there was no sex involved last night. Besides, I would *never* fuck you, Rae. A girl like you deserves so much more than that."

I clasped my hands over my eyes. This was too much. *He* was too much.

"I don't mean to embarrass you, Rae," he rattled on, "but it's the truth. I'm no saint, but with you things are different."

I heard the bed squeak as he sat up. Then he was crouched in front of me, prying my hands from my face.

"I don't know if it's because I'm technically a jock that you find me hard to believe, but I would never lie to you, Rae. I'm not a player, never was. Yes, I fooled around, but it was random hook-ups that were *rare*. I was hurt by what my first girlfriend did to me," it didn't escape my notice that he still didn't reveal her name, "but I'm not like these other guys that have a different girl in their bed every night. I'm not like that and I don't want to be."

"I don't need an explanation," I told him, "you just caught me off guard."

He shrugged. "I know, but I wanted to explain myself. You should know by now that this isn't me wanting to get in your pants," he chuckled. "Although, I am a guy so I want that too," he winked. "But I've told you stuff I've never told anyone else. Most people don't know about my brother and the shit with my dad? No one knows that." He reached out, smoothing a finger down my cheek. "Now, Rae," his voice dropped low and his eyes bore into mine, "are you my girlfriend or not?"

266

I took several deep breaths, trying not to think about the day when Brett asked me to be his girlfriend.

"I guess so."

"You guess so?" He chuckled. "It's kind of a yes or no question."

I thought about how much I cared about him already, so really there was only one answer. "Yes."

He grinned, his eyes crinkling at the corners. Instead of saying anything he took my face in both his hands and kissed me deeply, stealing my breath and maybe even a bit of my soul.

"Now, can we *please* go back to sleep?" He asked, pulling away.

I laughed as all my fear at what people would think fell from my shoulders and drifted away. "Sleep would be good."

***

"Why am I not surprised?" Thea slid into the seat across from me in the dining hall. Her gaze swiveled from me to her brother who sat beside me. "You know, you could've at least told me you weren't coming home last night. I was worried."

"I'm sorry," I frowned. I'd been horrible not to consider that Thea might worry when I didn't come back to the dorm. If it had been her out all night I would've been worried sick like a protective mama bear. I probably would've torn the whole campus apart looking for her.

"You better be sorry," she scolded. Smiling slowly, she said, "Now that that's out of the way, I have to say, it's about fucking time." With that said she picked up her yogurt and pealed back the top.

I looked at Cade and both of us were trying not to laugh.

"Glad you approve, sis," Cade chuckled, giving my hand a squeeze.

She stuck the spoon in her mouth, licking away the yogurt, and then pointed it at us. "Hey, I've been gunning for this from the moment I found out you two knew each other. My best friend and brother together forever? I mean, that's just awesome. But I better be the maid of honor at your wedding or I'll cut a bitch."

I snorted. "Um, it's a bit too soon to be talking about weddings. And, we weren't even friends when you found out that Cade and I knew each other."

"Logistics," she waved her hands wildly through the air. "I knew we'd be best friends one day and guess what? It happened." Grinning, she added, "It's like I can see the future or something."

Cade snorted. "Or something, sounds right."

She narrowed her eyes on her brother. "Do not make me flick yogurt at you. You know I will."

Cade chuckled, raising his hands in surrender. "This is my favorite shirt. No yogurt please."

"For that reason alone I should flick it at you."

Cade looked at me and sighed dramatically. "Little sisters are so annoying."

"And big brothers are a pain in the ass," Thea added. "Do you know that a guy from one of my classes was going to ask me out and this oaf comes along and scares the poor guy away? He'll probably never speak to me again."

"As it should be," Cade nodded. "Besides, what could you possibly see in a guy that wears skinny jeans? I mean, I don't see how he even has any balls in pants that tight." Cade picked up his bottle of water, spinning the lid around before taking a sip.

I snorted at his words and Thea looked mortified.

"They were not that tight!" She hissed.

Cade eyed her. "They were. I've never understood guys that think that looks cool. It's just weird. Your balls need room to breathe."

Thea clapped her hands over her ears. "Shut up! I don't need to hear you talk about balls. It's gross."

Cade chuckled, lowering the water bottle to the table. "Okay, okay. No more talk about balls of any type. Not bouncy balls, or hairy balls, or footballs."

Thea picked up her tray, glaring at her brother. "I'm out of here. Enjoy your breakfast."

With that declaration she moved to another table.

I swiveled to look at Cade. "You did that on purpose to get her to leave."

"Maybe I did," he shrugged, picking up the apple from his tray and taking a bite. "I wanted to enjoy breakfast with my girlfriend."

Girlfriend.

Cade had said that word a lot this morning. It was like he enjoyed saying it, which blew my mind. Wasn't the guy supposed to be the hesitant one in the relationship, not the girl?

As if he couldn't control himself, he leaned over and kissed my forehead. My eyes closed and a soft breath passed between my lips at the gesture.

"Oh, I wanted to talk to you about something," he started, taking another bite of apple. Once he'd swallowed, he continued. "Some of the guys on the football team are throwing a party. They share a house off campus and I'm supposed to go, and I want you to come with me."

"Uh..." A party at a bunch of football players house didn't sound like my cup of tea, but Cade was giving me that puppy-eyed look and it was hard to resist. "When is it?"

"Friday," he answered.

I didn't want to go, but I knew I needed to. Rachael wouldn't have hesitated to go. Besides, I'd be with Cade and that would make it worth it.

"I'll go," I replied, hoping I didn't regret this decision.

Cade smiled like I'd given him the best present ever. "Thank you."

"Do I need to dress up?" I asked.

"No, it's a casual thing, but I'm sure there will be some...barely dressed women there seeking attention."

"Oh," I laughed, "so I'm not an attention seeker?"

"Definitely not," he replied, leaning in close and nuzzling his face against my neck, "and that's a good thing."

I pulled away reluctantly and looked at my phone, sighing. "I've got to head to class and I need to call my mom. I'll see you later." I leaned over to kiss his cheek, but he moved his head at the last second so my lips collided with his. He deepened the kiss, drawing me close, and I was pretty sure someone whistled in the dining hall.

Breathless, he pulled away. "See you later."

Damn him. My legs were shaking now and he knew it. I grabbed my bag and tossed my trash. When I reached the door to exit I couldn't help turning back and peeking at him. Cade watched me with his arm slung over the chair I'd just vacated. He smiled when he caught my gaze and my stomach fluttered.

I finally tore my eyes away from his, knowing my cheeks were now colored a light shade of pink, and pushed the door open.

The air was cold and I immediately zipped up my jacket. I pulled my phone from the pocket and rang my mom.

She answered on the first ring, and that made me feel bad. How often did the woman sit around hoping I'd be a good daughter and call home?

"Rachael? How are you?" She rattled.

"I'm good." I reached up, catching a strand of hair that wanted to blow into my mouth. "School keeps me busy."

"Of course," she agreed. "I'm glad you called. We miss you. I really wish you had come home for Thanksgiving. Surely you'll be home for Christmas?"

I winced, scrubbing my free hand over my face. "Um, I'm not sure yet, mom. I'll keep you posted," I lied.

"Your dad and I were thinking about driving down there one weekend. A few hours in the car won't kill us and we want to see you. We could stay for a weekend..."

I didn't know what to say, so I settled on, "Whatever you want." Before she could continue I interrupted with, "So, I called because..." My throat closed up and I wasn't sure I could get the next words passed my lips. I'd contemplated this a lot, and I was sure of my decision, but that didn't make it any easier to confess.

"What is it?" She asked, sounding hesitant. "You're not pregnant are you?"

I snorted. "No, mom."

"Sorry," she laughed. "I had to ask. These things happen, and you're a good girl, but even good girls do stupid things."

Yeah, I guessed she was right about that. And I'd already made one stupid decision by looking at that text message instead of driving my car like I was supposed to.

I sighed, knowing I needed to get back to the reason I called in the first place. "I called you because I've decided that it's time I saw a therapist again. I know Dr. Snyder gave you a list of recommendations for people in the area. I was hoping you could email it to me." Dr. Snyder had been my therapist at home. I'd never thought he did me much good, but I thought it was worth trying again, especially since he'd been so disappointed that I refused to continue treatment with a new doctor when I went to college. He'd said I needed more time to talk to someone and work out my issues. I was thinking he was right.

My mom was quiet on the other end. So quiet that I thought maybe the call had been disconnected.

"Mom?" I asked.

"Sorry," she replied, "you surprised me."

It was pretty sad that the fact that I wanted to see a therapist again surprised my mom. Had she come to the conclusion that I'd always be fucked up? Had my own mom given up on me?

"I think it's great that you're ready to talk to someone again," she continued. "How about I call the people he recommended and see if I can find a good fit for you? I know you're busy with class and I'd like to do something for you."

I reached the building where my class was located and leaned against the stone exterior. Nova passed me and smiled, throwing up her hand in acknowledgement before disappearing into the building.

"That would be great mom," I told her. "Thank you."

"Anything for you, Rachael." She began to sniffle, the sound of my mom's tears breaking my heart. "I just want to see you happy again."

I leaned my head back and closed my eyes. It was all too easy to get caught up in the hell I'd been living in, and forget that the people around me were suffering too.

"I love you, mom," I finally said.

"Love you too, sweetie." The call ended and I stood there for a moment, breathing in slowly.

I hated to think about how much I'd broken my parents with what I'd done and how I handled the situation.

I never meant to hurt them, but I did.

I really hoped seeing a therapist would help fix things.

Maybe soon, I'd be ready to go home and face all my fears—close the book on this chapter of my life and start anew.

chapter twenty-two

"WHERE ARE YOU GOING?" Thea looked me up and down. "That doesn't look like something you wear for a night in with your roommate," she joked, sitting on her bed cross-legged. She was already dressed in her pajamas. Her iPad was propped on the bed and I figured the second I was gone she'd be on Netflix. Apparently she was addicted to Gossip Girl and had a crush on someone named Chuck Bass. According to her, I was missing out on greatness.

"Your brother asked me to go to a party with him." I straightened the shirt I wore.

"I wasn't invited? That isn't fair," she pouted.

I shrugged. "Sorry."

"Whatever. Chuck is waiting and he's so much more exiting than a party."

Somehow I didn't believe her, but in all honesty I would rather stay in than go to this party. I was going to be surrounded by Huntley University's finest, people I didn't know, and that gave me major anxiety since I was no social butterfly.

"Well, if there's another party, I'll make sure you can come." I added to appease her.

"Yeah, so I can feel like the third wheel," she grumbled, crossing her arms over her chest. "This past week has made me wonder why I wanted you guys to date. All the kissing is grossing me out."

I laughed, smoothing my hair back into a ponytail. "I'm sorry. I'll tell Cade to tone it down."

"Don't tell him anything," she warned. "It'll just make him kiss you more to gross me out. Brother's are assholes like that."

I finished my makeup and sat down beside her on her bed, since I still had some time before Cade was due to arrive.

"So, what's going on with you and Xander?" I'd asked her the same thing before, but I felt like we were better friends now and she might tell me more.

She shrugged. "Honestly, like I told you, nothing. I like him," she shrugged, "and I think he likes me, but neither of us has made a move. Besides, I'm kind of over him. There's this one guy in my English class that I really like and he seems interested."

I eyed her. "Thea."

"What? Why are you saying my name like that? I feel like I'm in trouble," she frowned.

"If you like Xander you should go for it."

She sighed. "We've been friends since we were kids, so that makes it weird, but he's also Cade's *best* friend which makes it complicated. I don't need that kind of drama in my life. Besides, I don't want to end up on 48 Hours when Cade kills us for...canoodling," she supplied, and we both dissolved into laughter.

I decided to let the topic of Xander drop. "Okay, so who's this new guy you like?"

Her cheeks flushed and I figured that was a good sign. "His name is Trevor and he's really nice."

"Trevor and really nice? That's all you've got?" I laughed. "Come on, give me more than that." I gasped, and grabbed her hand. "This isn't skinny jeans guy is it?"

"What?" She laughed. "No! Besides, like I said, I'm pretty sure Cade scared him away from ever talking to me again. It's okay, though. He was kind of odd and those jeans were a turn off."

"So, are you going on a date with Trevor?"

I marveled at how easy our conversation was. It was so normal and easy. Two girls discussing guys and dates. I never thought this would be my life again.

"Tomorrow actually," she admitted.

"Tomorrow?! And you didn't tell me?! Thea!" I shrieked, probably disturbing the girls in the room beside us.

"What?" She shrugged. "You didn't tell me about the party."

I frowned. "That was an accident, truly. To be honest, I don't even want to go, so that's why I didn't say anything."

Her face softened. "You're forgiven."

A knock sounded at our door. Thea shook her head. "That'll be my brother. No doubt he's sweet-talked yet another girl into letting him into the dorm. I swear, all he has to do his bat his eyes and they turn to goo. It's annoying." Reaching her arms out to hug me, just as there was another knock, she added, "Have fun, and call me if you're not coming back to the dorm. I don't want to worry."

"I will," I assured her, hugging her back.

A third knock sounded and I hollered, "I'm coming." To Thea I rolled my eyes and muttered, "He's so impatient."

I opened the door and found the reason for his incessant knocking. A girl that lived on our floor, I think her name was Jessica, was hanging onto his arm and talking his ear off.

"Sorry," I apologized, slipping out the door.

"Thank God," he muttered under his breath, taking my hand.

"Bye, Cade!" The girl called.

"Bye, Jessa," he groaned.

I poked his side. "I'm pretty sure it's Jessica."

"Jessica! I meant Jessica!" He yelled back as we started down the stairs. I couldn't help laughing. "She wouldn't shut up," he hissed to me, "and honestly, the talking was tolerable compared to how she kept feeling up my muscles. I was getting afraid that she might get adventurous and grab my junk."

"Oh, that would've been interesting." I laughed, picturing Cade getting mauled by the girls on my floor.

"Seriously," he flailed dramatically, "the girl's hands were relentless and it's not like I could forcibly remove her."

"Hey, you don't need to feel bad about it. I mean, I can't blame her," I winked. "Who wouldn't want to feel you up?" I asked playfully.

He laughed. "Apparently you."

I blushed at that and ducked my head. If only he knew how little experience I had in that department he wouldn't make jokes so lightly.

Cade held open the door for me and we strode out into the frigid night air. The sky was dark and cloudy, barely any stars shining.

"This way," he took my hand, leading me to his Jeep. "I couldn't find a parking spot close."

"How long do we have to stay?" I asked, my nerves skyrocketing as I realized I was about to attend my first real college party. It was already nine and I figured these things ran late. I felt like such a grandma for not even wanting to go in the first place. I'd rather hang out with Cade in his dorm or with Thea.

Cade shrugged. "An hour or two. If you absolutely hate it, then say so and we'll leave sooner."

He could read me so well it was scary at times.

I climbed into the Jeep, trying to think calming thoughts. My nerves raced and my palms grew sweaty. These were Cade's teammates I'd be meeting and their opinion of me mattered. I didn't want them to think I was some weird freshman just trying to finagle my way into the 'in' crowd.

"Your hands are shaking," he commented, turning up the radio.

I tucked them under my legs. "Sorry, I'm nervous."

"Don't be nervous." He rested one hand lazily on my knee, looking over his shoulder to back out of the parking space. "It's just a small party."

Small, I repeated to myself. I could handle small.

"Small?! You call *this* small?!" I shrieked, sinking my hands into the fabric of the Jeep's seat. I stared at all the cars lining the street and the large amount of people hanging around outside despite the cold.

Cade shrugged sheepishly. "I may have underestimated the size."

I felt like I was suffocating. Was this what a panic attack felt like? Oh God.

I clutched at my chest, dragging air into my feeble lungs.

"Rae?" He questioned. "Are you okay?"

"Give me a minute," I pleaded.

Even Rachael would've had trouble with a party this size, so Rae was in full on freak out mode.

What the hell had I gotten myself into?

I wanted to climb in the back and hide beneath the seat.

"It won't be that bad," Cade said soothingly. "I'll be by your side the whole time. There's nothing to worry about. It'll be fine."

I chewed worriedly on my fingernail.

"We won't stay long, I promise, but I have to show up or the guys will give me hell." He took one of my hands in his, rubbing it soothingly. "Whatever you're imagining I promise it's not like that."

He was making an awful lot of promises I was afraid he wouldn't be able to keep.

I looked at the house and back to him. "Okay."

If I didn't get out of this car now, I never would, and I think Cade sensed that because at my word he was out of the car and at my side in only a few seconds.

"Breathe," he told me, pulling me against his side.

Breathe? What was breathing?

Oh, yeah. That thing where you forced air in and out of your lungs.

Cade's hold on my hand was tight as we slithered between cars and up to the front door. The people milling around outside didn't seem to be paying us any attention. They were too busy smoking something that was definitely not a cigarette.

Cade didn't bother to wait for anyone to come to the door. He just reached out, took the knob in his hand and twisted it.

I immediately wanted to slap my hands over my ears from the deafening sound of the music playing. The rumble of so many voices didn't help my ears to feel any better. I realized as soon as the door closed behind us that there was no way Cade and I were going to hear a word the other said.

Cade pushed through the throng of people crowding the entryway, heading towards the back of the house. I could see the kitchen and figured that was his destination. I held tightly to his hand, afraid if I let go that I would be sucked into a black hole and lost forever.

He looked back at me and seemed to sense my fright, so he drew me closer to his body until I felt like I was glued to his side.

"Hey, Cade," someone I couldn't see called.

Then a chorus of, "Hi, Cade," and "Hey, Cade," started up.

He nodded, not really acknowledging a specific individual.

We finally made it to the kitchen and it was as packed as the living room and dining room we'd come from.

"Want anything to drink?" He asked me.

"Just water," I squeaked, lowering my eyes to the ground to avoid the stares of the people around us. And no, I wasn't paranoid, because they were definitely staring.

"What? Hanging out with jailbait, Montgomery?" A male voice from the corner of the kitchen called out. I looked up, locating him immediately. He was a monster of a guy, taller and wider than Cade with black wavy hair falling messily into his eyes. He was smiling, but there was something off about it.

"Shut up, Eric," Cade growled.

The guy named Eric chuckled, draping his arm around the shoulder of a blonde that looked like her boobs were about to pop out and say hello to all of us. "Ooh, someone's testy."

"Ignore him," Cade mumbled under his breath to me. "That's what I try to do."

Try being the keyword there.

"Don't worry, beautiful," Eric turned his gaze towards me, "I don't bite."

I stepped closer to Cade. I felt like at this point I was practically trying to climb him to get away from these people.

I suddenly wished I had my camera so I could hide behind its protective lens.

"Don't talk to her," Cade defended, moving his body in front of mine.

I might not have liked the guy, but I didn't need Cade to get all Alpha male defensive on me.

I moved so that I stood beside him once more. Eric glared at Cade, taking a few steps forward around the kitchen island that separated us. The blonde moved with him, his arm was still draped over her shoulders and every little bit he brushed his fingers over her breast. "What's your name, sweetheart?" He asked me, ignoring Cade's threatening glare. He smiled once more and I still found it threatening.

I didn't want to give him my name, but I knew lying wasn't an option. "Rae."

"Rae," he repeated my name slowly, like it was a flavor exploding on his taste buds. "Beautiful name for a beautiful woman."

Cade growled, his hold on me tightening.

"Don't get defensive, Montgomery. I'm just stating the obvious," Eric chortled. "Man, I've never seen you so worked up over a girl before. Haven't actually seen you with many girls. I was starting to think you were gay."

Cade jolted forward, his fist tightening.

I grabbed ahold of his arm, digging my fingernails into the skin. "Cade, stop," I warned. "He's just trying to get a rise out of you."

That made him stop, but he still glared at Eric like he was ready to kill him.

"Come on," I coaxed, "let's grab a drink and go back to the living room." *Or leave*, which I didn't say out loud.

He bristled, still glaring at Eric, but after a few more seconds his body relaxed and he turned away from the other guy.

"He's just trying to piss you off," I hissed.

"I know," Cade mumbled, staring down at his shoes, "but it's working."

Cade grabbed a bottle of water for me and a beer for himself. Taking my hand, he led me from the kitchen. I felt Eric's eyes boring into my back. I didn't tell Cade, but the guy gave me the creeps. There was definitely something off about him.

Cade found an empty space of wall in one of the hallways and pulled me in front of him, my back to his chest. Almost every surface in the house was covered with bodies, and those that weren't looked like they were covered in vomit and other mysterious stains.

I could feel a headache coming on from all the noise and reached up to rub my temples.

This was exactly what I'd pictured a college party to be like and I didn't want anything to do with it.

Even when I was still Rachael I'd never been the girl screaming, taking her top off, and dancing on a table. And yes, that definitely just happened.

I wasn't sure whether I should cover my eyes, Cade's, or both. Probably both—oh God, she was going to knock someone out with one of those if she kept swinging around like that.

I felt like maybe I should be the responsible person and step forward to try to stop her, but now a ring of people were forming around her, urging her on. Yeah, I wasn't going to try and break through them.

Cade's hands grasped my hips and I tilted my head back to look at him. "Is this what all your parties are like?"

He laughed. "This isn't my party, but yes most of them are like this."

"Well, that's...gross," I mumbled, trying not to watch the show being put on.

Cade moved from behind me and dragged me into the dining room where we couldn't see the girl anymore. I was thankful for it.

The dining room wasn't even decorated as a dining room. It was set up more like a den with a couch, chairs, and a TV with an expensive looking game box. The only thing that gave away the origin of the room was the chandelier in the center that must've come with the house, because there was no way college guys would've installed one.

I didn't want to sit on the couch, because it was definitely stained with something funky, so Cade and I stood against the wall like we had in the hallway. The room had cleared out, thanks to the striptease going on—although, I wasn't sure it could be considered *teasing* when you ripped off your clothes.

I noticed Eric was still in the kitchen with the same girl. She was basically humping his leg and her mouth was glued to his neck, leaving a slobbery trail.

But Eric seemed oblivious to the poor girl, who was clearly trying to get his attention. I knew this because his eyes were on me. His eyes scanned my body lazily, like he was memorizing every curve. Now I really did want to hide behind Cade.

"What are you looking at?" He asked, turning around to see for himself.

Eric had the good sense to look away in time, so Cade assumed I was just grossed out by the display.

Cade looked down at me, frowning. "Let's go."

We couldn't have been there more than thirty minutes, and I felt bad that he wanted to leave because of me.

"No, I'm fine," I assured him. "These are your friends. Go mingle. I'll be fine here." I gave his hand a reassuring squeeze.

He looked at me skeptically. "I think we should go."

"Cade," I said his name sternly, like I was scolding a child. "I won't be the girlfriend that keeps you from doing things. I'm *fine*," I assured him. "Don't worry about me."

He sighed, swallowing thickly. "Give me fifteen minutes and then we'll go."

I nodded as he lowered his head to press a soft kiss to the corner of my mouth.

As soon as he disappeared from my sight my anxiety sky-rocketed, but I knew I'd made the right decision. I didn't want to become a burden on him and keep him from his friends. I didn't need Cade to become my shield from life. I had to learn to deal with uncomfortable situations on my own.

I fiddled with my fingers, feeling extremely awkward to be standing there by myself. It was clearly only upperclassmen at the party, which only served to make me feel more out of place.

Maybe if I was still Rachael I'd plaster a fake smile on my face and introduce myself to some people. But I felt frozen to the spot.

To have something to do I fiddled with a loose thread on my shirt.

"Need some help there?"

I let out a startled squeak as I looked up and saw Eric. He stood there with his hands in the pockets of his jeans, angling his body towards me. He smiled in a way that I was sure was meant to comfort me, but only made me feel more unease.

"Uh," I let my hand fall away from the sleeve of my shirt, "no, I don't need any help." I took an unconscious step away from. If he noticed he didn't act like it.

His smile widened. I'm sure that smile had lots of girls swooning into his arms, but not me.

"That's a shame," he chuckled, his eyes zeroed in on my breasts.

"Well, if you don't need anything, I'll be going." I moved around him to leave, but he caught my arm, jerking me back in front of him.

"Ow," I groaned, rubbing the tender area where my shoulder and arm connected. "Was that necessary?"

"Sorry," he apologized, but there was nothing sincere in his voice. "I just didn't want you to leave."

I looked over my shoulder where the blonde who'd been hanging onto him earlier glared at me. "I don't think you're lacking for company. I'm leaving."

This time when I moved around him he grabbed both of my arms and shoved me against the wall so hard that it felt like my skull cracked against it. Tears stung my eyes and all air left my lungs as he glared down at me.

"I wasn't done talking to you, bitch," he spat.

I flinched from his words, his hold, and the scary look in his eyes. It was like he was possessed. They were so empty and lifeless.

"Wh-what do you want to talk about?" I stuttered, trying to appease him.

This was like the night at the club, but so much worse, because Eric was huge and I knew there was no way I was getting out of this situation on my own. I had to hope Cade came back soon or someone intervened.

Eric was clearly drunk, but his hold on my arms was so tight that I swore my bones rubbed together. I was definitely going to have bruises in the morning.

"Why are you here with Montgomery?" He asked.

I hadn't expected that question. "Because he's my boyfriend," I whispered.

"Boyfriend?" He chuckled, the stench of alcohol on his breath making me feel dizzy. "That's funny."

"It's not a joke," I glared. "Now let me go." I said the words with as much strength as I could muster, but there was still a slight quiver to my voice.

He chuckled. "That's cute."

"What's cute?" My whole body started to shake. This was so bad.

"That you think I'm going to let someone as pretty as you get away." He released his hold on one of my arms, but before I could make a move to wiggle away he pressed his body firmly against mine. I felt like I was suffocating. "You're not going anywhere." When my body bucked against his he smoothed his fingers down my cheek. "Shh, I won't hurt you."

I wanted to argue that he'd already hurt me, but I knew my words would only fall on deaf ears.

Glaring at him, I spat, "I never knew someone such as yourself had to force themselves on girls to get any action. That's called sexual assault."

His eyes burned and I had no time to react before his hand slapped against my cheek.

I saw stars and wiggled my arm, trying to get my hand to my cheek to soothe the burn, but I couldn't move.

I tasted blood in my mouth from the impact, and while I might have been scared I was also mad. I spat the blood out on his shirt and he chuckled in response.

"You have sass, I like that."

"Get away from her." An icy voice spoke beyond the mountain that was Eric.

Eric didn't step away from me, in fact I was pretty sure he drew even closer, tightening his hold to the point that I was sure my circulation was cut off.

Looking over his shoulder he chuckled menacingly. "Now why would I do that, Montgomery?"

With a roar Cade charged forward, ripping Eric from my body. Eric stumbled back and Cade maneuvered his body in front of mine.

"Stay the fuck away from her."

Eric held his arms out, chuckling. He seemed oblivious to the anger rolling off of Cade in waves.

"Do you really think I'm going to listen to you? I always get what I want, Montgomery, and I want her." He puckered his lips at me.

Cade lost it and there was nothing I could do to stop him.

He charged forward like a bull, tackling Eric to the ground as if they were on the football field and not in the middle of a party.

There was a collective gasp and then sounds of, "Fight, fight, fight!" broke out.

The guys rolled around, fists flying.

I didn't know what to do, but I did think it was best if I stayed out of the way. If I tried to break up the fight I'd only end up getting hurt worse in the process and my head was already throbbing from the impact of Eric shoving me into the wall. I was probably going to end up with a knot on the back of my skull the size of a baseball.

The crowd grew even more in size—apparently fights were more interesting than boobs now, or else the girl had gotten dressed.

When I couldn't see the fighting men anymore I eased out of the room heading for the front door.

I walked along the sidewalk and crossed into the street when I spotted Cade's Jeep.

He'd figure out where I went. Well, I hoped...and preferably soon. It was extremely dark and none of the houses near his car had any outdoor lights.

I made sure to stay hidden before I landed myself into any more trouble.

I wanted this night to be over. I hadn't expected much of tonight, but it had been even more of a disaster than I had anticipated.

As I sat on the sidewalk by myself tears sprung to my eyes.

This night felt so much like the one at the club, but I was far more afraid of Eric than I had been of Icky Guy. I got the impression that Eric wasn't used to girls denying him. And Eric had this mean glint in his eye that was worrisome.

I wiped tears from cheeks.

I hadn't even realized I was crying.

I dried my face but it was pointless. More tears replaced those. I was a blubbering mess. I always tried to be so put together, at least on the outside, but I was falling apart. Everything seemed to be catching up with me.

I guessed it was a good thing I'd told my mom I was ready to see a therapist again. My first appointment was tomorrow, and after this night I was going to need it.

I was shivering by the time I spotted Cade walking to the car.

"Rae?" He called into the night. "Rae? Where are you? Are you out here? Rae?"

"I'm here," I stood up, sniffling.

"Oh, thank God." He breathed a sigh of relief. He ran towards me and wrapped his arms around me. "I was so worried. I tore that whole house apart looking for you."

"I had to get out of there," I blubbered into his shirt. He was going to think I was a crybaby if I kept crying all over him.

"I'm so sorry." He kissed the top of my head, smoothing his fingers through my hair. "I'm so sorry," he began to chant over and over again. "I shouldn't have left you."

"I'm okay," I assured him.

"Are you sure?" He tilted my head back to look at me and that's when I winced. "What the fuck did he do?" Cade growled, his face transforming to an angry grimace.

"M-my head hit the wall," I stuttered.

He cursed unintelligibly under his breath.

"We'll go to the hospital and get you checked out." He pushed passed me and opened the passenger door.

"I really think I'm fine," I assured him.

"No." His jaw was set. "I'm not taking you back to the dorms until I know you're okay. We're going to the fucking hospital, even if I have to drag you kicking and screaming."

"Okay," I agreed, figuring it was better to be safe than sorry.

"Thank you," he said softly before I got in the car.

I didn't know why he was thanking me. I should've been thanking him. He saved me tonight...but really, he saved me before that.

"Everything is fine." The emergency room doctor assured Cade. To me she added, "There will be some soreness and a sizable bump, but you have no signs of a concussion."

"Thank you." Cade stood up and extended his hand for the doctor.

"Have a good evening," she said before exiting the room.

A nurse came in a few minutes later with some papers for me to sign. Once that was done we were free to go.

Cade kept a hand on the small of my back as we headed for his car. It was like he was still afraid I might fall over.

I climbed into the big vehicle and exhaustion flooded my body. I wanted nothing more than to sleep for the next three days.

"Do you want to go back to your dorm or mine?" He asked, pulling out of the hospital parking lot. An ambulance zoomed past us, illuminating the car with its flashing lights.

"Mine," I mumbled, fighting the urge to close my eyes.

"Are you mad at me?" He asked softly.

"No," I gasped, "why would you think that?"

"You said you didn't want to come back to my dorm," he shrugged, "so I thought maybe you were mad at me."

I wanted to go to my dorm, because frankly I wanted my own bed right now and I was seeing my new therapist early in the morning. I hadn't told Cade about it yet. I wasn't sure what he'd think and I was a bit scared to say anything to him.

"Nope, I just want my own bed," I assured him. He looked at me doubtfully so I added, "I swear, Cade. I'm not mad. Trust me, if I was mad you'd know."

He chuckled. "Okay, I believe you."

"What's Eric's problem?" I asked, suddenly. I'd wanted to ask before, because there was obviously more there than I knew, but there hadn't been a good opportunity.

Cade pinched the bridge of his nose, the red of the stoplight illuminating his face.

"Eric's just a fucking asshole," he spat. "He wanted to mess with you to piss me off. He's jealous because scouts are interested in me and not him, and of course the whole team knows I have no desire to join the NFL, so that only pisses him off even more." He sighed heavily. "I shouldn't have gone to the party. I only went because Adam and Brady were supposed to be there and guess what?" He laughed humorlessly. "Neither of the fuckers showed up, so it was pointless for me to even go." He looked at me sadly. "I promise not all of the guys on my team are like that."

"I believe you." I forced a smile because I was too tired to offer a real one. "You're not like Eric and neither is Xander."

He reached for my hand, entwining our fingers together. "I really am sorry about tonight."

"Cade," I said his name warningly, "you don't have to keep apologizing to me."

"I know," he glanced at me, "but I want you to know I mean it."

"I do," I promised. "Please, don't beat yourself up over this. Eric is just a shitty guy and that's not your fault."

"It's my fault for leaving you," he countered.

"And I told you to leave," I reminded him. "It happened and it's over with, okay?"

He sighed, tapping his fingers against the steering wheel to the beat of the song. "No promises."

I was too tired to argue anymore and drifted to sleep. When I woke up the next morning I was in my bed and Cade's scent lingered in the air.

chapter twenty-three

I STOOD OUTSIDE THE THERAPIST'S DOOR. It was my turn to go back but I was frozen. I was tempted to turn around and run out the door screaming, "I can't do this!"

But I never got that chance.

The door opened and I stumbled forward. A bright and cheery woman of no more than forty smiled at me. "You must be Ms. Wilder."

"R-Rae," I mumbled, my heart racing with fear. With the way I was sweating you would've thought the woman was trying to kill me.

"Rae," she repeated, "it's nice to meet you. I'm Dr. Daniels but you can call me Kathleen."

"Kathleen," I repeated, my pulse racing.

"Yes." She closed the door and sat down in a chair, not behind a desk like my old therapist had. "Sit, please." She motioned to the other unoccupied chair.

I scurried over and sat down. I figured to her I must've looked like a frightened rabbit.

She grabbed a notebook and pen off a table, depositing them in her lap. "How are you today?"

"Good, I guess." I mumbled, staring out the window where morning sunlight streamed in the window.

"You guess?" She repeated.

"I don't want to talk about it," I mumbled. I didn't know this woman, not yet, and no matter how kind she might look with her warm brown eyes and sweet smile she was still a stranger.

"That's fine. Why don't we spend this session getting to know each other?" She suggested.

"Excuse me?" I replied, my brows rising. My last therapist had made it very obvious that he was the doctor and I was the patient. But this woman was different.

"I think we should get to know each other," she repeated. Sliding forward in her seat she peered at me. "I'm here to help you, Rae, but that doesn't mean we can't be friends."

"Friends?" I snorted.

She smiled. "Yes, friends. I'm not your enemy. I want you to get better as much as you want to get better."

"How do you know I want to get better?" I countered, looking around the room at the framed photos and memorabilia. It looked like she was married to a nice man with two children. She had a lot of books and not all of them were medical books. Many were fiction. I even saw a set of Harry Potter books, which made me smile as I thought of Cade.

"If you didn't want to get better you wouldn't be here," she replied easily.

"What do you want to know about me?" I asked.

She smiled. "I think maybe you should ask me that first."

"Why?" My brows furrowed together.

She smiled, crossing her legs. "Because, I want you to see that I'm not here to analyze you."

I wanted to snort at that, but I kept myself in check. "Okay then...what are your kids names?" I pointed at one of the framed photos.

"Tessa and Tyler," she replied. "We adopted them."

"You couldn't have kids?" I asked, and then promptly felt bad for asking. It wasn't proper of me to pry and I wasn't sure quite how far I could take this question thing.

"Sadly, I couldn't," she frowned, her eyes growing distant. "But I love those two as much as if they were my own flesh and blood. They're my miracles." I could see the love she was talking about as she spoke. "You're in college, correct?" She asked. At my nod, she continued. "What are you studying?"

"Photography," I answered, my thundering heart slowing to a dull roar.

"Photography?" She repeated. "Wow. I'd love to see some of your photos sometime."

"I could bring some next time," I mumbled.

"That would be great," she clapped her hands together. "I always did have such an appreciation for the arts. I played the violin as a child."

The rest of the session went much the same way. She wanted me to come back on Monday after classes, and something told me that she'd be ready to get down to the gritty stuff. I hoped I was ready.

"Rae, wait up!"

I stopped at the sound of my name being called. Snow flurries fluttered around me, sticking to my lashes. I was glad I'd worn a beanie and scarf, even though the weather hadn't called for more snow.

Cade jogged up to me, his breath fogging the air with each exhale. "I've been looking all over for you. You didn't answer your phone and Thea said you left early this morning and didn't say where you were going. I was worried your head was bothering you and you'd gone back to the hospital."

"My head's fine," I assured him.

"I'm glad to hear that." He blew into the palms of his hands to warm them. "Where'd you go?"

I looked away, toeing the ground. I'd expected him to ask, but I wasn't sure I wanted to tell him. I couldn't lie though. Lying would only make my problems worse.

"I went to see a therapist." I looked into his eyes, waiting to see if he reacted in any way.

He smiled. "That's great, Rae. I think that will be good for you."

That definitely wasn't the reaction I'd expected. Most people, when you told them you were seeing a therapist, replied with, "A therapist? Like a shrink? Are you crazy or something?"

I should've known Cade wouldn't react that way. He never did what I expected him to. He was constantly surprising me and in the best ways possible.

"Thanks, I hope so." I reached up, grabbing a strand of hair that stuck to the gloss coating my lips.

Dropping the subject from my therapy session, he asked, "Are you hungry? I thought we could go out for lunch?" He rubbed his hand around his stomach absentmindedly.

Now that he mentioned it I was starving. In my haste to get to the therapist's office I'd forgone breakfast.

"Lunch would be great," I smiled.

"I know it might be too soon," he rocked back on his heels, "but do you think you'd be up to meeting some of the guys on the team afterwards? I'm supposed to meet them at the gym at one. Eric won't be there," he hastened to add.

"Uh..." I paused, thinking. "That would be fine."

He grinned and the dimples in his cheeks popped out. "They're going to love you, Rae."

I hoped so. The last thing I wanted was to be known as the weird girl by the football team. But knowing me I'd do something stupid to make them hate me. Or Eric had gotten to them and told them some disastrous lie about me.

"What's with that face?" He chuckled, reaching out to guide my chin up so that I was eyelevel with him.

"What if they hate me?" I frowned.

He grinned crookedly and lowered his head so he could whisper in my ear. "I'm going to let you in on a secret, Rae. You're impossible not to like."

I snorted at that. I disagreed completely with that statement. All I did was push people away.

But then why do you have friends now? A little voice in my head piped up.

"What? You think I'm lying?" He pushed strands of his hair from his eyes.

I shrugged. "I'm not the nicest person." Rachael had been nice. She loved everybody. Rae...not so much.

Cade reached out, tucking a strand of hair behind my ear. His fingers lingered longer than necessary against the skin of my cheek. "You're nicer than you think you are. You're way too hard on yourself."

Sadly, I felt like most times I wasn't hard enough.

"They're going to love you," he repeated. "Trust me."

Trust him? Didn't he know I already did? I would've never told him about the accident if I didn't. I trusted Cade in ways I'd never trusted another human being before.

I reached out, grasped his jacket and stepped closer. I tilted my head back and peered up at him.

His lips twisted into a smile. "What are you doing?"

"Getting closer to you."

"Why?" He drew out the word.

"So I can tell you that I trust you. You should know that, Cade."

His smile widened until it was almost blinding. His smile made my stomach flip. It was such an easy *happy* smile, despite the shitty things he'd been through. I wanted to smile like that again.

He didn't say anything in response. Instead he kissed me, and it was exactly what I needed.

His lips were slow and gentle against mine. Even though it wasn't a passion filled kiss where we were clawing at each other, I still felt it through my whole body. Slow could be good. Slow was sweet. Slow was perfect.

When Cade pulled away he placed a gentle kiss on my nose, the snow swirling around us.

It was a scene straight out of a fairytale, but I was no princess, and his kiss couldn't save me.

Only time could do that and my own desire to shed the pain that clung to me.

Step One of healing had been telling Cade.

Step Two, I knew without even discussing it with my therapist. I needed to accept the events of that day, and understand no matter what I believed I couldn't change it.

Step Three...well, that would be the hardest. I had to say goodbye to the people I lost. And goodbyes? Well, those were never easy.

Cupping my cheek and stirring me from my thoughts, Cade asked, "Are you ready to get lunch or do you need to go to your dorm first?"

"I can go now."

"Good, because I'm starving."

"This better not be the same restaurant you took me to for burgers before," I warned, trying to hide my smile. "If I end up with food poisoning again then I might have to reconsider your status as my boyfriend."

He threw his back and laughed, causing quite a few people to turn and look at us. "You're funny."

"No, Cade," I tried to sound angry, "I'm dead serious."

"Don't worry, Sunshine," his hand found the small of my back, "we're not going there."

"Thank God." I was actually relieved. If he'd taken me to the same place I would've run away screaming. Food poisoning was no joke, even if you did have a hot football player to take care of you.

He chuckled. "Did you really think I'd take you back there?"

"Well, you seemed to like their burgers," I shrugged.

"I still feel bad about that," he admitted with his lips twisting. "But I don't regret getting to spend the next day with you. I don't regret anything with you."

"Not even knocking me down?" I laughed, my hair blowing all around my face from the wind.

He stopped walking and took my face in his large hands. "Definitely not that, because without that moment I might not have ever met you, and that would've been a real tragedy."

His words got me to thinking about how certain events in our lives lead to another and another. Take one of those events away and a whole new scenario would play out.

If I hadn't met Cade, I might never have been able to accept that I had to get better.

That was pretty crazy to think about.

We came to the Jeep and I clambered inside, curious as to where we were headed.

Twenty minutes later and I still had no idea.

He pulled in front of a Subway and I gave him an odd look. "Subway?"

He chuckled, lowering his head. "Are you disappointed, Sunshine?"

"Well, it's better than that burger place," I shrugged, ready to hop out of the massive Jeep.

"Don't worry, we're not eating here...well, we're getting our food here, and then we're leaving."

"Leaving?" I questioned, raising a brow. "And going where?"

"It's a surprise."

Of course it was.

With a sigh I headed for the sub place.

It took us no time to get our food and drinks. Another five-minute drive and Cade exclaimed, "Here!"

I didn't know where *here* was. I looked around and all I saw was an empty field of grass.

"What are we doing here? Isn't it kind of cold to be outside?" I asked, afraid to leave the warmth the Jeep provided.

"We won't stay long," he promised, reaching into the back for a blanket. "You can wait here until I get everything set up." He surprised me by leaning over and kissing my cheek, well more like the corner of my mouth. Cade had no problem expressing his affection while I was a little more reserved.

He got out of the car and I watched him wade through the tall grasses and spread out the blanket and lay the food on top. He came back to the car for the drinks and grabbed yet another blanket. I looked behind me wondering what else he had stored back there and saw a duffel bag and football.

"You coming?"

I jumped, realizing he was still standing there waiting for me to get out.

"Yeah," I mumbled, my cheeks heating at getting caught being nosy.

It was cold, after all it was practically December, but luckily it wasn't windy.

Cade led me to the blanket spread out over the dried brown grass. He set the drinks down and shook out the other blanket he'd tucked under his arm. He wrapped it around both of us, which meant that when we sat down we were impossibly close. My heart sped up and my breath stuttered. Cade affected me like no guy had before. From the first moment I met him deep down I knew he was different.

Cade handed me my food, his eyes lingering on the side of my face. "So, you think it went well with the therapist?"

I should've known he'd bring it up again. I shrugged, staring out at the grass and trees beyond. It was easier to look at it than him when I spoke. "I do. She was nice and wanted to get to know me instead of trying to diagnose me or pry information out of me. I didn't expect that."

"I'm glad to hear that." The way he said the words I knew he meant that genuinely. "I just want to see you happy."

Cade Montgomery was infinitely too sweet for me, but I was too selfish to let him go now.

"I am happy," I replied. "Right now, with you, I'm happy. I'm not happy every second of every day but who is?" I took a breath, gathering my thoughts. "I'm trying to learn to appreciate the little things, those brief moments where..."

"Where what?" He prompted.

I turned my head towards him, my hair blowing around me. "Where I feel peace."

His lips quirked into a smile, and he reached forward to grasp my chin between his thumb and index finger. "Do I also bring you peace?"

"You do," I admitted. "When I'm with you everything feels right." I hoped I hadn't given away too much of my feelings with my words, but with the way he smiled it had been the perfect thing to say. I hated to ruin the moment, but I had something I needed to ask him. "Have you ever considered seeing a therapist? You know, to talk about your brother and what your dad does to you."

Cade looked away, his jaw clenching, and I worried that I'd made him madder than I predicted. After a few moments of breathing deeply he looked back at me. "I probably should, but I don't know if I can. That's why I commend you for having the guts to go. I just...I don't know if I can admit to a stranger that my dad hits me. It makes me feel so pathetic."

*

I leaned my head on his shoulder. "You're not pathetic, Cade. Far from it. You're strong, loving, a protector, and so many other things. Pathetic, is definitely not one of them. What your dad does, that's a reflection on him, not you. I...I want you to know," I reached for his hand, playing with his fingers, "that you can trust me. I'm here anytime you need to talk about things."

"Back at ya, Sunshine." He cupped the back of my head and drew me closer so he could kiss my forehead. I closed my eyes, soaking in the feel of him against me.

I worried about Cade. I knew what keeping pain bottled up inside had done to me, and I didn't want the same to happen to him. After all, if I hadn't seen his dad hit him he would've never told me. But Cade was a different person from me, with a different personality, so maybe he could cope with things better than I could.

"Don't worry about me," he whispered, like he knew what I'd been thinking about.

"I can't help it. I don't want you to hate yourself for things that aren't your fault. That's what I've done and I know how miserable it can be." I looked up at him and found him staring beyond at the trees.

"I'm okay, Sunshine. Really." He lowered his head to look at me. "Sometimes I want to blame myself and think that it must be my fault that my dad hits me, but then I stop and think, and I know that I'm wrong. I don't ask for it. He's just angry. But he's still my dad, as stupid as that sounds. If he wants to use me as his punching bag, that's fine." Cade's face became fierce all of a sudden. "But if he ever lays a hand on my mom, then we'll have a problem."

Reaching up I curled my fingers against his shirt. "Does she know?"

"No," Cade sighed. "I think she wonders, but she doesn't want to believe it's possible. So, I let her think nothing's wrong," he shrugged. "Sometimes we have to protect the ones we love, and for me that means keeping my mouth shut."

I tried a different approach, not wanting to let it go. "What if you saw a little boy on the street corner and his father hit him?"

He winced. "That's different."

"No, it's not and you know it," I spoke fiercely, determined to get him to see my point. "You need to stick up for yourself. If you won't seek help then I think you should at least confront your dad about it."

He sighed, scratching his stubbled jaw. After a moment he turned and gave me a small smile. "When did you become the one giving me advice?"

"When I started thinking like a normal person."

He chuckled, resting his chin on top of my head. "You were always normal, Rae, just a little sad."

He tilted my head back and covered my lips with his. The kiss was slow and sweet, but still managed to leave my toes tingling.

He brushed his nose against mine when he pulled away. "We better eat before we freeze to death."

"It was your idea to eat out here," I laughed. "And you've yet to tell me where exactly here is." I looked around the field. The grasses were dry and brittle looking, but I was sure in the spring and summer it was bright green and soft. Maybe flowers even bloomed.

"I'm not sure exactly," he shrugged, taking a bite of his sandwich.

"You're not sure?" I laughed. "What if this is private property?"

"Well, in the four years I've been coming here no one has chased me off so I'd say we're safe. Now eat," he pointed at my food.

"Okay, okay," I obliged.

"Sometimes I come here when I want to get away from school and think..." He paused. "And get away from the football field. Out here, there's no one to bother me. I can sit for hours and just be me."

"You spend a lot of time by yourself, don't you?" I questioned.

"I guess so," he shrugged. "I learned that it was easier that way."

I laid my head on his shoulder and inhaled his familiar scent. "But you brought me here."

"I know." He laid his food down and wrapped his arms around me. "I've begun to realize that no place holds any meaning without you."

My breath faltered.

"Where do you see this going?" He asked. "Us, I mean?"

"I-I don't know." I stuttered. "I'm not like other people. I can't imagine myself five years down the road. All I can focus on is the here and now, and you're a part of that."

"I'll take it," he whispered.

Breaking the seriousness of the conversation, I said, "Shouldn't we be getting back to campus so you can go to the gym?"

Cade cursed under his breath. "You're right. We'll finish eating and head back."

By the time we packed everything up and got in the car my fingers and toes were numb.

"I think you should come to the gym with me." Cade glanced at me out of the corner of his eye.

"Uh...isn't that what I'm doing?"

He chuckled. "Yeah, sorry. I should've worded that better. What I meant is, I miss our runs. Why don't you change, meet the guys, and stay for a while?"

I didn't know what to say. It made me nervous, that was for sure. I didn't know these guys and what if I hated them? At least if I was only going to meet them I could escape when I felt like it. Staying to work out with Cade would leave me trapped there. "I don't know, Cade," I mumbled.

"Hey, if you get there and decide you don't want to stay then you can leave."

When he put it that way I didn't see how I could argue with him. "Okay," I relented. It was hard to tell Cade no, but I also knew I needed to put myself out there.

His smile was huge which instantly made me feel better for agreeing.

We reached campus and Cade waited in the Jeep while I rushed inside my dorm to change. Thea was gone and I was kind of glad for that, so I didn't have to explain anything to her.

I hurried back outside to the Jeep and clambered inside.

"That was fast," Cade chuckled, driving over to the building the gym was housed in since it was too chilly to walk that far—and I still felt a bit frozen from eating our lunch outside.

"I thought you were running late," I shrugged, "I didn't want to hold you up anymore."

The closer we got to the gym the more nervous I became. I wiped my damp palms on the black material of my pants.

I'd spent my last year of high school alienating myself from all human contact, and now I felt like I was constantly putting myself out there. College had changed me for the better, molding me into the person I needed to be. I still had a long way to go, though, but I now believed I'd get there. I didn't feel so hopeless anymore.

When Cade parked at the gym I hopped out of the car before he could try to give me a pep talk. I was okay. Nervous? Yes. But I wasn't freaking out.

Cade grabbed his duffel bag from the back and took my hand. I breathed out slowly, trying to calm myself. I hoped Cade was right and Eric was nowhere to be seen. I might run out of the building if I spotted him.

Cade led me around the equipment and to a back part of the building where the football players trained separately.

He opened the glass door and I thought the amount of testosterone swirling in the air might suffocate me. Hot, half-naked, sweaty guys everywhere. It was every girls dream, but I found myself clinging tighter to Cade as my eyes landed on every face searching for Eric. Cade was right though, and he wasn't here. I breathed out a sigh of relief.

"Guys," Cade called in a loud, authoritative voice. They all stopped what they were doing and looked at us. I kept my shoulders squared and my chin high, refusing to be intimidated by the large men. "This is my girlfriend, Rae. She's going to hang out with us today."

Someone whistled and then I heard a slap. Apparently someone wasn't happy with the whistler.

The guy nearest to us stood up from the bench press he'd occupied. His shirt was drenched with sweat and his dark hair was damp too. "Nice to meet you," he grinned, his brown eyes crinkling. Dimples, deeper than Cade's, popped out in his cheeks. "I'm Brady."

Brady...I remembered Cade mentioning that name.

I smiled at the big bear of a man. "That's Adam." He pointed to another guy and this one had coppery brown hair. "Dane. Jesse. Rob. And Tyler."

"Hi," I waved weekly.

"Go change," Brady clapped a hand on Cade's shoulder. "I'll watch her."

I wrinkled my nose. Watch me? Like I needed a babysitter? Great.

"I'll be right back," Cade kissed my cheek. "Five minutes tops."

He eased out the door, giving me a reassuring smile.

Brady threw an arm around my shoulder. "We don't bite. You have nothing to be afraid of. Contrary to popular belief, most of us are quite lovable. Like big, muscular teddy bears."

I laughed and he smiled.

"See? Nothing to be afraid of." He dropped his arm and stood in front of me. "I remember you," he stated.

"Remember me?" I asked, laughing. "But we've never met."

"I distinctly remember lover boy tackling you on the sidewalk," he smirked. "Who would've thought that would've spawned a relationship. The guy hasn't dated anyone in all four years he's been here. We would've thought he'd taken a vow of chastity if it weren't for the...well..." He winced.

"It's okay," I laughed. "We've talked about it. I know he's had hook-ups."

"Well, then, that's good. Otherwise this conversation could've been very bad for Cadie boy."

I liked this guy. The others looked on curiously as Brady continued to talk. He was obviously the chattiest of the bunch.

I was surprised when Adam spoke up, sweeping his hair from his eyes. "We heard about what happened with Eric. That wasn't cool."

I flinched. I didn't want to be reminded about Eric.

"Coach heard about it," Brady informed me, sitting on the bench again. "Eric won't be playing in our last game next week."

My eyes widened in surprise. I hadn't expected that.

Cade returned, changed into his workout gear. "You better not have scared her way," Cade warned good-naturedly.

I smiled up at him. "Not at all. Your friends are great."

"So," Brady chuckled, "does this mean I can bring my girlfriend to workout?"

Cade snorted. "Yeah, if you can get her to stop talking about her nails for five minutes."

Brady shook his head, smiling. "Yeah, she does talk about them a lot."

Cade chuckled, bumping his friend's shoulder with his fist as he passed. I followed him over to the row of treadmills.

"It's not as good as running outside," he shrugged, and waved a hand at the treadmills, "but it will do."

I stood on one of the treadmills and he climbed on the other.

Once we started running there was no room for conversation, but that was okay. With Cade I didn't need to fill every moment with chatter, being with him was enough.

chapter twenty-four

"*I WANT TO KISS YOU.*" Brett's voice skated over my skin. My heart fluttered like a little bird trapped beneath my ribs. My first kiss. It was finally going to happen. I'd always known it would be Brett. Even as a little girl I'd known the boy next door was the man I was going to marry. He was my best friend, my everything. We shared everything together so it seemed natural that we'd share the rest of our lives too.

I stepped closer to him and draped my arms around his shoulders. Other couples swayed around us at the school dance but I was oblivious to them.

Brett lowered his head and his lips glided lightly against mine. It wasn't even a kiss, just a simple brush of his lips, but I already felt my knees weakening.

His hand at my waist tightened and he deepened the kiss, slow at first, and then with more urgency.

He pulled away and murmured into my hair, "I love you, Rae."

Rae?

I looked up and saw Cade smiling down at me. The dance was gone and we stood on the football field. A sparkle caught my eye and I gasped at the ring on my finger.

"Thank you for giving me forever..."

"And then I woke up," I told Kathleen. "What do you think it means?"

"It doesn't matter what I think," she sat back, crossing her legs. "All that matters is what it means to you."

I bit my lip.

"You can tell me," she continued. "This is a no judgment zone," she waved her hands around, encompassing her office. I'd been coming to see Kathleen several times a week for three weeks now, so I knew she wasn't kidding.

"I think it means I love him, that Cade's the one...maybe Brett and I were never meant to be." I fiddled with my fingers to have something to do. "I had my whole life planned out and then the accident happened and nothing made any sense."

"Could you tell me more about the accident?" She pushed.

I sighed. There was no point in beating around the bush. Besides, I'd been whining to her about my woes for nearly a month now—might as well get to the point of all my problems.

"I was driving, got a text message, looked at my phone, crashed the car, and essentially murdered my boyfriend and best friends." I tried to say the words casually, like it had no effect on me, but of course Kathleen knew better.

She tapped her fingers against the arm of the chair she occupied. "And that makes you feel guilty?"

"Of course it makes me feel guilty!" I exploded, the anger I felt rearing its ugly head. "I didn't have to look at my phone! But then I go and have dreams like that and I hear my mom's voice in my head telling me everything happens for a reason. So, then I wonder if I couldn't have prevented what happened. But then I think that's crazy, of course you could've prevented it by not looking at your fucking phone!" I gasped for air and sat back.

Kathleen watched me, not saying a word. "Texting and driving is a horrible thing, but it happened, Rachael. It happened, you've dealt with the consequences, and it's time to move on. Hanging on to the past is pointless. It's the past for a reason. It's gone. Done. Over." It was like she was trying to drill the words into my head.

"Sometimes I feel like they should've put me in jail."

"Do you really think that would've solved your problems?" She countered with a raised brow.

"No," I mumbled.

"It's good that you feel remorseful for the accident, Rae. You're not a killer."

I closed my eyes. That's exactly what I'd thought of myself for far too long.

"You were a girl who made a mistake. A mistake you've learned from."

My lower lip began to tremble as sobs racked my body. "Sometimes I can still hear them screaming. I just want it to stop." I wiped at my tears.

Kathleen reached out and clasped my hand. "You know how you make it stop?"

"How?" I asked, my voice shaking.

"You lay them to rest." She said simply.

"Huh?"

"You have to accept that they're gone," she clarified. "Go to where they're buried, say what you need to say, and be done with it."

"I don't know if I can do that," I stared at a water stain on the ceiling. Lowering my gaze, I mumbled, "What would I even say?"

"I can't tell you that," she shook her head, tapping her pen against her lips. "That's something you have to figure out on your own."

⁓ℯ𝓈⁓

Thea buzzed around our dorm room with excitement. Nova sat on my bed watching her with an amused expression on her face. Even though we'd recently finished our project we still hung out anytime we could.

"Is she always like this?" Nova asked me, brushing her long purple hair over one shoulder.

"Pretty much," I replied as I finished lacing my Converse.

"It's the last game of the season and Cade's last game *ever!*" Thea exclaimed. "How can I not be excited? This is going to be epic!"

I looked at Nova and shrugged.

"It's football," Nova stated in a deadpan voice.

"And it's amazing," Thea countered.

"At least I can take pictures." Nova held her camera close.

"Pictures? There's no time for pictures!" Thea grabbed a Huntley University sweatshirt and shrugged into it. "You have to watch the game!" She grabbed a beanie and put it on as well.

"Yeah, Nova, you have to watch the game," I laughed.

"Is Jace going to be there?" She asked, brightening.

"No," Thea grabbed her shoes from the closet, "he never goes to the games."

"Well I didn't either until today," Nova countered. "How did I get suckered into this again?"

"Well, Thea bribed you with coffee and suckered you into it," I replied, pulling my hair into a ponytail. It was windy and the last thing I wanted was my hair whipping my face through the whole game.

"Dammit," Nova laughed, "coffee is my weakness."

"I'm ready," Thea finally declared.

The three of us headed over to the stadium and while I'd attended most of the games I'd never seen one as crowded as this.

"Are there going to be enough seats for all of these people?" I asked Thea under my breath.

She laughed. "Of course, silly."

I was still doubtful despite her positivity.

We took our seats and my body got that familiar hum of excitement.

"Hey, look," Thea pointed, "it's my dad!"

I leaned forward, craning my neck to see the man she pointed at. Yeah, that was definitely their dad. I hoped he didn't do or say anything to Cade. Cade was such a positive and happy person. He didn't need his father trying to cut him down.

Nova lifted her camera, taking pictures of the crowd, the field, everything really.

"I'm so excited," Thea rubbed her hands together.

"I can tell," I mumbled under my breath. Thea was always super hyper at football games, sometimes annoyingly so.

"I'm going to go talk to my dad and I'll be back." Before I could reply she slipped out of her seat and down the steps.

"Is she going to be like that for the whole game?" Nova asked, lowering her camera to her lap.

"No."

"Thank God," she breathed a sigh of relief.

"She gets worse," I laughed.

"Fuck," Nova groaned.

My thoughts exactly.

When halftime came and the players left the field I couldn't help watching Cade's dad leave his seat and I wondered if he was going in search of his son.

Despite the thrill of the game and the packed bodies I was still freezing in the December air. Even though I wore gloves my fingers were frozen. I tried to wiggle them but they wouldn't move. I wished I had a hot cup of coffee to hold. Yeah, coffee would be fantastic right about now. Or a small fire.

"I'll be right back," Thea told us, standing and going to talk to some girls she knew.

Blowing warm air into her hands Nova looked at me. "I think I picked the wrong game to come to. I'm so cold."

"We should've brought blankets," I agreed, and we huddled closer together like penguins.

Halftime passed quickly and Thea joined us once more.

The score was so close that I feared we might actually lose this game.

"You see that guy there by my dad?" Thea tapped my shoulder and pointed.

"Yeah," I nodded, squinting my eyes so I could see the man more clearly.

"He's a scout." She clapped giddily, her cheeks flushing.

"Like for the NFL?" I clarified. I was clueless when it came to this kind of stuff.

"Yes," she cheered. "Isn't it exciting? Cade could be on a professional team next year!"

I frowned, and didn't comment. I knew that was the last thing Cade wanted, but Thea clearly didn't know that. It made me worried that Cade might pursue that path just to please his family. It wasn't something we'd discussed in depth. I knew he didn't want to be a part of the NFL, but he'd never told me if he knew for sure he wasn't pursuing it.

Thea seemed to sense my change in mood and left me alone—although she still cheered obnoxiously loud. The girl put the cheer team to shame.

"Are you okay?" Nova asked.

I opened my mouth to answer her, but gasped instead.

Cade went down, his knee slamming into the ground. He rolled over clutching his leg.

"Oh my God!" I gasped, my hand flying to my mouth. "Cade!" I cried, trying to push by Thea to reach him—like as if they'd actually let me onto the field. "Cade! I have to get to Cade!" I pleaded with Thea when she grasped my shoulders.

Panic swarmed through my body at seeing him lying on the field. I wanted to get down there and do something. I needed to help him—even if it was just to hold his hand.

"Rae, he's okay, see?" She pointed to the field where a teammate was pulling him up. He was walking with a limp, but appeared to be shaking off the injury.

"Oh, thank God," I breathed, hugging her.

My moment of panic began to fade. I'd clearly over reacted, but the thought of Cade being seriously hurt had been crushing, and it was within that moment that I finally grasped the depths of my feelings for Cade and the truth my dream had been trying to reveal to me.

I was in love with Cade Montgomery

Not the kind of puppy love of someone infatuated.

This was true, deep, irrevocable love.

I knew it was probably too soon to feel that way, but these things couldn't really be controlled. When something is meant to be it's unstoppable.

"You can check on him after the game, but I promise he's okay," she assured, urging me to sit down.

I watched his teammates guide him to the bench and I wished desperately that I could be there for him the way he was always there for me.

But I had to wait, and that really fucking sucked.

My eyes flickered for the rest of the game from Cade on the bench to his father in the stands. Even from this distance I could see the hard set of the man's shoulders. He was pissed. I was terrified that the man was going to inflict even more damage to Cade, both physically and mentally.

When the game ended I had no idea who won, but from the cheers on our side I assumed it was us. I pushed Thea out of my way so I could get to the aisle. I didn't care if I offended her with my gesture or not. I had to get to Cade. Now.

I glanced behind me and saw his dad racing for the exit as well.

I knew I needed to beat him.

I was able to cut him off and ran for the locker rooms.

I reached the locker room door, ready to burst inside. I slammed my shoulder against it and flinched when it didn't budge. Fucking locked.

Tears pricked my eyes and I whimpered in desperation.

I looked behind me and saw his dad approaching.

Double fuck.

I stood against the opposite wall of the locker room door and slid down until my butt touched the floor.

His dad stopped, looking from me to the door. He gave no indication of recognizing me. Just looking at him was getting my blood boiling.

"You're an asshole, you know that, right?" The words bubbled out of my mouth before I could stop them.

"Excuse me?" He stopped pacing and stood in front of me. His hands were shoved into his pockets.

"You heard me," I sneered. "I know what you do to him."

"Do to who, sweetheart?" He chuckled, completely unaffected.

"To your son, Cade. Remember him? The son you like to hit? I saw you," I seethed, standing up once more. With my height I was eye level with him and I refused to cower from his domineering presence. "I saw you hit him, so don't even deny it," I spat. "He's a good guy, which is more than I can say for you," I looked him up and down. "You're scum and like to take your anger out on your son. Who does that?"

"You have no idea what you're talking about." His face grew red and a squiggly vein on his forehead threatened to burst.

"I'm not stupid, so don't treat me like I am," I glared at him.

Anger radiated off of both of us as we stood staring, neither of us willing to back down.

His fists clenched at his sides and I briefly wondered if he might hit me.

We startled apart when the locker room door opened.

"Rae?" Brady asked, taking in the scene in front of him. "Is everything okay?"

"I don't know," I answered honestly.

Brady hesitated. "You want to come see him?"

I nodded, brushing past Cade's dad. Before the door to the locker room closed behind me I caught it with my hand. I turned back around and spoke calmly but with authority. "Watch what you say to him, I mean it. I won't watch you tear him apart." He didn't say a word, just stood there. I pushed the door open wider. "Are you coming?"

He finally cracked a smile...a small one, and not very nice, but a smile nonetheless. "Am I allowed or will you yell at me for that too?"

I rolled my eyes. God, this man was a piece of work.

I turned around and let the door swing closed. It locked behind me, barring Cade's dad from entering the locker room.

Brady stopped me, his eyes wide. "What the hell was that about? Did you get into it with Malcolm?"

"We were having a discussion." I straightened my clothes. Brady looked at me like he didn't believe me. "Honestly," I added.

"Mhmm," he hummed, not believing me at all. "He's this way." He turned down a different hall and pointed to a room. "You can go on in."

I pushed the door open and found Cade sitting on a padded bench like you'd find in a doctor's office. He had already changed into sweatpants and a sweatshirt. His pants were rolled up exposing his right knee. A doctor gently probed the area and Cade didn't flinch so I hoped that was a good sign.

"Hey," I whispered, and he looked up at me.

He smiled beautifully, like I lit up his whole world. He reached his hand out for me and I stepped closer.

"How bad is it?" I asked, and I wasn't sure if I was addressing him or the doctor.

"Not too bad," the doctor answered. "There's some swelling and it will bruise, but I don't think anything was torn. It's going to require rest and elevation to help with the swelling. Don't overdo it, I mean it," he warned Cade. He turned to the freezer in the small room and grabbed an icepack. "Sit tight for a little bit," he directed. "I'll be back in a few minutes."

Cade sighed and rested his head against the wall, the icepack on his knee.

"Come here," he patted the empty space beside him.

I hopped up, afraid to get too close in case I caused him more harm.

"Closer," he growled, wrapping his arm around my waist and drawing me fully against him. "I'm not going to break if you breathe on me."

I laughed, leaning my head on his shoulder. "You scared me."

"I did?" He seemed surprised.

"Yeah," I whispered, and tears started to fall.

Seeing Cade injured on the field had reminded me of the helplessness I'd felt seeing my friends dead in the car. When you love someone, and I knew I loved Cade, it was terrifying to see them hurt. You want nothing more than to take their pain away.

"Don't cry, Sunshine." He reached over and swiped my tears away.

"I can't help it."

He pressed his lips against my forehead and my eyes closed. "I'm okay."

"But it could've been worse." My voice shook with emotion.

"But it wasn't," he countered, rubbing his hand up and down my arm.

I looked up at him, staring into his kind blue eyes. In five months this man had become my friend, my boyfriend, and so much more. He saved me.

"I love you."

His eyes widened and his mouth parted, like he didn't quite believe I'd said it.

I wasn't ashamed for having admitted my feelings. Instead, I felt stronger. Love didn't make you weak, it gave you strength and a purpose, so when you found it, it was only proper that you shout it from the rooftops.

"Love is a very powerful word," he whispered, cupping my cheek. He brushed his nose against mine. His hair tickled my forehead and his lips were dangerously close. If I was a braver person I would grab his face and kiss him until we begged for oxygen. Instead, I was still slightly terrified of his rejection.

"I know, that's why I used it, because what I feel for you is a very powerful thing." My hands began to shake and I was tempted to runaway. But I held my breath and stayed, waiting to hear his reply.

He grinned, pressing his forehead against mine. "I love you too, Sunshine."

I gasped, but he silenced the noise with his lips. He tilted my head back, his tongue finding mine.

My hands wound around his neck and I squeaked when he grasped my thigh and pulled me onto his lap.

We moved against each other and I could feel him pressed against me, his desire evident, which only increased mine.

He moaned into my mouth, gasping my name.

"I love you," I murmured again and again. Now that I said it I never wanted to stop. I wanted him to know that I meant it and I wasn't going to retract my words.

He bit my bottom lip lightly, his hand cupping the back of my neck. He pulled away and our gasps for breath became the only sounds in the quiet room.

"What did I do to deserve you?"

I reached up, brushing my fingers over his slightly stubbled cheek. "I'm the one that should be asking that question," I murmured.

"You underestimate yourself, Sunshine." He ran his thumb over my bottom lip. "You can't see what I see, and that's a damn shame."

The clearing of a throat had us breaking apart.

The doctor tried to hide his smile behind his hand. "That doesn't look like resting to me."

My cheeks flamed with color, but Cade was unaffected.

"My lips may have been moving, but my knee was stable doc. Don't worry."

The doctor shook his head, muffling a laugh. "Get out of here."

Cade tossed the icepack at the doctor and took my hand.

After grabbing his duffel bag we headed for the exit. I couldn't stop myself from looking for his father.

"What?" He asked, noticing that I was distracted. "Are you looking for someone?"

"No," I whispered.

I was silently thankful that his dad had left. It meant I'd spared Cade from being hurt by cruel words and maybe even a fist to the face. A small part of me hoped that maybe my words had affected the man somehow and he could find it in his heart to seek Cade's forgiveness.

Forgiveness could heal immeasurable pain, and it was time that I forgave myself.

chapter twenty-five

"ARE YOU GOING HOME FOR THE HOLIDAYS?" Kathleen asked before I could even sit down in the chair. "I'm sure your family would love to see you."

Her words screamed ambush, but I kept myself calm. After all, I had no proof that she talked to my mom, but with a question like that it sure sounded like it.

"I haven't decided yet," I shrugged, picking a piece of lint off my black jeans. "Maybe."

And that was the truth. My mom had started calling me every day and it was becoming harder and harder to say no to her. My parents had been nothing but supportive since the accident, so I had no real reason to stay away except for my own insecurities.

"Have you thought about visiting your friends?" She questioned, chewing on the cap of her pen.

I knew what she was asking. Did I decide to visit the cemetery where they were buried.

"I haven't made up my mind," I sighed. "I didn't even go to their funerals. I was still in the hospital and afterwards it just...it felt wrong," I mumbled, closing my eyes at the onslaught of memories. Oh God, the hate I'd received had been crippling. My friend's parents needed someone to blame and I was the only person they could fault, and rightfully so. But I was only human. I had feelings. I bled. I cried. I hurt. But they didn't think about what I was going through, only themselves. Going back to school had been just as bad. People looked at me differently, whispering under their breath as I passed. It had been horrifying and I was completely alone. But I always felt so selfish anytime my thoughts strayed down that path. I was *alive* and I should be thankful for that, any rude comments thrown my way shouldn't even matter, but they did.

Kathleen stared at me, twisting her lips as if she thought deeply about her next words. I held my breath, waiting for what she might say.

"You act as if because you were responsible for the accident that you don't have a right to grieve their deaths."

I flinched, turning away.

She continued, "You're allowed to mourn them, Rae. You lost them too."

My hands began to shake and I felt the telltale burning in my eyes that indicated the threat of tears, and lots of them. Kathleen was exactly right.

"You have to let yourself mourn them," she reached out, gently placing only the tips of her fingers against my knee. "Say goodbye to them and put this all to rest. I'm not saying you need to forget them, or that this will magically heal you, but it is a huge step. This will always be a part of you, Rachael, but it doesn't have to define you."

She sat back and grabbed a tissue. She held it out to me and I accepted it, dabbing at my now damp face.

Right after the accident I cried all the time, especially when I woke up in the mornings and realized it wasn't a nightmare. My tears had dried up about six months after the accident, but coming to college seemed to have stirred them up again.

"It's okay. Let it out."

And I did.

A year and half's worth of tears burst forth and nothing else had ever been so cleansing.

~es~

"I can't believe Cade isn't coming home for Christmas," Thea whined, neatly folding her clothes and packing them in a suitcase. "It's Winter Break! Who wouldn't want to go home? Well...except for you two apparently." Her mouth fell open with a sudden gasp. "Oh my God, are you two planning like a romantic getaway or something?"

I snorted. "Absolutely not. I don't have a romantic bone in my body."

"But my brother does." She eyed me with a hand on her hip.

I raised my hands in surrender. "Honestly, we have no plans. I just don't feel like going home and he doesn't either."

"Whatever," she huffed, zipping her suitcase. "You're both so boring." Her phone beeped with a text message and she read the screen. "That's my mom. She's picking me up since Cade obviously won't be taking me home. I need to get my own car," she rambled. "Anyway," she walked over to me and held her arms out, "I'm going to miss you and I'll see you when break is over."

I hugged her back. "I'll miss you too," I said and meant it. I'd become so used to seeing Thea every day, and listening to her prattle on about random nonsense that it would be weird to be without her for two whole weeks. Maybe while she was gone I could have a ceremonial burning of all the pink shit on her side of the room. With the way she was dressed—leather jacket, torn jeans, and boots—I doubted she'd mind seeing the stuff gone.

"Text me!" She called over her shoulder as she left the room.

I wasn't prepared for the amount of loneliness I'd feel the moment Thea was gone. She was always so fun and energetic and while at times it was annoying I had grown comfortable with her exuberance.

I spent a few hours editing photos, talking to Nova on the phone—she'd flown home to California—and watching Netflix.

College life. What could I say?

I wasn't surprised when there was a knock on my dorm room door around dinnertime.

I opened the door to find Cade holding an armful of food and other bags.

"Moving in?" I joked.

He laughed. "If you let me."

I closed the door behind him and he set the bags on Thea's bed. He began unpacking them and I saw that he'd brought Chinese and... "Candles?" I questioned. "Why did you bring candles?"

He turned to me and smiled, that same smile that always made my knees quake. "I may be a guy, but I thought girls liked candles."

"Candles are fine, I just wondered why you brought them," I shrugged, my stomach rumbling as I inhaled the scent of the food. "Besides, I think it's against school rules to light candles in the dorms.

"Rules were made for breaking," he countered.

He grabbed the fluffy blanket I kept on my bed and spread it on the floor along with several pillows. He then set the food on the blanket and scattered the candles around. He pulled a lighter out of his pocket and lit all the candles before dimming the lights in the room.

He surveyed the room with his hands on his hips. "What do you think?"

Cracking a smile, I said, "I think we're going to burn down the building with all these candles."

"I guess we just can't roll around," he winked, causing my insides to squirm. The last week, ever since I told him I loved him, things had changed between us yet again. The intensity between us had become electrified like we were combustible.

He stepped forward, closing the distance between us and ghosted his fingers along my cheek. I was sure he could feel the heat there from my blush.

"Don't get shy on me," he whispered, brushing his lips softly against mine.

A small moan escaped me and I grasped his shirt in my hands, pressing up on my toes so I could kiss him fully.

I always tried to keep things from getting too out of hand between us, but it was growing increasingly difficult to do that. I wanted Cade in every possible way and I wasn't sure how much longer I could wait. But I knew Cade, and he wouldn't be the one to initiate things in that direction. He thought of me as a skittish cat that might run if he made one wrong move. If things were going to go farther than kissing, I would have to be the one that pressed for more, and that scared me. I'd always been more comfortable letting someone else take the lead.

His hand that rested at my waist skated beneath my shirt and I shivered at the feel of his hand against my bare back.

He backed up and my legs hit my bed. I sank down and he followed. The bed was far too small for the two of us, but I didn't mind.

He was careful to hold his weight above me. Always so gentle with me. Sometimes I missed the Cade that he was when we first met, the one that wasn't afraid to joke with me. I wasn't as breakable as I used to be. I was growing stronger every day and I wouldn't be able to say that without having him in my life. I wished he could see that.

"I love you," he growled, his fingers tangling in my hair.

I didn't respond. My lips were otherwise occupied.

My body grew warm with the heat we were generating and I pulled my shirt off. He hummed in approval, peppering small kisses over my breasts.

I closed my eyes, soaking in the moment.

The room could burn down around us and I would never even know.

⁓

I curled my body around Cade's and laid my head on his chest. His warmth wound around me.

Our make-out session had ended long ago. We'd eaten and cleaned up, and now were ready to go to sleep.

There was no discussion about whether or not Cade would stay the night, we both just knew it would happen.

I'd changed into my pajamas and Cade had stripped down to his jeans—like I'd pitch a fit if he wore his boxers.

He rubbed his fingers lazily against my arm, humming under his breath.

He cleared his throat suddenly and I lifted my head to look at him. My hair brushed against his bare chest and he shivered.

"I was thinking that maybe we should go somewhere tomorrow." His voice was soft and hesitant.

"Sure," I agreed readily. "Where do you want to go?" Getting away for a little while sounded like a good idea—even if it was only a day trip. A change of scenery would be nice.

"Xander's dad has a cabin close to here. I was thinking maybe we could stay there for a few days," he suggested, tangling his fingers in my hair.

"A cabin? Is there plumbing?" I wrinkled my nose, envisioning some shack in the woods.

Cade started laughing and then couldn't seem to stop. Tears streamed down his cheeks. He wiped them away. "Of course it has plumbing, silly girl," he grinned.

"Hey, it was a fair question," I defended, giggling.

Lying there wrapped in his arms, laughing about plumbing, I felt like Rachael again.

Cade gave me myself back and I would never be able to repay him for that. I only hoped that my love was enough.

chapter twenty-six

I STARED AT THE OUTSIDE OF THE CABIN, wondering if it was really as nice as Cade claimed it was. It seemed so tiny—and I was now questioning whether or not he lied about the whole plumbing thing.

Cade looked at me over his shoulder with a small smile as he slid the key into the lock. As the door swung open he used his large body to block what lay beyond from my view.

Finally, he took a step to the side to let me pass.

I stepped into the cabin and my jaw dropped. "Cade! This is amazing!" I gasped in awe. I hadn't expected this, not at all.

While small, it was stunning.

A fire already roared in the stone fireplace, where two leather chairs were angled to face it.

The bed was in the corner and covered in fluffy white bedding.

There was a closed off area that I assumed was the bathroom and there was even a small kitchenette area.

"You like it?" He asked, sitting our bags down.

"I love it," I spun around, taking in the wood clad walls and rustic chandelier. "I can't believe you thought to bring me here."

He shrugged. "I knew it was close and I felt like we both needed to get away. Breathe fresh air, that kind of thing." There was a sadness to his voice that had me worried.

"Cade?" I probed. "What's going on? Is something wrong?" I asked worriedly. I loved this man and I didn't like seeing him so heart broken. I wrapped my arms around his neck, forcing him to look at me. "Talk to me."

"I feel bad..."

"For what?" No way was I letting him off that easy.

"For not going home, for not going pro and disappointing my dad, for lots of things," he frowned. "But despite that," a slow smile curved his lips as his hands wound around my waist, "I don't regret being here with you right now."

I closed my eyes, leaning my head against his chest where his heart beat. "You don't?"

"No," he kissed the top of my head. "This where I belong, but that doesn't stop me from feeling guilty."

I looked up at him, staring into his eyes. "Don't ever feel bad for making the choices that are best for you. When you start living your life for someone else, it's not your life at all."

"You're right," he agreed with a sigh.

"You're a good man, Cade," I moved my hand to cup his stubbled cheek, "too good, sometimes."

He chuckled. "You flatter me."

"No," I shook my head, "I'm honest."

He grinned, giving me a quick kiss on my lips. "You know, a few months ago I never thought we'd be standing where we are."

"Really?" I laughed, lightly poking his ribs in jest. "You sure were relentless in your pursuit to make me like you."

He threw his head back and laughed. "Yeah, I guess I was," he agreed. Lowering his voice and running his fingers lightly over my cheek, he said, "But that's only because I knew there was something between us—something that was once in a lifetime. I wasn't going to let you get away so easily."

Before I could respond he crashed his lips to mine.

There was nothing sweet about this kiss. This was pure passion and I loved it. I wanted more, so much more, with him.

"Cade, please," I begged, hoping he knew what I wanted and needed. I was too scared to come right out and say it.

He tilted my head back, his tongue flicking against mine. "Tell me what you want, Rae," he nipped at my bottom lip. "Whatever you want I'll give it to you."

"You," I breathed, slowly blinking my eyes open, "I want you, Cade."

"You have me," he murmured, taking my lips once more.

I pushed lightly at his shoulders and he pulled away enough to look at me.

"You know what I meant." My breath came out in soft pants. In this moment I felt so young and inexperienced, like a blushing twelve-year-old girl.

He brushed his thumb over my bottom lip, his blue eyes darkening. "Are you sure?"

"Yes," I gasped, hating that there was an almost begging quality to my voice.

Cade stared at me, and it was like he was giving me a chance to change my mind. When he saw that I was certain he picked me up and my legs wound around his waist. Our lips melded together. I smoothed my fingers through his hair as he carried me to the bed.

I knew he hadn't brought me here with this intent, but this place was perfect. I wanted to give him this final piece of my heart and not in some dorm room. This...this was *right*. This was the moment I hadn't known I'd been waiting for.

He laid me down carefully on the bed's surface. His movements were tender, like he was afraid I might crack or break.

He kissed me slowly and sweetly, but I could feel the desire building.

My hands found their way under his sweater and he tugged it off, throwing it somewhere behind him.

He spent minutes just kissing me, and I wondered if he was trying to torture me on purpose.

I removed my shirt and when his hands went to the button on my jeans my hips bucked.

"Cade," I moaned his name, whimpering. My body was a bundle of nerves and his touch set me on fire. I'd never experienced anything like this in my life. This was one moment where no memories from my past would linger, because there was nothing to compare it to. This moment was ours.

His eyes flicked up to meet mine and his gaze was so intense that Goosebumps broke out across my skin.

He moved up my body, sprinkling small kisses along the way.

His lips joined mine in a sensual dance and my hips lifted to meet his. Sweat dampened my skin as I wrapped my arms around his neck.

When he pulled away for a breath, a confession tore from my lips. "I'm a virgin," I panted.

His whole body stilled and he moved his head to look at me. His breath tickled my face as he weighed his words carefully. "Are you serious?"

I wanted to laugh at his silly question. "Why would I joke about that?"

He stared down at me with a mixture of awe and confusion. "H-how? You had a boyfriend."

Running my hands up his solid chest, I confessed, "I was never ready, but I am now." I leaned up just a little bit and whispered in his ear, "It was always supposed to be you. I see that now."

"Fuck," he groaned, his fingers grasping the fabric of the bed covers beside my head. "Are you sure about this? I can wait, Rae. I swear to God, if you tell me to stop I will."

"I'm ready," I spoke with surety.

He removed the rest of my clothes slowly, covering every inch of my body with kisses.

His touch was infinitely gentle.

When we came together there was a little pain at first, but Cade was patient with me, letting me get used to it.

Once the hurt disappeared I knew there had never been anything more magical in the world than sharing this moment with him.

I rocked my hips against his and clung to his damp shoulders.

Tears pricked my eyes—not because I was sad, but because I was so *happy*.

Later, when I lay wrapped around his body, I didn't feel like Rae or even Rachael. I felt like me and that was pretty great.

~~~

"This is nice," I murmured, leaning my back against Cade's solid chest. The heat from the flames in the fireplace warmed my outstretched hands. I felt content, there was no part of my mind lingering on the past. Right now, I was living in the here and now. I hadn't been able to do that in a long time. Cade gave me my life back.

"You think so?" He nuzzled my neck, making me laugh when his scruff tickled my skin.

Sitting here with him I felt so free. Like I could do and be anything—like I had a future that was no longer defined by an accident.

"This is perfect. *You're* perfect. How'd I get so lucky?" I leaned my head against his shoulder and looked at him.

His eyes grew serious. "Most people would argue that we've both been very unlucky in life, but I often find myself asking the same thing, and it's all because of you. You're my Rae of Sunshine, and I mean that. Before you, I was a ghost in my own life. You woke something up in me."

I felt like I'd done nothing for him, but seeing the sincerity written all over his face kept me from rebuking him.

We'd both been through a lot in our lives, and our time together had changed us for the better. It wasn't by sheer dumb luck that I met Cade. It was fate, pure and simple. I owed a lot to that fumbled football and the man that crashed into me. He said I woke something up in him, but he'd done the same for me. My life had changed the moment Cade stepped into it. I wasn't that girl hiding away from prying eyes anymore. He made me want to *live*, because I got this second chance at life. My mom had been right a long time ago when she told me just because my friends were dead it didn't mean I was. I couldn't see it then. I'd been too sullen and depressed. But now everything made sense.

"What are you thinking about?" Cade asked, brushing his fingers through my hair. It felt good, and I leaned into his touch.

"My mom," I replied, closing my eyes, "about how she was right about so many things and I didn't want to see it at the time."

"We rarely want to listen to our parents, but the truth is they usually know what they're talking about." His lips brushed against my ear with his words.

"I want to go home," I confessed, scooting away from him. It was something I'd been considering since my last appointment with Kathleen. "I want to see my parents and spend Christmas with them." He saddened at my words and I hastened to add, "I want you to come with me. They'd love to meet you." Actually, my parents knew nothing about Cade, but that needed to change. I had to stop trying to block them out of my life. We'd been close before the accident, but I'd pushed them away.

"Really?" Cade brightened.

"Yeah," I nodded, smiling. I was growing more excited by the second as I thought about getting to see them again. "They'll love you." While they might not know about Cade right now, I knew I wasn't lying. They'd both be thrilled that I'd moved on and Cade was such a good guy.

He rubbed his hands together. "I'm thinking I should wear my sweater vest to meet them."

I paused, holding in laughter, unsure if I heard him right. "Sweater vest?"

He frowned. "Don't parents' like a guy in a sweater vest? It means he has his priorities in order."

I had no idea what to say to that. Finally I responded with, "Why do you even own a sweater vest?"

"Halloween party a few years ago," he shrugged. "I went as a nerd."

I snorted. "Of course you did." Patting his shoulder like I would a child, I said, "I think you should leave the sweater vest here."

He chuckled. "Fine, no sweater vest. Bummer." He stood up, reaching his hand down for mine. "I think it's time we ate some dinner." Lowering his voice and grazing his lips against my ear, he added, "You know, restore our energy."

My cheeks colored as my mind was flooded with images of Cade above me and the feel of his body moving against mine. Despite the pain, it had been better than I imagined.

He took my hand and led me to the kitchen. The refrigerator was fully stocked and he placed the items he wanted on the counter. He directed me to chop the vegetables while he made his 'secret sauce' and slathered two chicken breasts with it.

It was all so normal. It made me imagine more moments like this with him, maybe one day at our own place, and even further in the future with cute blue-eyed children running around.

I couldn't help smiling at the thought and then tears pricked my eyes.

From the moment of the accident I'd stopped thinking about a future for myself. I thought there was no life left for me, but I was so wrong.

I could have it all.

And just like everyone was always trying to tell me, moving on didn't mean forgetting my friends, or Brett, or even my actions, it meant *acceptance*.

"Hey," Cade murmured, noting the single tear coursing down my eye. "What's wrong, Sunshine?"

I knew I could lie and tell him it was the onion making the tears, but I didn't want to. I always wanted to be honest with Cade.

"They're happy tears, Cade," I told him, leaning up to kiss his cheek right where his dimple was when he smiled wide. "I know now that I'm going to be okay and it feels so good to be free of it. I chained myself to that broken car and for a long time I thought my life couldn't move past that, but it can. I know now that I'm going to be alright," I rambled. "I don't feel like I'm a horrible person anymore."

He wiped the tear away and tilted my head back to place a small kiss on my lips.

"You're a remarkable person, you know that?" He leaned his forehead against mine. "I'm so glad you can finally see what I've seen from the beginning. You deserve to see your true beauty, because it shines through in everything you do, Rachael."

Beauty.

Happiness.

Sunshine.

It was all sort of the same thing, wasn't it?

They'd been masked by a dark cloud for me, for a long time now, but the storm had passed and now this Rae of Sunshine could truly *shine*.

chapter twenty-seven

WAKING UP NEXT TO CADE was something I could get used to, especially when he made me feel so good. My body felt languid and relaxed. I was so comfortable in fact that I completely forgot about our plan to visit my parents until he mentioned getting ready.

It was so nice in the cozy cabin that a small part of me was sad to leave. I hoped we could come back one day.

We cleaned up and headed back to campus. If we were going to be gone at least a week we needed to pack more than we'd brought to the cabin. Cade dropped me off at my dorm before heading to his. He told me he'd be back to pick me up in twenty minutes.

I hurried around my dorm room, packing everything I thought I might need. Really, I was just busying myself so I didn't worry about going back home and what I knew it meant.

I had to visit the graves.

Kathleen was right, saying goodbye and acknowledging that they were gone was what I needed to gain true closure. I still felt terrified, even though I knew in my heart that this was the right thing to do.

I didn't bother to call my mom and tell her we were coming. I just couldn't seem to bring myself to do it, even though I knew she would be thrilled. A part of me was still scared that I'd get there, panic, and demand that Cade turn the car around and take me back to campus.

I sat on my bed, taking deep breaths.

You can do this, Rae. There is nothing to be afraid of.

My little speech seemed to help and I finished packing. I slung my duffel bag over one shoulder and my camera bag over the other.

Cade was already waiting in the parking lot and he jumped out of the Jeep to help me with my bags.

"What the fuck are you wearing?" I stopped dead in my tracks.

He looked down at the blue shirt and sweater he wore. "What's wrong with this? I didn't think it was appropriate to meet your parents in my jersey. I was trying to dress up."

I could tell I'd offended him so I immediately felt bad. "It's just...I've never seen you dressed like that before. I like it." In fact, the dorky sweater was actually growing on me. There was something about it that was very much Cade in a weird way.

He put my bags in the back and I climbed in the car. Bags of Cheetos, Trail-Mix, and Doritos covered the middle console.

"Where did you get all this?" I asked.

"My room," he shrugged, messing with the radio station. "Sometimes I get hungry and I like to have options."

"I can tell," I laughed, eyeing all the bags.

"I brought drinks too," he pointed to the cup holder.

"You've thought of everything."

He grinned, his dimples showing. "Of course. What road trip would be complete without snacks and hydration?"

"It's only a three hour drive, that's hardly a road trip."

He raised his brows at me before flicking his gaze back to the road.

"It is when you're a guy and you're hungry all the time. Now hand me the Cheetos."

I handed him the bag, and he started munching.

Between bites, he said, "And since this is a mini road trip, I think we should sing at the top of our lungs to every song on the radio."

"I can't sing," I warned him.

"Neither can I," he flashed me a smile, orange flecks of Cheetos clinging adorably to his lips, "so it will be perfect. One of us won't outshine the other."

"Alright, fine," I agreed, not wanting to dampen the happiness between us.

He turned the radio up and we started singing.

I had to admit that it was pretty fun, even if we were both horrible.

Life should be filled with more of those simple moments, where for a few minutes everything is perfect.

✎

Cade parked his Jeep in the driveway of the two-story brick home. It looked exactly as when I left, just a little more festive. My dad had hung the multi-colored lights and wreaths dotted every window.

My hands shook with nerves, but I didn't feel like running away, which was good. This was my home and I'd been wrong to think it was anything but.

Cade glanced at me, but didn't say a word.

He was waiting for me to make the first move.

I couldn't help glancing to the right, where beyond the stretch of field lay Brett's house. We used to run through the fields as children, laughing, scraping our knees, and enjoying life.

I placed my hand against the window and closed my eyes. If I thought hard enough I could hear his laugh as we fell and rolled around in the tall grass.

I startled when I felt the slight pressure of Cade's hand on my knee.

I looked back at the house and without saying a word slipped from the car.

Cade followed me as I trekked up to the front door, his hand hovering comfortingly at my waist. I could've gone in through the garage, or used my key at the front door, but it didn't feel right. They didn't even know I was coming.

I felt horrible for not coming home for Thanksgiving, and not calling enough.

I'd been a lousy person and I had a lot of making up to do.

I raised my arm and pressed my finger to the doorbell. Even from the outside I could hear the loud ringing.

I held my breath as I waited.

I heard footsteps approach the door and I reached for Cade's hand. He gave mine a reassuring squeeze and I knew everything would be okay.

The door opened and I looked straight at my mom. She gasped, "Rachael! Is that really you?"

Before I could reply, she jumped at me, throwing her thin arms around me. I closed my eyes, inhaling her familiar scent of sugar cookies—of *home*. I started to cry, my tears soaking into her shirt. It had only been four months since I left home, but it really felt like so much longer than that.

She finally pulled away and grasped my face between her hands, just looking me over. "You look beautiful, sweetie."

I knew what she was really saying; I looked like myself.

"And who is this?" Her smile was wide as she reached up to hug Cade.

He seemed surprised by the gesture, but was quick to return it.

"This is Cade my...boyfriend." It still felt weird to say that. Maybe it always would, because Cade was so much more than that to me. He was my savior.

My mom's eyes widened in surprise and she clapped her hands together. "That's wonderful! Come on in," she waved Cade inside, and then grasped my arm. It was almost like she was afraid if she let me go for too long I'd disappear.

We headed to the back of the house where the kitchen was.

Baking ingredients cluttered every surface, with cupcakes, pies, and cookies, all in various stages of completion. I hadn't noticed before, but she even had some flour in her hair and on her cheek.

"I like to bake," she shrugged, when Cade kept staring at the mess.

"She makes the best cookies," I boasted, "have one." I pointed to a plate on the table. "You'll never want another cookie ever again."

Cade chuckled and moved over to the table.

I looked at my mom, who kept glancing between Cade and I with a look of awe. "Where's dad?" I asked, half-expecting him to pop out from behind me.

"He ran to the store to get more flour. I dropped a bag."

Well that explained why she had flour on her.

"These are delicious!" Cade exclaimed, reaching for another cookie.

"Told ya." I moved away from my mom to wrap my arms around him. He grinned at the gesture.

My mom watched on happily with a smile on her face.

She sat down at the table and gestured for us to sit down as well. She launched into a million and one questions like the typical mom, about school, friends, and particularly how Cade and I met. She found that part quite funny.

The door leading into the house from the garage opened and I jumped up with excitement.

When my dad turned into the kitchen I practically knocked the poor man down.

"Rachael?" He peered down at me, in shock that I was actually there. "I didn't think you were coming home for Christmas."

"Change of plans," I grinned.

He hugged me again. "I'm so glad you're home."

"Me too," I agreed, squeezing him tighter.

After he gave my mom the flour it was time to introduce Cade.

Even though I knew my dad would approve of Cade, it was still nerve wracking. I'd only ever brought one guy home.

"Nice to meet you," my dad extended his hand to Cade.

"Nice to meet you too, sir," Cade cleared his throat, shuffling his feet nervously. It was cute to see Cade so uncertain when he was normally so confident.

"Cade plays football," I blurted, knowing my dad would be thrilled with that information.

"Really?" His eyes widened.

"Yes, sir," Cade responded.

"Let's go talk in the family room," my dad clapped Cade on the shoulder, leading him out of the room. Cade looked over his shoulder, pleading with me to save him. I laughed, shaking my head. My dad was harmless.

"Can I help?" I asked, stepping up to stand beside my mom.

"You can frost those cupcakes for me." She pointed to a plate of cooled chocolate cupcakes. "Frosting is over there," she pointed again.

I took off my jacket, tied an apron around my waist, and went to work.

We were both quiet, focused on the task at hand.

Eventually, she asked, "So...Cade?"

"What about him?" I asked.

"How do you feel about him?" She asked, crossing her arms over her chest.

"Honestly?" I smiled, tucking hair behind my ear. "I love him."

She didn't say anything for a moment, just stared at me, as if weighing her next words carefully. "I saw it, but I wondered if you were aware of how you felt about him."

"Very aware." I ducked my head, feeling a bit embarrassed. "I never thought I'd love anyone else after Brett, but then I met Cade and everything changed. He scared me but exhilarated me all at the same time. I told him the truth and..." I searched for the right words. "It didn't matter to him. He still saw me as...well, *me*."

"I like him," she smiled. "I can see that he's good for you, and that makes me happier than you'll ever know. I love you, Rachael, and I've only ever wanted the best for you. I worried after the accident that we'd lost you." She reached out, touching my cheek in a gesture that made me feel like a little girl again. "In a way, we had, but seeing you today...laughing, smiling, looking at him with so much love...it's wonderful. I'm glad you've been able to move on."

I reached out and hugged her, probably getting frosting on her shirt but she didn't seem to care.

"Cade has helped me so much, just by being him. Kathleen, my therapist, has helped too. She's the real reason I was able to come home, and because of her I'm going to say goodbye." I didn't need to elaborate further. My mom knew exactly what I meant when I said I needed to say goodbye.

She took a steady breath, and her eyes filled with tears. "You're a strong girl, much stronger than you believe." She reached up and tapped her forehead. "Mental strength is harder to come by than physical. You have it, and don't ever forget it." Touching her fingers to her heart, she added, "You feel deeply and care immensely, that makes you a beautiful person inside and out. I would've been more worried about you after the accident if you acted like you didn't care. Sometimes we all have to suffer through terrible things to find the light in the dark."

I couldn't help looking over my shoulder, almost as if I felt him, and found Cade standing in the doorway.

Staring at him, I whispered, "I finally found my light."

I wasn't surprised when my mom put us in separate rooms that night. I was even less surprised when Cade snuck into my room a little after midnight.

"My dad might like you, but I'm pretty sure he'd still kill you if he found you in my room." I warned Cade as he slipped into bed beside me. The bed was a queen size, but even then it felt too small for Cade's large body.

Wrapping his arms around me he pulled me onto his chest. He ran his fingers through my still damp and tangled hair from my shower earlier. "We'll just have to make sure he doesn't find out." He chuckled, cupping the nape of my neck and leaning up to kiss me. "Thank you," he whispered against my lips.

I blinked my eyes open, and gave him a quizzical look. "For what?"

"For trusting me, for loving me, for giving me you." He rolled us over again so he was now above me. "I never knew what I was missing until you," he murmured, nuzzling my neck. "You make me see the world in a whole different way."

Warmth soared through my body. It felt good to hear him say that. I never wanted to be a weight tied around his ankles. I wanted to lift him up the way he did me.

He ran his thumb over my bottom lip, his eyes darkening with lust. "Thank you for showing me that my demons don't define me."

"Cade," I reached up, putting my hand on his arm, "I didn't show you anything."

He shook his head. "You did. Before you, my life was so dull. I played the part but I didn't *live* it. Now, I do. Everyone else saw what they wanted to see when they looked at me, but you? *You* always saw *me*."

With only a few words he stole my breath. I would never understand how I'd been so lucky to have this man come into my life, and I hated how badly I'd treated him at times. I vowed in that moment, to spend the rest of my life—or as much of it as he'd take—making it up to him.

"I love you," I whispered.

"Not as much as I love you, Sunshine."

~❧~

"Does your mom ever stop baking?" Cade whispered in my ear, as we sat at the kitchen table watching her whip up more treats.

"Nope," I laughed, "I'm pretty sure she even bakes in her sleep. Our house is always overflowing with sweets."

"If we don't leave soon I'm going to gain fifty pounds," Cade warned, reaching for another cookie.

I lightly slapped his hand. "Lay off on the cookies. It's not even noon."

He grinned. "It's not like they have alcohol."

"True," I agreed, "but I've also lost count of how many you've eaten."

He frowned, lowering his head like a little boy in trouble. "Okay, no more cookies...until after dinner."

I giggled, shaking my head at him. "I think I'm going to have to hide them."

"No!" He cried.

My mom peered around her mountain of baking supplies and said, "Why don't you two find something to do. Bundle up and go outside for a bit."

I looked over at Cade and cracked a smile. "That's code for she wants us out of her way and we're getting on her nerves."

"It is not!" She protested.

"It is," I whispered. "Don't worry mom, we'll get out of here." I started thinking about what my mom suggested, and said to Cade, "I'm going to grab my camera, I'll be right back and then we'll go outside."

"Sure, I'll be here," he pointed to the table, eyeing the cookies.

"Don't even think about it," I warned, before running out of the room and up the stairs.

I grabbed my camera bag, and shrugged into a jacket, and bound back down the steps. I was surprised to find him standing at the bottom of the stairs tossing a football in the air. Noticing my look, he explained, "Your dad found it."

"Don't expect me to play football," I warned, grabbing a blanket from off the back of the couch, "You know I can't catch."

"I said I'd teach you," he winked.

I knew that Cade's form of 'teaching' would involve lots of hands on activity. Not that I would mind.

"Besides," he added, following me to the back door, "you're probably better than you think you are."

"Well, I guess you'll have to actually teach me this time instead of rolling around in the grass," I joked.

He grinned wickedly and winked. "Ah, but rolling around in the grass with you is so much fun."

I laughed, shaking my head as a light wind stirred my hair around my shoulders.

For the time of the year it wasn't that cold and luckily there was no snow, so we wouldn't freeze to death.

Cade followed me down the deck steps and into the yard.

"I like it out here," he said, staring beyond the yard to the field of tall grass.

"I think you hate being cooped up inside," I joked, watching where I stepped so I didn't trip.

"That would be an accurate statement," he looked over his shoulder at me, grinning. "I blame it on the fact that my dad kept me outside playing football all the time and..." He paused, his face twisting with pain. He took a deep breath, as if bracing himself. "Before Gabe died we were an active family. You know, skiing, snowboarding, swimming, always outside and on the go."

I kept quiet not sure what to say. Cade didn't talk about his brother a lot, and I knew it was a testy subject, so the last thing I wanted to do was say something to upset him. I hated seeing him hurt, though, and I wondered if he often felt the same way when he looked at me.

I spread the blanket down on the ground, set my bag beside it, and lay down staring up at the sky.

Cade joined me, lacing our hands together.

He turned his head towards me and I looked over at him. "When I think about Gabe, and the years after that, and all the shit I went through, it makes me so grateful to have found peace—to be able to enjoy this moment, right here, with you." Bringing my hand up to his chest he continued, "I no longer feel scared to defy my dad. I know I'm ready to do my own thing, be my own person, consequences be damned."

"What are you saying?" I whispered.

"I'm saying that when I graduate I'm going into architecture. I won't pursue football. I want it to remain a hobby that I love, but not something I'm forced to do." He reached out, grabbing a piece of hair that had blown across my face, and tucked it behind my ear.

"It makes me happy that you're doing what you want," I admitted. True, it was scary that Cade was graduating in the spring and I didn't know where things would go, but life didn't come with a map for a reason. You weren't meant to know where your future would go, but you were supposed to enjoy the journey—even when you had to climb mountains.

"It does?" He questioned, seeming almost unsure.

I nodded. "I will always want you to do what makes you happy, Cade. I'll support any decision you make because I love you, and when you love someone you don't hold them back from their dreams, whatever they might be."

Before I could take a second to breathe he crashed his lips to mine.

His kiss was consuming, his touch electrifying.

Despite the chilly air, I felt warm all over as my body flooded with heat.

Cade pulled away, his breath fanning across my cheek. His stare was intense and I found myself drowning in his blue eyes.

Cracking a smile, he said, "Let's go exploring."

I couldn't dim my smile. "Sounds good."

I hopped up, but Cade was a little slower. His knee was still healing and a part of me worried that he might always have problems from the injury. But Cade was confident that it only needed more time.

I left the blanket where it was, but grabbed my camera bag. I pulled my camera out, following Cade into the brush. He was ahead of me, with the football clasped in his hand. I couldn't help taking a picture of him.

He looked over his shoulder and smiled, so I took another.

"You're lucky I'm not shy," he warned with a laugh, "because you're kind of intimidating with that thing."

I lowered the camera, sticking my tongue out at him.

"I'm serious," he chuckled, reaching out to shove some of the tall dead grass out of his way. "You're kind of a bad ass." He stopped and turned around, waving his hand at me.

I rolled my eyes. "I'm definitely not a bad ass," I shook my head.

He grinned crookedly and stepped forward, cupping my cheek. "You are...and you're also my Rae of Sunshine."

"Cade," I laughed, "I thought you forgot that shitty nickname."

"Never," he gasped, faking that he was offended. "It's an awesome nickname and I will use it as often as I can for the rest of your life, so get used to it."

"Oh, really? For the rest of my life?"

"Yeah," he smiled, leaning his forehead against mine. "Did you think you were going to get rid of me or something? I want you, always, Rae. I mean that."

I closed my eyes and laid my head on his chest. I could hear the steady beating of his heart and I knew he meant what he said. Sometimes it was still hard for me to believe that he loved me and saw a future for us. I wanted those things too, but sometimes it was all too easy to doubt that he'd want them too. It felt good to hear him say it.

I stepped back and smiled up at him. "Come on." I started forward and he followed.

He nodded his head towards the house beside ours. "Is that where...?" He trailed off.

I nodded. "Yeah." Steeling myself, I added, "We used to run through these fields playing as children." I forced the words passed my lips. I didn't want to be afraid to talk about Brett, Hannah, or Sarah. I wanted to remember them and be okay with it all. Pointing to the swing set that sat broken in our yard—and honestly I didn't know why my parents hadn't gotten rid of dingy thing yet—I said, "Sarah and Hannah used to come over when we were little and we'd play out here for hours and run over to Brett's house to make trouble," I laughed.

Cade gasped. "Rachael! Were you chasing after a boy?!" He joked.

I laughed. "Hey, it was only one boy," I bumped his shoulder. "I wasn't one of those girls that had a new crush every week. It's only ever been...well, you and Brett," I shrugged.

"And selfishly," he lowered his voice, "that makes me very happy." His lips grazed my chin and I shivered from the feel of his stubble rubbing against my skin. "Enough serious talk," he grinned, backing away from me. "Let's play some catch."

"Cade," I groaned.

"Come on," he coaxed, "it'll be fun."

I set my camera down where it wasn't in danger of being stepped on, and prayed to whatever God was listening that I wouldn't get hit in the face with the ball.

"Ready?" Cade asked, lifting the ball.

"I think so..." I screamed when he threw it before I finished speaking. I jumped up, catching it, and then turned to run when he started chasing me.

He caught me around the waist and spun me around, before we promptly fell to the ground, and rolled until he hovered above me.

"I win." He kissed my nose.

"You didn't even give me a chance," I frowned.

"My bad," he grinned crookedly. He stood up slowly and offered me his hand. "This time you can throw first." He lowered and picked up the football, handing it to me.

He jogged away and I tossed it to him. He had to run forward to catch it since I didn't throw it far enough. He turned away from me and ran.

I jogged after him and when I got close enough I jumped onto his back.

He started laughing, reaching back to grab my legs.

"I got you," I chimed, pressing a kiss to his neck.

"You got me a long time ago, Sunshine."

I smiled widely at his words as he headed back to where we left the blanket. He dropped the football on the ground and I hopped off his back. I jogged back to where I left my camera and as I approached, I called, "Smile!"

He grinned and my stomach fluttered. Cade's smile did crazy things to me.

After snapping a few more photos he took the camera from me. "My turn."

I blushed, lowering my head, suddenly shy at having the tables turned.

"Don't hide from me," he warned, his voice husky.

I looked up slowly and found that he'd lowered the camera.

"You have nothing to be afraid of, Rae."

"I know." I stood up straight, squaring my shoulders and leveled him with a smile.

He grinned. "Now that's more like it."

I took the camera from him then and sat down on the blanket, going through photos. Cade leaned over my shoulder looking as well.

"Hey, you made me look good there," he pointed to one.

I laughed, leaning against his chest. "That's because you look good no matter what and you know it."

He chuckled, lying on his back. "That's true."

I set the camera aside and curled my body around his.

We grew quiet and Cade stroked my hair.

"Are you ready?" He asked softly.

I stopped breathing and my heart skipped a beat.

It was time. I knew it. He knew it.

I had to take care of what I came here to do.

"Yes."

⸳ℯᴈ⸳

Cade held my hand as we walked through the cemetery. My mom had told me where they were buried, so I didn't have to search the headstones.

The closer we got the faster my heart raced.

I knew this was it.

The beginning of something new for me—a life without fear.

"I want to go alone," I told Cade.

He nodded and released my hand. "I thought you would. I'll be over here," he pointed a few feet away." I knew what he was saying, if I needed him he'd be close.

"Thank you." I leaned up and kissed his cheek.

I gave him a reassuring smile as I headed to Brett's grave. Hannah and Sarah were just as important as Brett, but he was the one I needed to speak to and say goodbye.

Kathleen and Cade might've given me that final push to gather the strength to come here, but I'd known all along that this was what I had to do. I'd fought the inevitable for far too long.

As I strode through the graveyard I took several deep breaths to calm myself. I could do this. I was strong and I would not break—not anymore.

I stopped in front of the grave, a choking panic overcoming me.

Brett, the boy I'd grown up and loved once upon a time was gone and what was left lay here beneath my feet.

I suddenly felt bad for not bringing flowers or *something* to leave for him.

I sunk to my knees, tears coursing down my cheeks as I reached out to touch the cold stone surface of the headstone.

"Hi, Brett," I choked. "I'm so sorry it took me so long to visit. I'm sorry about a lot of things, actually," I laughed humorlessly. "I'm sorry I stole your sweatshirt when we were ten and lied about it...I really wanted it." I laughed, and this time it didn't sound forced. I reached up and dried my face with the sleeve of my shirt. "I'm sorry for eating all of your cotton candy when we went to the carnival. I'm sorry for ruining your art project in eight grade when I tripped and fell on it. I'm sorry for making you pose for hours while I took your picture. On second thought I'm definitely not sorry for that. You know what, forget it, I'm not sorry for any of it. I'm not sorry for being your friend or for loving you. I *am* sorry that because of me you're not here right now," I sobbed, "but I wouldn't take back any of the memories I have of you for anything. I'm thankful I got to have you in my life for as long as I did. I will always regret what I did, but I won't let it rule my life anymore. I wish things were different, but wishing gets you nowhere. I know one day I'll see you again, so even though I came here to say goodbye I was wrong. This isn't goodbye, Brett. This is me telling you I'll see you later." I took a deep breath and stroked my fingers over his name. "I have to live my life and I know you'd want that for me."

I sat there crying. There was so much more that I wanted to say, but I couldn't find the words. I knew in my heart they were unnecessary.

I pressed my lips to my fingers and placed them against the headstone.

I stood up and dusted the grass off my jeans, before I walked forward and was met by my present, my future, my forever.

epilogue
six months later...

"THAT'S THE LAST ONE," Cade grinned, setting the cardboard box on the floor. He came around the kitchen island and wrapped his arms around my waist from behind. I leaned my back against him, smiling. "Now we have our own place."

"*Almost* our own place," I reminded him.

After graduation Cade and I decided to move in together, but since Cade wanted a house, not an apartment, and we couldn't afford a house on our own we were going to have roommates.

But not just any roommates.

He groaned. "Way to burst my bubble, Sunshine."

About that time Xander and Thea strolled in. Each of them was renting a room from us so they could live off campus. Thea still insisted that nothing was going on between them. I guessed only time would tell where those two ended up.

Thea wrinkled her nose at us. "Am I going to have to watch you grope my best friend all the time?"

Cade chuckled. "Probably." He nuzzled my neck and I giggled.

"Bleh," Thea gagged. "I think I liked her better when she was mopey and didn't talk to anyone, because this," she pointed at us, "is getting majorly gross real fast."

Xander started to laugh and chimed in with, "Well, what do you think is going to happen when they start having loud, obnoxious, bang the walls down, sex."

"Oh my God!" She slapped her hands over ears. "I didn't even think of that!" She ran from the room and up the steps. "Moving in here was a *bad* idea!"

The three of us laughed at her over dramatic antics.

"I'll finish unpacking the stuff in the family room," Xander tossed his thumb over his shoulder and backed out of the room, leaving us alone.

"Are you happy, Sunshine?" Cade asked me, cupping my cheeks in his large hands. His eyes were serious, almost worried, like he thought I might say no.

As cliché as it sounded, he made me happy when my skies were gray. With Cade by my side, even the bad days didn't seem so bad anymore.

I placed one of my hands over his. "I couldn't be happier," I promised. "I'm ready for whatever the future holds for us."

"Like babies?"

I started laughing. "How about you let me graduate college first and *then* we'll talk marriage and babies?"

"Deal," he grinned.

And we sealed it with a kiss.

acknowledgements

I don't even know where to begin with the acknowledgements for this book. Rae of Sunshine wasn't an easy book to write. I was terrified to write a book about texting and driving and the consequences, because it is so pertinent in the world we live in. Many teenagers—and adults—are guilty of texting and driving. Even looking down at your phone while you're behind the wheel can have lasting consequences, like in Rae's case. When you're driving your sole focus should be on the road. Personally, I've never lost anyone because of texting and driving, but I've wanted to write a story about it for a while. I know many of the people who read my books are young, and I thought if I could stop one of them (you) from texting and driving, then I'd accomplish something. When I started Rae's story I knew the accident would be her fault and that she'd carry immeasurable guilt because of it. I wanted to show what it would be like to be the "villain" in the story, not the victim...but in a way Rae is very much a victim. One of her own making. She has to come to terms with what she caused and learn that she's not a monster. She made a mistake—one she'll carry for the rest of her life. Oftentimes we all think we're invincible and nothing will happen to the ones we love or ourselves, but the fact of the matter is it can happen. So always be thankful for what you have, because you never know when it might be gone.

Cade. Cade. Cade. He was exactly what Rae needed, despite his own tragic past. When I got the idea for Rae of Sunshine I knew he'd be a football player, but not your typical one. Cade is very sweet and humble. Life has shaped him into a guy that thinks beyond his years and I love him for it. I know many of you are probably mad that I didn't delve further into his story and have a resolution with his father, but this is Rae's story, so I felt it was important to focus on her overcoming her issues.

Okay, now that I have rambled for a page in a half I guess it's time that I thank some people.

Thank you to my wonderful author friends: Regina Bartley, Harper James, and Valia Lind. You're all always there to support me and I don't know what I'd do without you. Thanks for listening to my many breakdowns and dealing with my panic attacks.

Thank you to my lovely beta readers, Haley, Becca, Kendall, and Stefanie. You guys were an immeasurable support system throughout this book.

Regina Wamba, I can't thank you enough for the stunning cover. It's exactly what I wanted.

Monica and Michael, thank you so much for bringing Rae and Cade alive! You both did amazing and I'm blown away by how well the pictures match up with the book.

To all the bloggers that have/will read and review Rae of Sunshine, THANK YOU. Without bloggers most books would fall through the cracks. Thank you for taking time away from your busy lives to read my books. I've become really good friends with many of you and I'm so thankful for that.

I can't forget to thank YOU. The readers! You guys blow my mind! When I started this journey three years ago I NEVER expected the amount of support I have today. Every time I get a message or email from one of you I can assure you that there's a smile on my face.

Enjoy two excerpts from Live for Her by Harper James
& Causing Heartbreak by Regina Bartley.

Live For Her
Harper James

Prologue
NATE FIVE MONTHS EARLIER—SENIOR YEAR

Nate turned the lights off on his bike as he approached the Marshes' home. He didn't want to draw attention to himself and wanted a minute to prepare what he would say when the door was answered. No matter who it was, there would be explaining to do. He had left when he and Scott had fought about being caught with that stupid beer so long ago, and he had made it a point to never come back. Chloe was the one girl he was willing to break that vow for. As he straddled the bike at the end of the driveway, his heart sank. Her car was nowhere in sight. She wasn't here, and he was no closer to making sure she was all right. He couldn't ask her if the stories all over the news were true or if she could handle what was sure to come her way the next day.

"If you're here to give my brother a piece of your mind, then punch him and bail, you're a day late. Little brother, Josh, took care of that last night." Olivia walked out from the shadows at the far end of the house where he knew she must have just crawled from her window.

"Little Livvy, long time no see." Nate smiled.

"No, that's not true. You have definitely seen me. You just choose not to talk to or acknowledge me, even though I'm pretty sure the thing that crawled up your ass and died has nothing to do with me." She walked up so she stood a few feet from the bike he had turned off. "If you're looking for the main attraction, she's not here."

"I figured that out: no car, no Chloe."

"And here I thought you were the dumb one all this time." Olivia gave him the same smile she had when they were getting in trouble as kids. After a second, she chuckled and wrapped her arms around his neck, hugging him. "I've missed you."

Nate was taken aback. He had gone so long hating Scott that he had forgotten he had also been friends with Olivia. Slowly raising his hands, he wrapped them around her waist and hugged her middle. "Me too."

"Sorry she isn't here. I'll let her know you came to check on her if I see her tonight, okay?"

"Thanks, Liv. You know, just because I hate your brother doesn't mean we have to be mortal enemies. I remember plenty of times when we were little that it was the two of us taking him on. We can always try that again."

"You just now figuring that out?" she asked, tilting her head to the side to study him. "Too bad you took so long. Bridges have been burned; hearts have been broken." She took a step back and shrugged her shoulders. "Besides, at this point, Chloe's either going to break your heart or his. You won't want her best friend around if she breaks yours, and I can't hurt Scott by coming around you or bringing you around here if she breaks his."

"Yeah." Nate sighed.

"See you around, Fennell."

"Later, Livvy." He waited until she had crawled back in her window to start his bike up and head home.

CAUSING HEARTBREAK

a novel

regina bartley

CAUSING HEARTBREAK

regina bartley

PROLOGUE
Dane

"I need to talk to you." Wren stopped me at the front door as I was leaving. Talking was out of the question. I hadn't slept in days. I had some place to be, and it wasn't there.

"Not now, Wren."

"It's important Dane. I need to talk to you now." She followed me down the steps and towards my car.

"It can wait." I open the car door and started to get inside.

Just as the door was shutting, I heard her say, "I'm pregnant."

When I looked back at where she stood, I saw a serious look in her eyes. My head was already jumbled with everything that was going on. I hadn't been able to deal with finding out that the people I'd thought were my parents weren't. It had weeks now, and I still couldn't get past it. The damn pills weren't killing the pain, and now this. My freaking head couldn't take anymore shit.

"You sure it's mine." You could never be too sure about these things. The only time we'd slept together was at that party. That was months ago. My hands clenched hard against the steering wheel. I rocked back and forth in the seat. When I looked back at her she had tears running down her face.

"What did I ever see in you?" She dropped her chin to her chest. My eyes scanned her body until they landed on her stomach. I could plainly see it. Her stomach was clearly sticking out under her shirt.

"I'm trying to figure that out myself." I stared at her once again willing her to say something. I knew she wouldn't though. She knows as well as I do that I am a piece of crap that not even the dogs would take a second look at. I didn't need this crap. Not now, not ever. If she was expecting me to act like this was great news and that I should be forever excited, then she truly didn't know me at all. Just add this effing great news to all the others. My life was a bowl of fucking cherries.

"Are we through?" I snapped at her.

She glanced up at me once more and I watched a single tear slide down her pale white face, but I didn't let it get to me. It was about time someone felt as broken as I did. Why did I always have to be the one to suffer?

"A small part of me expected you to react different. I wanted you to care about one little thing in your miserable fucked up world Dane." She swiped her hand across her cheek. "If your own child can't make you care, then I don't know what else will."

I huffed out a breath and smirked in her direction. "I still don't even know if the kid your packing is mine." I barked, but didn't look in her direction. I knew I was hitting below the belt, but I wanted her off my ass.

"Go to hell." She stomped off towards the house.

Funny, that's the exact place I was headed.

I started the car and backed out of the drive. My eyes followed her as she quickly made her way inside the house. *Good Wren. Runaway. You don't need someone like me in your life.*

～✦～

I stood there in front of the grave of the people I thought were my parents. The ones who'd spent their whole life telling me they were. The realization was that every piece of my life up until this point had been a lie. Parents... What fucking parents? The feeling in the pit of my stomach made me want to claw out my insides. It was creeping up my throat and it felt like I could vomit up everything inside.

Make it go away. I let my lips linger on the glass bottle before turning it up again. The burn of the alcohol wasn't helping the pain in my chest. Neither were the two pink pills I swallowed over an hour ago to kill the pain. They used to help. They used to make every conscious thought and abrasive feeling go away. Not this day. First my parents and now Wren. I can't imagine that anyone would want me to be the father of their baby. I don't know how to be a dad. Now looking back, I realize I never had one, so this baby would be just fine if it didn't have one either. Better none, then some phony. No one wants a man saying "I love you son," if he obviously didn't mean it.

I blamed everyone. When Sawyer said she needed to talk, this wasn't the conversation that I was expecting. I would never have expected this, in a million years. How is it possible that I didn't know that these people were my parents? Looking back now I realize that I shared no physical traits with them. I am the tallest one of the family, and I have blue eyes. Fucking blue eyes. Not brown. Ugh... All lies.

You can't make this shit up. Poor Sawyer didn't want to tell me, and I couldn't blame her. It wasn't her secret to tell. She was just trying to help, and I flipped my shit when she told me. I called her a liar. "Oh God, I called her a liar."

I pinched the bridge of my nose to hold back the tears, but it was no use. There was no fighting this pain. With enough alcohol it would all go away. Wouldn't it?

I slammed the bottle down on the edge of the headstone, and watched it shatter into a million tiny pieces. I picked up the full bottle next to my feet and opened the top. I put the rim to my lips and tipped it back, welcoming the burn once again.

"Why," I stared at the stone, willing it to say something anything. Nothing but silence answered me back. It pissed me off even more. "Why didn't you tell me? Why did you let me believe this stupid lie my whole life? Why didn't you trust me enough to tell me the truth? Why did you die? Why do I still love you? WHY?" I screamed just before I dropped to my knees. I rocked back and forth before resting my head on the ground. My eyes were shut tightly, but the tears still fell. I could almost hear my mother's voice, urgent and clipped telling me to straighten the hell up. But how could she expect that from me, she wasn't even my mother.

I reached in pocket and pulled out another pill. The pain had to stop. I washed it down with the whiskey, and laid down on the cold ground. The earth was spinning, and I just wanted it to stop. Closing my eyes, I rested my arm across my face. Flashes of mom, dad, and a pregnant crying Wren were wracking my brain. Over and over.

Finally I could feel the fuzziness from the pills or the alcohol. My fingers went numb first, and I took a deep breath and I could feel the air entering my body and leaving. The silence of my breathing calmed me and I wanted to just drift off to sleep and let it consume me completely.

about the author

Micalea Smeltzer is a bestselling Young and New Adult author from Winchester, Virginia. She's always working on her next book, and when she has spare time she loves to read and spend time with her family.

Follow Micalea:

Facebook: **https://www.facebook.com/MicaleaSmelt zerfanpage?ref=hl**
Twitter: @msmeltzer9793

Instagram: micaleasmeltzer

Made in the USA
Middletown, DE
21 January 2015